Anne McCaffrey, the Hugo Award-winning author of the bestselling Dragonriders of Pern novels, is one of science fiction's most popular authors. She lives in a house of her own design, Dragonhold-Underhill, in County Wicklow, Ireland. Visit the author's website at www.annemccaffrey.net

Elizabeth Ann Scarborough, winner of the Nebula Award for her novel *The Healer's War*, is the author of numerous fantasy novels. She has co-authored eight other novels with Anne McCaffrey. She lives on the Olympic Peninsula in Washington State.

Book Two of The Twins of Petaybee, *Maelstrom*, is now available from Bantam Press.

Ann McCaffrey's books can be read individually or as series. However, for greatest enjoyment the following sequences are recommended:

The Dragon Books
DRAGONFLIGHT
DRAGONQUEST
DRAGONSONG
DRAGONSINGER: HARPER OF PERN
THE WHITE DRAGON
DRAGONDRUMS
MORETA: DRAGONLADY OF PERN
NERILKA'S STORY & THE COELURA
DRAGONSDAWN
THE RENEGADES OF PERN
ALL THE WEYRS OF PERN
THE CHRONICLES OF PERN: FIRST FALL
THE DOLPHINS OF PERN
RED STAR RISING: THE SECOND CHRONICLES OF PERN
(published in US as DRAGONSEYE)
THE MASTERHARPER OF PERN
THE SKIES OF PERN
and with Todd McCaffrey:
DRAGON'S KIN
DRAGON'S FIRE
By Todd McCaffrey:
DRAGONSBLOOD

Crystal Singer Books
THE CRYSTAL SINGER
KILLASHANDRA
CRYSTAL LINE

Talent Series
TO RIDE PEGASUS
PEGASUS IN FLIGHT
PEGASUS IN SPACE

Tower and the Hive Sequence
THE ROWAN
DAMIA
DAMIA'S CHILDREN
LYON'S PRIDE
THE TOWER AND THE HIVE

Catteni Sequence
FREEDOM'S LANDING
FREEDOM'S CHOICE
FREEDOM'S CHALLENGE
FREEDOM'S RANSOM

The Acorna Series
ACORNA (with Margaret Ball)
ACORNA'S QUEST (with Margaret Ball)
ACORNA'S PEOPLE (with Elizabeth Ann Scarborough)
ACORNA'S WORLD (with Elizabeth Ann Scarborough)
ACORNA'S SEARCH (with Elizabeth Ann Scarborough)
ACORNA'S REBELS (with Elizabeth Ann Scarborough)
ACORNA'S TRIUMPH (with Elizabeth Ann Scarborough)
ACORNA'S CHILDREN: FIRST WARNING
(with Elizabeth Ann Scarborough)

Individual Titles
RESTOREE
DECISION AT DOONA
THE SHIP WHO SANG
GET OFF THE UNICORN
THE GIRL WHO HEARD DRAGONS
BLACK HORSES FOR THE KING
NIMISHA'S SHIP
A GIFT OF DRAGONS

The Petaybee novels
written in collaboration with Elizabeth Ann Scarborough
POWERS THAT BE
POWER LINES
POWER PLAY
CHANGELINGS
MAELSTROM

CHANGELINGS

Book One of

THE TWINS OF PETAYBEE

Anne McCaffrey

Elizabeth Ann Scarborough

CORGI BOOKS

CHANGELINGS
A CORGI BOOK : 9780552154406

Originally published in Great Britain by Bantam Press,
a division of Transworld Publishers

PRINTING HISTORY
Bantam Press edition published 2006
Corgi edition published 2007

3 5 7 9 10 8 6 4 2

Set in 10/12pt Plantin by
Falcon Oast Graphic Art Ltd.

Corgi Books are published by Transworld Publishers,
61–63 Uxbridge Road, London W5 5SA,
a division of The Random House Group Ltd,
in Australia by Random House Australia (Pty) Ltd,
20 Alfred Street, Milsons Point, Sydney, NSW 2061, Australia,
in New Zealand by Random House New Zealand Ltd,
18 Poland Road, Glenfield, Auckland 10, New Zealand
in South Africa by Random House (Pty) Ltd,
Isle of Houghton, Corner of Boundary Road & Carse O'Gowrie,
Houghton, 2198, South Africa,
and in India by Random House Publishers India Private Limited,
301 World Trade Tower, Hotel Intercontinental Grand Complex,
Barakhamba Lane, New Delhi 110 001, India.

Printed and bound in Germany by GGP Media GmbH, Poessneck

Papers used by Transworld Publishers are natural, recyclable
products made from wood grown in sustainable forests. The
manufacturing processes conform to the environmental
regulations of the country of origin.

This book is dedicated to Mary, Ke-ola,
and Keoki Poole

We'd also like to acknowledge the contributions of Lea Day for her memories of Hawaii and her research of both print and televised sources of information about volcanoes, otters, seals, and sea turtles.

Richard Reaser provided valuable feedback and inspiration as well as consultation on scientific matters, while Andy Logan provided dinner.

Mary, Ke-ola (the hula consultant), and Keoki Poole provided valuable information about Hawaiian culture, language, and customs and generously shared their own resources with us.

CHANGELINGS

Prologue

Petaybee was changing. It was always changing. The quakes and eruptions, avalanches and slides, great winds on land and sea, even the ebb and flow of the tide, brought about fundamental changes in the planet's surface, in the way it *was*. The people who lived on Petaybee knew and accepted this. If it had not been for the changes, jump-started and accelerated by a terraforming process begun only a few decades before, no one would have been able to live on Petaybee. The people made songs about the changes, celebrated them.

Their planet, once a cold ball of cosmic rock, was an awakening giant. Each shift, slide, rumble, storm, or explosion was a sign that Petaybee was stretching, growing, continuing to re-form its being into something even grander than it already was. The people and their songs celebrated the changes.

A lot they knew.

If they had bothered to ask their sentient planet just once how *Petaybee* felt instead of always bringing their own hopes and fears, joys and sorrows, into the communion caves where they spoke to the planet and the planet responded, Petaybee would have told them that it sometimes hurt.

All of that grinding of plates, cracking the surface, sloughing away here, washing away there, pushing some bits out and pulling others back, could be painful. Most worlds could take millennia to do what Petaybee did in hours, days, weeks, at the most, years. It was really quite a hectic pace, all this change in such a short time, and Petaybee was not always sure just what was happening to its great self or why.

The planet did know that its function was to be a home for its creatures, its two-legged, four-legged, winged, shelled, finned, and flippered fauna; its leaved, flowered, vined, barked, or grassy flora. It not only made homes for these life forms, it helped them adapt to its conditions so that their fragile husks did not die. The cycle of life formed by all of these living creatures fed Petaybee's vitality even as the planet nourished them. The two-leggeds who had become part of Petaybee's own great being returned its care by keeping the more destructive members of their species at bay, in space, away from their world.

No one was allowed to drill into it or set explosions on its surface to take away bits of its body it might have a use for later. If life was taken, it was replaced by new life.

Though a small planet whose surface consisted of little more than two ice caps and a sea between them, Petaybee had nevertheless made a lot of progress since its terraforming.

But it wasn't enough. Petaybee had to – *had* to –

make other kinds of places where more life forms could live. There was too much sea. Too much ice. If there were warm places, dry places, where life could begin, that life could become part of the cycle too and would add its own special gifts to its world. Though Petaybee was a world that could, as humans understood it, think, this idea was not a thought or even a true idea as such. It was a compulsion that expressed itself as a buildup of pressure in one particular area. Here. Land belonged *here*. The sea felt particularly empty and limitless at that point, but moreover, Petaybee actually felt as if it contained a continent within its core. A continent that belonged in this place where now waves rolled on and on. Some shoreline was needed. Some beach. And eventually, some trees and flowers, perhaps, other plants and animals. Yes. As industriously and deliberately as a two-legged dweller might move the furniture inside a house, Petaybee began rearranging its own interior to create what belonged on the surface.

This was not easy, even for an entire sentient planet with a sense of purpose. The landmasses were too far to move them to the empty spot without destroying all of the other life. Besides, the ice would melt and upset everything. The only efficient way to get land in the right spot was to bring it up from the inside, up through the bottom of the sea. And so Petaybee hacked and coughed and spewed and spewed and shot its red hot inner essence up into the sea bed, where some of the minerals within the hot sulfurous gas and magma turned into hollow rock towers that became chimneys for other eruptions.

As the hot vents opened like red mouths, Petaybee swallowed great gouts of seawater. It mixed with the minerals in the molten rock, then, superheated and full of nutrients, it shot back into the sea. When it cooled, it was a warm nutrient for new life. New species of plants and animals sprang up all over. They were not bothered by the sulfurous waters, but thrived in them. Petaybee thought this was as it should be, but then, Petaybee had a very large view of things. It took no particular notice of the *other* life forms lurking near its new cauldron, the ones not of its own creation.

Until that point, the planet's creation had blossomed in relative obscurity – the people had neither navy nor civilian fleets, no boats, in fact, but those used for subsistence fishing and hunting. Fly-bys were rare. There was no satellite surveillance. Once, a seal had swum by, pausing to observe the volcano's birth with interest. But he was on his way elsewhere. Only now, with the newest of the life forms in place, was Petaybee's work monitored, though it was done so unobtrusively that the preoccupied planet took no notice.

Gradually, the lava built up the floor of the sea around its chimneys. It was good, but too slow.

Heaving and squeezing, Petaybee pushed magma and gas up through the center of the elevated sea bottom. Once the pressure built up, it would blow a hole big enough to gush rivers of lava out into the sea. It would build up and up and up until it rose above the waves, then begin spreading out until it was a new place, a new home. Though it would be hot and hazardous at first, the seawater and air would cool it until it too was a warm place for life to flourish.

Though volcanoes had created landmasses on Petaybee shortly after terraforming, it had happened very quickly, while the planet was barely awake. This new volcano, this new island, was a conscious effort, Petaybee's greatest work to date. But work it was, a lot of work. As birthing mothers everywhere knew very well, the process of bringing life into the world was called 'labor' for a reason.

1

The Shongili twins gave almost simultaneous burps of repletion – the boy on his mother's shoulder and the girl on her father's – and were carefully laid on their backs on their fur-lined cots. Sean and Yanaba made no move to leave the nursery, unable to leave the sight of their offspring, safely delivered just a few hours earlier. The babies looked up at their parents, their dark pewter eyes as brightly focused as those of any bird. Each already wore a soft crown of deep brown downy hair, but Yana would have been hard pressed to decide whose nose or cheeks they had. Everything was still rounded and squashy, unformed and utterly adorable.

Even their contented gurgles sounded for all the world like the chortle of a small and active brook swirling among stones.

'Listen to them,' Yana said fondly. 'They sound as if they're laughing.' Then, 'I thought it took longer than that for babies to do things like laugh.'

Sean shrugged. 'Babies who are always and entirely human perhaps. But a selkie's development is a bit different. Faster in some ways. I don't recall when exactly I developed what, but I do recall being aware of my surroundings almost at once. But as to the details, well, too bad my parents aren't still around to advise us.'

But Yana, lost in wonder at the perfection of her children, answered him only with a dreamy glance. 'It's almost too much joy for one person to bear,' she murmured, feeling tears come to her eyes.

Sean took her in his arms. 'Then let's share it. I smell food, and you're still feeding two – one at a time.' He gave her a hug and a cuddle and, one arm draped on her shoulders, propelled her gently toward the door of the cube they had hastily attached to one side of the cabin to serve as a nursery. It was spare and spartan except for the furred cots, for it was the custom in Kilcoole to refrain from giving expecting parents items for their unborn children. A superstition really, but since Yana, before conceiving, had thought herself well past childbearing age, it seemed wise to encourage every sort of good luck.

As Sean opened the door, Nanook, his black-and-white track cat, and Coaxtl, his niece Aoifa's snow leopard, slid into the nursery. Nanook took a place under the boy's cot, while Coaxtl, after one long look at her charge, flopped beside the girl's.

'The sentries are on the job,' Sean said, and continued to push his wife to the door.

'I just never thought I'd have children,' Yana said, looking back over her shoulder at her twins even as Sean closed the door behind her. He left it slightly ajar so they could hear the babies if they cried out or if one of the cats needed to go out or get their attention.

No smells had been able to penetrate the cube from the main part of the house, Yana's old one-room cabin. Now, however, delicious odors of pepper and snow onions, roasting fish and unidentifiable savory spices, wafted from the stove. Over it stood the substantial and comforting bulk of Clodagh, the village's shanachie, singer of songs, bearer of culture, rememberer of history, settler of disputes, healer of wounds, and dispenser of medicines. She had also served as Yana's midwife.

'It's about time,' Clodagh said, closing the lid of the pot she had been seasoning. 'I thought you'd never think of yourselves. Now, sit and eat. And Yana, use that longie thing,' as she pointed a ladle at a chaise longue that had recently made its appearance in their home. There was no proscription against giving an expectant mother a gift for herself. The chaise, which took up a good half of the wall next to the woodstove, had seemed too large and in the way before, but now Yana found it inviting. 'Get your feet up and relax. As much as you can, that is,' she added in an affectionately derisive tone.

Major Yanaba Maddock-Shongili was quite willing to assume the seat and stretch her legs. Her overtaxed muscles carried her that far mostly because of Sean's support. He rearranged her feet a trifle and sat on the end, folding his arms over his chest and giving a sigh.

'Don't you dare look at your desk,' Yana said sternly. 'Even from here I can see the pile of orange flimsies, and they mean urgent.'

'Nothing is so urgent as feeding the pair of you up,'

Clodagh said staunchly, 'and there really isn't anything *that* damned pressing that someone else can't handle or defer – preferably until next year.'

'But those hydroelectric engineers were supposed to touch down today . . . and you know how eagerly Sister Igneous Rock is awaiting them.' Sean referred to the planet's geological expert and its self-proclaimed acolyte. The woman and her fellow would-be Petaybean cult followers had surprised Petaybee's longer-term residents by turning out to be quite useful once they discovered they could be of more service to Petaybee practicing their hard-science specialties instead of their misguided attempts at theology.

'Iggierock has 'em and she's dealing with them.' Clodagh gave a deep chuckle. 'She's near as good as I am . . . at some things. But this stew will give you much-needed energy. And we've more urgent matters to consider, such as the babies' naming song and the latchkay. I'm thinking that tomorrow will be none too soon, if Yana can make it back to the lodge and the communion cave to properly introduce your young by name to their people and their world.'

'She can and she will, if I must carry her,' Sean said fondly.

'I can handle it,' Yana said. Fortunately, those aching muscles of hers were well toned and trained from her years in the Company Corps. 'It's the babies we'll need to be carrying.'

'Good,' Clodagh said. 'All of Kilcoole has been waiting for these young ones, but there's a time and place for their gawking and well-wishing and filling your house up with doodads for the babbies. The sooner the better, though. Have you thought of what you'll call them at all?'

She dished up three huge bowls of her concoction, and after serving the new parents, she pulled up one of the new spare chairs to the new huge kitchen table they'd been given by friends who evidently thought they were going to have dozens of children instead of just two. Clodagh passed rolls just out of the oven, and steaming through the white napkin she had covered them with.

Yana chewed quickly but deliberately, thinking hard. 'Of course we've thought about it, but now that they're here, no name seems special enough. Among my mother's ancestors, you know, babies weren't named right away. High infant mortality rate was one reason, but also, her people believed a child didn't get its soul until the first time it laughed.'

She and Sean looked at each other over their full spoons and smiled. 'Which they've already done, and them only a few hours old,' Sean said. 'I can tell they're going to be quick, but then, it's well-known that all of the children born to my side of the family are very precocious.'

Yana made a face at him. 'Oh, in my family too, but our babies are also taught to be modest.'

'You two are too giddy by half!' Clodagh mock-scolded, shaking her spoon at them. 'Naming is a serious business. It should fit the baby's bloodlines – perhaps we could have names from your mother's people, Yana. There'd be a bit of novelty. It should also tell the world what the child is all about.'

'This world knows what the children are about,'

Yana said. 'It's responsible for their selkie nature, after all – well, it and their father,' she added with a roll of her dark eyes at her husband. 'And how advisable it is to tell the rest of the universe about *that* is debatable.'

'No debate about it,' Sean said in a tone that brooked no argument. 'The universe at large does not need to know that our children mutate into seals when they submerge themselves in water any more than it needs to know that the kids inherited that trait from me.'

'Well, the names don't need to come right out and say, "I'm a selkie",' Clodagh said. 'But they should, for instance, indicate that these children have an affinity for water.'

'Born for Water,' Yana said with a swallow of soup.

'What?'

She gestured with a piece of roll. 'I'm just thinking perhaps we should call them after the Hero Twins my mother's ancestors revered, Born for Water and Monster Slayer. Except at the moment they both seem to be Born for Water and it isn't yet clear who would be Monster Slayer.'

'My money is on the wee lassie,' Sean said. 'She's got something of the look of you in the glint in her eyes and the set of her chin.'

'She's barely *got* a chin,' Yana said, shaking her head. 'No, I think we'll have to go with the Irish side of my family this time. Here in Kilcoole where you're all Irish and Inuit, they'll blend in better with the other children that way anyway. Besides, among the Diné – my mother's people – girls all have war names like mine, and war is the last thing I want my daughter named for.

Water's a bit difficult too. The sacred land of Mother's people had very little rain, or standing water either, and so they were extremely short even on fish, not to mention seals and selkies.'

She stopped with her spoon halfway to her mouth. 'I just had a thought. *Will* the babies be transforming every time they get into water? Any water? If so, I'm going to have a fine old time trying to bathe them and it won't be easy keeping their nature a family secret.'

'I used to have the same problem,' Sean grinned. 'Until I taught myself not to fur up the moment a drop touched me. But I had no da to show me the way, and they do. Meanwhile, if you need help with the family secret, well, we've plenty of family here who know all about it. They'll help. And the four-foots will watch to make sure no outsiders come close enough to learn more than they should.'

'You say that, Sean,' Clodagh said, speaking quietly into her soup bowl, 'but there are outsiders who've seen *you* change, and one of them may take it upon himself to wonder if the twins inherited the ability and need studying.' She looked up, her moss green eyes fathomless and deep as one of Petaybee's many artesian springs, seeming troubled. She hated bringing up such worries on what should be a flawlessly happy day. 'You know how much scrutiny this planet is under.'

'Well, how the hell could they possibly interfere with my family peculiarity when Yana and I have the final say as governors of this planet?' Sean asked.

Clodagh shrugged.

'As long as the four-foots are their guards, no one

will get near them,' Yana said with far more conviction than she felt. 'And Nanook and Coaxtl will keep them from being seen, won't they?' A nervous tic started in her cheek. She rubbed it. 'Will the cats follow them into the water?'

'Yes,' Sean said positively. '*If* the little ones elude them long enough to get near water, Nanook and Coaxtl would follow them into the mouth of a volcano if necessary. The cats do converse. We just have to make it plain to them how dangerous it would be for the kids to be caught half in, half out. Like I was.'

'We'll hope they don't take arrows in their anatomy to induce such a condition,' Yana said, referring to what was nearly a mortal wound for him. 'And I thought leading training troops on landing parties for the Company Corps was a heavy responsibility!' She shook her head as if to clear it. 'We're borrowing trouble. It's not as if shape-changing is a viable occupation.'

'Oh, selkies would be real useful on water worlds,' Sean argued.

'Yana's right, Sean. There's trouble enough right here and now without borrowing any,' Clodagh said in a cajoling tone. 'Don't fall into *that* water until the ice breaks up. For now your biggest problem is to decide what these babes of yours are to be called. I will think on it, remember the stories of our peoples, see if there's some appropriate names there. You and Yana should sleep while you have the chance. The cats can't take care of all the needs those babes will have.'

* * *

The drumming began shortly after sunrise. Inside the nursery cube, the twins opened their eyes to the brightness pouring in through the piece of sheeting that covered the cube's single small window. The babies whimpered and wiggled.

Nanook's ears were the first part of him to wake up. They pricked to attention. Coaxtl's tail lashed restlessly before the snow leopard stretched a sleepy paw. The kits had awakened. Both cats stretched and rose, poking their noses over the sides of the cots.

'Rrrow,' Nanook told his friend. 'I'd cry too if I smelled like that. Where are those humans when you need them?'

'These cubs leak,' Coaxtl agreed. 'And they've got these things tied around their haunches to hold the leakage in. One wonders how humans come up with such ideas. This arrangement keeps the nest clean but the cubs dirty.'

'Sean would not want his kits to be dirty,' Nanook said.

'Can one pull these haunch harnesses off so one can clean them?' Coaxtl inquired.

'Yes, they are meant to be removable. But take care with fang and claw. We want to remove the harnesses only, not the kits' pelts. Humans, lacking proper coats, have very sensitive hides.'

Nanook's nose touched the kit's leg as he grasped a pinch of cloth in his teeth. The kit stopped whimpering. He looked at it anxiously lest it was merely saving its breath for a good howl, but it was staring at him, wide-eyed and curious. Disconcerting, these human younglings, born with their eyes all open and gawking.

'Hee,' the kit said aloud, quite distinctly giggling.

'Hee,' the female kit echoed, pumping a plump fist in the air.

Tickles, one of them – the female? – said.

Ma? the other inquired.

No, child, I am Nanook, your keeper. Your mother sleeps. And this one is Coaxtl, also your keeper.

'*Nook.* Nanook realized suddenly that the boy's more advanced utterances were mental and that it understood as well as transmitted thoughts.

Co'. The female kit was also transmitting thoughts.

Co-ax-tl, the snow leopard said with a dignified fluff of his tufted cheeks. *You may as well get it right to begin with, youngling.*

Co'.

Nanook sat back on his haunches. The harness was too close to the tender skin. 'Don't growl, leopard. They will learn. When I was their age, my mother had to lick me to teach me to do what they've already done in their harnesses.'

Coaxtl sat back too. 'This harness removal is for those with thumbs. The drums call. The time has come to wake the parents. *They* can cope with haunch harnesses.'

2

Just in case a seventy-five-pound track cat standing over her was not enough of a hint that she should wake, Sean was saying, 'Yana, love, it's time to rise. The drums have begun and the babes are hungry again.'

'Yes, I got that idea,' she said, looking up into Nanook's black-and-white marked face before Sean shooed the cat back to the floor. He had been so good, getting up to change the babies during the night and tucking them in with her so she could breast-feed without disturbing her rest unduly. She attempted to roll out of bed with her customary agility, only to find it sadly lacking. The birthing had not felt too traumatic, thanks to the underwater method Clodagh had employed to ease the way of the children into the world. But what pain had been spared her yesterday seemed to be catching up with her now.

A muted buzz went off in the adjoining cube, which was the main office of the Shongilis. Sean paused halfway to the nursery cube, waiting until a second mechanical noise clicked in.

'It's working?' Yana asked in surprise. This was not

the latest or most up-to-date answering machine, but it was the one that worked on their planet. They all listened for a second click, and then a red light appeared on the bar above the door into the cube, indicating a message was waiting. More efficient communication was one of the 'improvements' that almost had to be implemented with all of the attention – most of it unwanted – Petaybee received from offworld interests. One com shed could no longer handle all of the messages, now that Intergal communications had pulled out when Space Base was dismantled. The landing area and fueling station had been left intact, and for a small consideration and a trade agreement regarding the fuel for visiting vessels, Kilcoole was allowed to retain it as a civilian concession.

'That thing can wait,' Sean said. While recognizing the need for the 'labor-saving' device, at the same time he resented its intrusion into what had once been their comparatively peaceful life. 'I'll help you with the twins.'

First he had to help her hobble into the 'nursery'. Coaxtl looked up, yawned, stretched, and padded out. One's shift was over, one presumed. Nanook joined the snow leopard, and the two stood by the door until Sean retraced his steps and opened it for them to go out.

The blast of cold air that blew in when the cats departed chilled the overheated room that had been so efficiently warmed by the woodstove and the hot burning Petaybean alder wood. The nursery cube, like the office cube also attached to the cabin, had its own temperature- and humidity-controlled environment, which was why they had chosen it for the twins, in spite of its lack of the individuality that characterized Petaybean dwellings.

Both twins were wide awake and smelly. The little girl held up a fist full of white fur. 'Coaxtl got too close to you, I see, my little Monster Slayer,' Yana said, pulling off the dirty diaper and cleaning the child with the moistened moss compresses Clodagh recommended for the job. 'You need to choose your monsters more wisely, though, my love. Coaxtl is a friend.'

'Hee,' the little girl said.

'Hee,' echoed her brother, spraying his father with urine the minute the diaper was removed and air touched his skin.

'Here now,' Sean said. 'I think your mummy said your role model was called Born *for* Water, not Born *to* Water!'

'Hee,' the baby said again, so of course his sister had to say it again too, so as not to be outdone.

Sean held the boy and walked him around the cabin, talking to him while Yana fed her daughter. Then they switched babies. Finally the little ones were fed, changed, rediapered, and swaddled in clean furs.

Yana had finished washing up and pulled on a pair of old uniform trousers and a fleece top when someone knocked on the door.

She opened it to admit Bunny Rourke, Sean's niece and her closest friend since she had first arrived on Petaybee. Beside Bunny was Aoifa, Bunny's sister. Coaxtl considered Aoifa her twolegged cub.

'Clodagh said we should come to help with the babes while you and Sean get ready.'

'Clodagh's reputation as a wise woman is richly

deserved,' Yana said thankfully. 'You missed the messy bits for the time being, but they can use distraction for a moment.'

With the help of the girls, the entire family unit was ready to mobilize within an hour. Yana and Sean carried the twins, while the girls followed with their changes of diapers, their packets of moss wipes, and extra furs in case the twins messed the ones they were wrapped in. 'We look more like an expeditionary force than a family,' Yana remarked.

Sean smiled. 'You've not been around all that many families up till now, love. Families with new babies can make expeditionary forces seem underpacked.'

'Good thing we brought the snocle,' Bunny said. 'And a curly coat to carry the gear.'

'Have packhorse will go next door,' Yana quipped when the girls loaded the supplies on the shaggy little Petaybean horse with its thick curly coat. Sometime during the night it had begun to snow. A blanket three or four inches deep covered the well-tramped path to the river road. Snow still sifted down from a light pewter sky. Soon the sun, which had just risen, would be setting again.

Aoifa led the horse, while Sean and Yana – who were clad in parkas, snow pants, hats, mittens, and mukluks – squeezed themselves and their fur-wrapped offspring into the snocle beside Bunny.

Smoke poured from the smoke hole of the latchkay lodge, a great plume among the pinion feathers emitted by the chimneys of Kilcoole's other houses. In front of the lodge, men stirred soups and stews in sterilized fuel drums over open fires. The smells didn't travel far in the air, which was so frigid it froze the hairs inside people's nostrils.

The drums drowned out all other noises now, calling the people together. Their beat was so strong the snow seemed to fall in time to it.

The babies wiggled in their parents' arms, wanting to see what all the noise and fuss was about. The thing in which they had been squeezed, the thing that roared and slid, stopped, and suddenly they felt cold air rush in through their furs. It felt wonderful!

Strange and familiar voices mingled all around them. Their parents walked forward until the cold went away and the babies were enveloped in great warmth and felt themselves being passed from their parents to other people. When they were handed back, their furs were removed and their mother had changed from the furry beast she'd transformed into outside back to the soft-slender-dark-haired-sweet-milk-smelling giver of food and cuddles who spoke to them in long utterances and smiled often.

Many faces peered down at them, touching their cheeks and chins, toes and fingers, all of the features of their land shapes. People spoke in odd voices that had 'ooo' sounds.

They had slept well and were as curious as the cats who prowled among the people sitting and standing in the hall. The drums stopped for a while as people ate. During the eating, several people stood and spoke, saying things that seemed to make their mother happy.

Then they were both in their father's arms as the one

drum began again and their mother stood and danced with other mothers, a slow pacing dance around the center of the big space. Father spoke to them then. He was easier to understand than anyone else, and half of what he said was inside their heads, his meanings confusing and mysterious but clearly important clues to what lay before them. His silvery eyes shone happily down at them as he spoke, and his voice held a lilt of laughter and good feeling.

'Children, we are at your naming latchkay. What's a latchkay? I'm glad you asked. The people of our village and I come from two peoples of Old Earth – the Inuit and the Irish. When something wonderful or important happened, the people would gather to eat and speak, dance and sing together. Among the Inuit, this was called a potlatch. Food and gifts were given to all. Among the Irish, it was a kay-lee, where there was much music and food and drink. We on Petaybee celebrate our occasions with something that mixes the two customs and we call it a latchkay. At this one, people will give us gifts for you. When you are five, we will hold a latchkay to redistribute the baby gifts you no longer use, and you will add gifts of your own to ones we make or barter for. Today your mother and I shall sing and dance with you, and everyone will suggest names and explain why they are good names. Clodagh will probably come up with the best ones. Clodagh was the lady you both saw yesterday, before you saw your mother's face or mine. Your mother has finished dancing now and it is my turn. Any questions?'

'Hee hee,' the twins said. Then, ''Kay.'

But their father, passing them to their mother again, didn't hear.

Then Father picked Her up and mother picked Him up and they all danced, a happy jiggly rhythm such as the parents had used to put them to sleep. Two drumbeats, twin hearts, moved the people up and down, back and forth, up and down.

After that there was some more fun. Mother and Father sat down, each still holding one of them, and a round lady not Clodagh brought bright-colored soft things with shiny little round things in pretty patterns all over the front.

'Thank you, Aisling,' Mother said. 'Carry pouches are exactly what we need. Now the twins can see what's going on too.' Mother handed Him to Father and stuck her arms into the bright soft thing she said was 'kind of a cobalt blue.' Father handed Him back to her, and she put Him into the thing, so that His legs were apart but stuck through the front, His middle held in by the strip with the shiny round things that sparkled in the light, and His head, though cradled between Mother's food-givers, faced forward. He could see everything! Everything!

Father handed Her to Mother too. Mother had a hard time hanging on to Her, because She wanted to see too and tried to twist in Mother's arms. Mother's cuddle wasn't as comfortable as usual because He was in the way.

But Father put on his new soft bright thing, which he said was 'Hot pink, not my color, but Hers,' and then She too faced forward.

Thus they were able to see all of the gifts. Soft warm

things, not furs, for covering during sleep. Moss wipes and haunch harnesses, as the cats called them, though Mother and Father called them diapers. Small versions of Mother's fur-faced thing that made her big when she went outside. Other things like that, garments, clothes, they were called, that their parents held against them or stuck over their arms and legs a little ways to show.

The pile in front of them grew and grew until they couldn't tell one thing from another. Then two men came forward, 'Seamus' and 'Johnny.' If the first thing was the best so far, these last things were best too. They brought between them a cot surrounded by a box that had images of fishes swimming all around it. The bottom had things they took off and put on again.

'Rockers for in the house,' Johnny said. 'Runners for sledding them over the snows,' Seamus said. 'Wheels for when it's dry,' they both said, attaching round things to the front and back and taking them off again. 'And when you're near water and you don't want them in it, use nothing at all on this and it will float tight and dry as any boat.'

Best of all, it was not one cot but big enough for two. Mother and Father laid the twins together in it, so they could see each other and snuggle together. It was very nice but the twins did not let them get away with it, of course. Sleep could not come without food.

Before the latchkay adjourned to the communion place for the Night Chants, the singing was interrupted by the howls of the dogs tethered outside and answered by dogs running toward them. The lodge's doors were flung open and three figures, heavily covered in fur parkas, snow pants, and boots, stamped inside. Bunny and Aoifa Rourke, Diego Metaxos, and young Chugiak rushed out to tend to the newcomers' teams.

'Friends, we're so pleased you've come to honor these children and their parents!'

The first person, now stripped of his parka, was a small dark-haired man. In his plaid shirt and snow pants, he walked in among the celebrants and said, 'We are not the only ones to honor them! For weeks the seals have been gathering along the beach, thick as snowflakes. Dolphins and whales come too in great profusion, not to their killing grounds but near our settlements, as if waiting for something to happen. Then yesterday the ice began to crack and break up as if it were spring. Finally, a giant wave came rolling in and crashed onto the shore, carrying fish and other creatures, some we have never seen before, and washed away half the village. We heard twins were born here in Kilcoole at the same time the wave rolled in, and the three of us, who have the fastest teams in our area, were sent to greet the children and bring them naming gifts.'

The twins, seemingly oblivious to the noise, were asleep in their new cradle when the coastal people arrived, but by the time the visitors stood dripping melted snow from their hair in front of Sean and Yana, the little ones had awakened again.

One man pulled out a length of string and began making figures with it a few inches above the twins' faces. 'A story string to amuse them and help them trap the best stories in its net. It is made of good strong synweb too, so they can use it to snare rabbits if they want.'

The next person, a woman, handed Yana two knives: a dagger, and a blade that looked as if it were a quarter cut from a circle, the point removed and replaced by a bone handle. 'A hunting knife and an ulu, so they will never go hungry or cold.'

The third person, also a woman, handed Yana a large-eyed steel needle with a cutting end. 'My mother always said a needle was the true magic of our people because without a needle, we would not be able to make the clothing we need to survive. Actually, my mother wanted me to bring you her old treadle sewing machine, but there wasn't time to load it, even if there had been room on the sled.'

Yana and Sean laughed and thanked them all.

The baby girl reached up and snagged the story string in her tiny fingers.

The man who had been demonstrating its use beamed.

Then the food was served, musicians brought out their rusty instruments, and people began dancing the reels and figure dances from long ago, separated by occasional waltzes.

Marduk, the orange and white striped cat who had adopted Yana when she first arrived at Kilcoole, hopped into the cradle and wrapped himself around the twins' feet, purring when a baby hand patted his magnificent bushy tail. Nanook and Coaxtl reappeared and sat on either side of the cradle. Nanook looked expectantly up at Sean.

'I think that's my cue to ask the mother of the honorees to dance.'

Yana was still sore and stiff from sitting so long, but the happiness of the occasion gave her something only a little less earthbound than wings. Taking her husband's arm, she slid to the dance floor and they half waltzed, half polkaed to the plunk and wheeze of instruments that had been frozen and thawed many times and played through many latchkays.

'This has all been a lot of fun, Sean,' she said. 'Exhausting, but fun. But even though everybody's had suggestions, I still don't know what to call the kids. Do you?'

'Not really. I sort of liked Seamus and Siobhan, but it's a bit too much like Sean and Sinead, and we're not even twins.'

'Aisling suggested Murray, which is a sea name, I'm told, and Mairead, but that's not a water name. Muriel is, but I'm afraid we'd confuse them. Murray and Muriel sound awfully close.' She dropped her voice so he could barely hear her above the drums. 'To tell you the truth, I think those alliterating names for twins are just a bit on the cutesy side.'

'It will come to us, love. There's still the Night Chants.'

Shortly afterward everyone took a break in the festivities while the dog teams of people from distant villages were hitched up again, the little curly coated horse was loaded with the gifts to be deposited at the cabin on the way, and local people returned home and hitched up their dogs or saddled their curly coats for the trip to the hot springs where the Night Chants were held.

The drummers arrived ahead of everyone else so that drumbeats greeted each new party.

Yana as always was struck by the beauty of the hot springs. You saw the steam first, rising above the snow, and then, between ice-encrusted banks, the curtain of water pouring from the top ledge into a deep pool that cascaded into a second, then a third pool, the water through the steam like jewels behind a sheer veil. That this was the place where she had first made love with Sean and only yesterday birthed her babies added immeasurably to its beauty for her. But the most powerful enchantment it held lay beyond the waterfall, in the communion place.

People stood aside to allow Yana, Sean, and the twins to slip into the cave behind the upper falls. Clodagh was there ahead of them and, surprisingly, the three newcomers from the coast. Soon the cave was crowded with the bodies of neighbors and friends. Yana was a bit surprised to realize that all of these people were from Petaybee, most from Kilcoole. None of their offworld friends were here. She wondered if the naming ceremony wasn't hastened in order to prevent the attendance of offworld folk. It seemed a bit discriminatory, especially when some of them would never have survived some recent events without the help of those friends.

When everyone arrived and settled, Clodagh said, 'Desmond here is the shanachie of his village. He heard how we were looking for sea names for the babes and said he has a song to share.'

Desmond spoke so quietly everyone had to be still to hear him. He also seemed to be well aware of the special nature of the cave.

'The seals came to remind me of my mother's song

from her mother. The song she sang in its original tongue, so I will tell you about it before I sing. It tells of a lonely widow who had lost her husband and her only child to the sea. Every day she walked the beach and watched the seals play. One day when she could not go to the beach because of the rain, a strange mute girl came to her door to be her daughter. The woman called her Murel, Bright Waters, and for seven years the mother and daughter lived together. Then one day when they walked the beach, a seal called from just off-shore. 'Ork ork ork!' he cried. 'That is Ronan, the little seal,' the woman told the girl. But the girl knew already. 'Ork ork ork!' she cried, and the widow knew it was time for her daughter to return to the sea.'

He then began singing quite a long song in a language that bore only a distant resemblance to the Gaelic people sometimes sang.

Yana didn't pay too much attention, after the translation, because she was pondering the names of the seal children, Murel and Ronan. Bright Waters and Little Seal. They had a ring to them that she liked. Of course, when the kids got older, she supposed she'd have to figure out how to change the boy's name so it meant big seal, but that could wait. She exchanged a look with Sean over the heads of the twins. By the bioluminescence that made the stone cave walls glow softly and the water wall glimmer, he smiled and nodded.

The cave was warm and cozy, and the bioluminescence had begun to scribe patterns on the cave walls. Desmond's song had a bit of a drone, but the children all liked it when he made the seal sound, which seemed to figure in the chorus. Her own children were no exception. With every ork, the babies squirmed, and for the first time ever she wished the ceremony over and them back at home.

When the song was done, Clodagh turned to them, smiling, her brows raised in question.

'You have the names then, do you, Yana? Sean?'

Yana and Sean nodded once to each other. Then Sean took the little girl from Yana's arms and held her out to Clodagh, who had taken a place of prominence in front of the waterfall. 'Right then, pet,' Clodagh said softly to the baby. Then she raised her head, her voice still quiet and calm enough to keep from alarming the child but carrying above the roar of the waterfall to everyone in the cave. 'People of Petaybee, and our beautiful home, here is Murel Monster Slayer Shongili born to us to live among us.'

Yana had been struggling to pay attention but now her eyes snapped open in dismay. 'I never . . .' She began to say that she had not seriously meant for Monster Slayer to be part of her daughter's given name, but Clodagh was passing Murel Monster Slayer Shongili to Aoifa, who sat next to her, and accepting Yana's son.

'And this fine one here, people of Petaybee, is Ronan Born for Water Shongili, born to us to live among us.'

But as she turned to hand Ronan to Aoifa, who had been trying to pass Murel to Bunny Rourke, sitting beside her, Aoifa fumbled. That seemed to be the chance Murel had been waiting for. With a fishlike twist, the infant spurted from Aoifa's grasp and into the waterfall. In the confusion, Ronan escaped Clodagh's embrace and dived in after her. 'Heeeeee,' they cried, followed in a moment by 'Ork.'

Before anyone could start breathing again, Sean eeled past them and dove into the water himself.

Yana slid to the cave's entrance and ran out, snatching up furs from the snocle as she ran downstream. Behind her, Clodagh commanded everyone to stay put.

By the snowball moon she saw the large sleek head of a seal break water in the lower pool. Using his nose and mouth, he shoved two tiny silvery white seals onto the shore, then climbed out himself, blocking their way to the water while they orked merrily at the prank they'd played on everyone. Yana reached them and flung the furs over her family. Inside the furs, Sean shook himself like a large dog and the little ones instinctively followed suit.

Yana's heart began beating again. Being the only full-time biped in her family was going to take some getting used to.

3

As usual, it was midday of the following day before the latchkay ended. Yana and her family returned home, accompanied by Clodagh, who came armed with left-overs from the feast.

To her surprise, Yana found she was ravenous again. After she fed the twins – Murel and Ronan – she sat down at the table with Sean and Clodagh, knowing that if she stretched out on the chaise longue she would drown in her soup.

Clodagh served the rolls and soup. She looked exhilarated, as she always did after latchkays, even though Yana thought they must be somewhat draining for her too.

'Your message light is still on,' Yana observed idly, nodding to the red light above the door to the office cube.

'It can wait,' Sean said gruffly, and almost savagely took a bite from his roll, an expression of extreme delight on his face as he chewed. 'Featherlight, Clodagh.'

'I can't take credit for those. That Aoifa has a real light hand with bread.'

'Indeed. More, please?' And Yana used the last of her third roll to sop up what little gravy remained on her plate before handing it to whomever would take it.

'Drink that blurry too, Yana. Makes good milk,' Clodagh said as she rose to refill her plate and Yana's. The blurry was a special sort of Petaybean beer. One could not drink enough of it to get drunk, but did get pleasantly – well, blurred.

Obediently, Yana took a sip of the dark brew. Actually, it was not her favorite beverage by any means, but she knew of its benefits to a nursing mother, having been told so ad nauseam by every person who had noticed her protruding abdomen in the last nine months.

On the other hand, if she drank enough of the stuff, she might forget which twin she had last breast-fed, though actually she was getting the hang of the rotation bit. Excusing herself from the table, she sought out the chaise and leaned gratefully against its back. Large as it was, it still was the perfect couch for her . . . and even fit her tall body, with room for Sean.

They finished the meal companionably, with Clodagh reciting a list for Sean to write down of the people who had sent messages and congratulations to the new parents from other parts of Petaybee, and another list of the gifts and givers.

'One thing's sure,' she finished up, rising to her feet and collecting plates, 'they won't lack warm blankets and fur rugs! Nor babysitters. Your nieces have offered their services as their baby gifts. Aoifa said she'd had a lot of experience with babies and kids in Vale of Tears.'

Clodagh gave one of her disapproving sniffs for the trials and tribulations of the poor Aoifa, who had been rescued from a most barbaric enclave and the untender mercies of its leader, Shepherd Howling.

Yana scrunched her shoulders into a more comfortable position and sighed with repletion.

'That was splendid, Clodagh.'

'Indeed. A fitting end to a very fine naming latchkay, in spite of that little show of independence from the guests of honor.'

'I suppose it's just something we'll have to get used to,' Yana said. She closed her eyes and saw imprinted on the insides of her lids the incredible patterns the planet had created in the walls of the cave when the twins were recovered and the communion ended. 'Even Petaybee seemed proud of them, though.' A yawn overtook her and she stretched, jerking her knees up as abused muscles in her abdomen resisted.

'C'mon then, Yana, and get a good night's sleep . . . on your side or your tummy . . .' Clodagh said, and Sean slid his wife's legs to one side of the chaise so she was in a position to rise easily.

'On my tummy, oooh, it feels so good. Yesterday I was too knackered to notice how I lay,' she said with a cautious hand on her now unoccupied belly.

'I'll come tuck you in,' Sean said, knowing she disliked being too fussed over. 'And let you know if that message was anything important.'

She gave him a loving smile and stuck out her tongue at his offer to share the message as if it would be a treat. She had already slid into her gown and a dressing robe, so getting ready for bed took little time. Once there, she experimented with positions denied her during her pregnancy to find the most comfortable one. She'd have to get up in about three hours to feed her ravenous babies.

As tired as she was, she found her mind would not quit whirling as she settled down to sleep. There was so much to think about that she had put on hold the last few days while preparing to birth her babies.

Her babies . . . She was forty-five, and although she had always kept herself fit in the Company Corps, conceiving had been a minor miracle she attributed entirely to Petaybee's healing influence . . . another reason she blessed the planet and resolved to protect it to the best of her ability as joint governor of this fascinating world.

Many of the problems she and Sean had originally faced were sorting themselves out, especially now that Petaybeans, who had been recruited by the Intergal Company for lack of other employment on the planet, were resigning their commissions and returning to their native world, where the training they'd had made them invaluable and very employable in Petaybee's new business ventures.

She would be so relieved when the novelty of the planet faded and it stopped being invaded by all kinds of groups – esoteric, exotic, and daft – who felt they would benefit by time spent here in some capacity or another. Sooner or later word would get around that the planet's wonders were hardly a free lunch for all and sundry. Petaybee took care of its people, keeping them healthy and well fed, but the recipients of those benefits had to endure very cold winters with deep snows and a short and very busy summer with swarms of biting insects attacking any visible flesh. The planet itself had stern criteria that newcomers had to meet.

Yana grinned in the darkened room and twitched a blanket over her shoulder. Where was Sean? Maybe the message was a good one. He said he'd come tuck her in. She'd need to get as much sleep as she could with the feeding schedule she was now facing.

Sister Igneous Rock had suggested that the planet itself interview candidates. There were several problems with that, but the downside – the candidate had to spend the night in one of the communion places, and some people had very intense reactions to the experience – was sometimes a problem: negative for the applicant, very helpful in weeding out those who had no talents or abilities that the planet needed. There had been some protests by people rejected . . . but that was their tough luck. As word got around that Petaybee was not an easy mark, fewer duds arrived for their entrance exam.

The latest bunch, hydroengineers, had passed with flying colors, and spent more time with Sister Iggierock – as she was called with affection and admiration – who had spent hours reading to the planet so it could decide which types of modernization it would accept.

Now that folk were becoming accustomed to what Clodagh called the 'Rock Flock,' they were proving invaluable. There had been other 'religiously' inclined visitors who'd had to be disillusioned by fact and their interview with the planet on their arrival. So far, of those with determined evangelical zeal, only the Rock Flock had been acceptable to the entity Iggierock still referred to as the Beneficent.

Much had changed, besides the seasons, since Yana first set foot on her 'retirement' planet. She hadn't known, but secretly suspected, that her damaged lungs were incurable. That is, until she met Clodagh and had lived through her first winter on the planet. Its curative powers – good food, clean air, and exercise – had restored many to complete good health. The clinic, inaugurated by Farringer Ball, the CEO of Intergal Company and a confirmed sicko who had once been one of the most critical of the company executives, had to increase its beds yet again to accommodate those seeking treatment on organic Petaybee. That clinic promised to be a profitable business now, with the laboratories adjacent to it to have state-of-the-art in equipment. Highly qualified physicians and researchers and equally qualified men and women lined up to take any position available. On his long list of to-do's, Sean added similar clinics for the southern continent and perhaps another facility on the western coast of the main continent.

She heard her door being carefully opened and knew Sean was there to 'tuck' her in.

She turned over in the bed and heard his chuckle.

'You were supposed to be asleep,' he teased.

'Not until you came to tuck me in. So who was it and what's the new problem?' she asked, having taken a look at his face. She knew him so well now that his expression indicated he needed to talk about whatever that message had been. She pulled her legs to one side so he could sit on the bed, and then she curled her body around his.

'Marmie is coming,' he said, as if that explained everything. Perhaps it did. Marmion de Revers Algemeine was one of their most devoted and shrewdest new friends, having been part of a team sent initially to examine the 'sentient' claim Sean and Yana had made for their planet. 'And she's bringing a top-class lawyer and legal team.'

'Why on earth do we need a top-class lawyer and a legal team . . . apart from those already resident on Petaybee?' Most disputes among the residents were solved by the intervention of shanachies or people like Clodagh who were respected as leaders and wise mentors. The Collective Interplanetary Societies – or CIS – under the guidance of Phon Ton Anaciliact, had helped prove that Petaybee, the planet, was a sentient entity, and Sean and Yana had scrupulously held to the tenets provided by the CIS. So far the planet had been more sinned against than sinning.

'Well, complaints have been lodged by individuals of discrimination by the employer . . .' Sean began, after clearing his throat.

'Oh, those who got rejected,' Yana said.

'Exactly.' His grin was dour.

'They were interviewed by the main employer and found unsuitable for the tasks available,' Yana said, which was basically what the people were told as they were transported to the departures lounge.

'They said the interview was biased and they had not taken any written tests to prove their skills nor asked to produce documents or recommendations to prove their competence. Ergo, they were denied their right to seek employment here.'

‘Oh, Lordy,’ Yana said, pushing her hair back from her forehead. ‘Half of them didn’t have working skills but had heard that life on Petaybee was dead easy.’

‘Most of them also had diseases we do not wish to see circulating here,’ Sean added. ‘I asked Petaybee when she started wholesale rejections. Some of the diseases were social, which could be communicated to the entire population. A lot of them were mentally unstable, some criminally insane. Oh, and the discrimination on religious grounds is cited all too often.’

‘But Petaybee is not religious,’ Yana said. ‘I thought we’d cleared that up when we had to limit the number of pilgrims. Mind you, Iggierock and Shale and the others have proved more than useful, but certainly not in any religious circumstances.’

‘And Marmie says we have to clear that up in legal terms, which must then be presented to would-be immigrants before they take passage here. That won’t be hard to do since we control the only transport that is technically admissible in Petaybean space. But we have to set it up, or be continually set upon by lawsuits.’

‘Who’s behind that notion? I thought we’d got rid of Luzon and company.’

‘Marmie says we’re not out of the woods so easily . . . especially since our population is mainly composed of other i.p.’s – inconvenient people. As an Earth-type planet, we are still supposed to accommodate i.p.’s.’ He grimaced.

‘First they have to prove they are not going to remain inconvenient, and so far none of those rejected could.’

‘There are some iffy cases, Marmion went on to say,

which is why we have to sort this problem now. Oh, and more Nakatira cubes are on their way.'

'How does she manage that?' Then Yana waved off the need for an answer. She was only too grateful to get all they could of the useful buildings. They came equipped with all mod cons, as Clodagh called it, and required no special foundations or extra facilities, coming complete with solar heating and sanitary bio-conveniences. Their only drawback was a certain characterless sterility, which with a little imagination could easily be imprinted with the individual style of the occupant.

The cubes were manufactured and distributed by a Japanese known to Marmion, and Yana and Sean suspected she had financial connections there as well. They had arrived in what Bunny called the 'niche' of time. Building materials alone were precious on Petaybee, and energy to heat them even more so. The cubes were the perfect answer to provide accommodations for an overwhelmed planet that had never expected so many visitors or the need for such things as hotels, schools, offices, and storage space. One of the first to be placed was the cube that was next to Yana's old house and provided the couple with office space and occasional living quarters for legitimate visitors. A second was Kilcoole's school, and others had been placed at the Space Port for essential services and finally for the beginnings of the new hospital. Another cube was now the nursery.

Marmion had warned them that eventually Mr. Soshimi Nakatira wanted to visit this incredible planet and meditate in one of the communion caves. He hadn't yet taken Sean and Yana up on that invitation, but Marmion was certain that he would.

'He's the kind of guy you want to visit and to stay as long as he likes,' Marmion had assured them.

At the time, plagued with importunate visitations, Yana had remarked with irony, 'Which means he'll arrive in the midst of one of our crises. We'll have to save one cube for him alone.'

'Oh, he'll probably bring his own accommodation,' Marmie had replied negligently. 'He's like that. A truly gifted man.'

'At least we have Soshimi's cube available for the lawyers,' Yana said cheerfully.

'Probably the time he'll come for that visit,' Sean remarked.

'Now, let's not borrow more trouble,' she said soothingly, stroking his hand where it was on her pillow.

'True, love. We'll be looking back on these as the grand old days soon enough. Once Petaybee's midsea volcanoes build up the landmass in the temperate zone, we'll be besieged with even more folk wanting to come to this unspoiled planet to "improve" it. Without the cold climate to deter them, every planetless soul in the cosmos will be wanting to live here.'

'That's far off in the future, Sean,' she said. 'From what you told me of your journey through that area before, everything is still well below the surface. These things take eons.'

'In the natural way of things, that's true. But on a terraformed world like this one, even latent development is much accelerated. I give it a decade, tops.'

'For someone not borrowing trouble, you're deep in debt now,' she teased.

'Sorry, love, you're quite right. Now you get some sleep,' he urged, leaning down to kiss her tenderly. 'I want to do a bit more work before I join you. I've let things slide the last few days. Can't think why I've been so distracted.'

Yana smiled and squeezed his hand.

'However did I find you in all the worlds I could have gone to?' she asked with a grateful sigh.

'I know you looked long and hard, love,' he said, half teasing, half serious, as he pulled the soft fur around her shoulders and kissed her forehead. 'Remember, it'll be Ronan gets the source this morning.'

'I did remember that.'

'I'll remind you,' he whispered as he left the room.

Closing the door behind him, Sean looked in on the twins before returning to the office cube. Asleep in their new dual cradle, they looked as sweet and peaceful, as peachy and golden, as if they had never turned into little silvery seals. That trick of theirs this evening showed him that he would need to be on his guard with these two slippery characters. He was glad to see the cats had taken notice too. Marduk had planted himself across the twins' legs, making a living fur blanket, and Nanook and Coaxtl stretched out beside the cradle. Nanook opened one eye, and Sean nodded and closed the door.

He was glad that Yana had been too tired to take in the end of Shanachie Desi's song, where after seven years Murel changed back into a seal and swam out to meet her brother, neither of them ever to be seen again by her foster mother. It was nonsense, of course. That was a fairy tale told back on earth about a supernatural species, not a genetic mutation like himself. All of those stories involved seals temporarily turning into people and, when they became seals once more, never being able to return. They were wild creatures, not part of families like his. Of course if his children swam away, they would return. He always had, hadn't he? Becoming a seal was a gift, an ability, a talent, actually, that allowed him to do certain things others could not.

Still, he was grateful that Yana had not heard the rest of that song, and he hoped no one would ask her about it. She had enough to worry about without bringing in folk tales that had nothing to do with the mutation brought about by Shongili genetic engineering, accident, and Petaybee's own tendency to adapt species to its own needs. With the big cats for baby-sitters when he himself could not be teaching them about being seals, the kids would be fine; sure they would.

4

Murel and Ronan were quite advanced in most ways. They learned to walk very early, and to run almost as quickly. By the age of three they could sit on the back of a curly coat without being held there. They started school when they were five, and learned to read and write, demonstrating their abilities by reading to each other at home. But by the time they were seven, they were in and out of trouble all the time, the mildest problem being that the teacher was unfairly suspicious when they kept turning in identical test papers written in nearly identical left-handed printing.

The teacher also noted in their student evaluation that Murel and Ronan did not reach out to befriend the other students, especially the newcomers, and spoke mostly only to each other unless asked to recite.

The truth was, they not only didn't reach out to newcomers, they didn't like or trust them much either.

'They come to *our* world because they're sick or other worlds won't have them, and act like they're better than us,' Ronan told their mother.

'They're just scared,' she said. 'It's rough for them,

you know. They realize that they're not as well adapted as you are, so they have to act as if they know more in other areas.'

'I don't see why,' Murel said. 'If they were nice, we'd try to teach them stuff about Petaybee, but some of them, especially the older ones, are just nasty and mean. All they do is moan and groan about how bad the com stuff is around here and how they can't always depend on it to reference their lessons or talk to their friends wherever they were before they left. They want to know why we don't have a decent satellite so all the stuff that needs a satellite works better. They don't care about learning about *here*.'

When Ronan came home with a black eye and Murel with a cut lip, their father said, 'Fighting, were you? Murel too?'

'It wasn't our fault, Da. That Dino Caparthy is a bully. He's really big and he has a gang and they jumped Ronan – I mean all of them. I sorted – I helped Ronan sort them out and sent Dino away with a bloody nose, grabbing his bollocks with both mittens, but they're really a problem.'

'So you *did* win then, did you?' he asked. They looked at each other, shrugged, looked back at their father and nodded. He said, 'Well, good. I'll speak to their parents and teachers but I'm not sure how much good it will do. They came here from Romopolis on Mingus Prime. It was one of the earliest terraformed worlds and it's not in very good shape. The cities are filthy and the air has been recycled so many times inside the domes that you can cut it as quick as breathe it. Their folks applied to us so they could get their kids out of that environment to someplace more wholesome, and since they've skills we can use, we accepted them. But they're going to have to talk to their kids about cooperating.'

'To hear Dino tell it,' Ronan said, 'Romopolis is a wonderful funfair of a city, and Kilcoole is at the end of the universe and the bottom of the food chain. He said we were all so breaded our chrome was broken and we were mutes with scales.'

'Is that insulting?' Da asked, looking puzzled.

'What he *meant*, of course,' Murel said in a very careful and grownup voice, 'is that we are *inbred* and our *chromosomes* are broken so that we're mutants on the *evolutionary* scale, but he's too dumb to even know how to call people bad things.'

Da looked like he was trying to keep a straight face and not smile. He liked it when they used big words, and because he and Mum used them a lot to talk about their work, Murel and Ronan knew how to say the words. And because they wanted to join in the conversation but had to keep asking what things meant, and Mum and Da always told them to go look it up – now – they knew what the words meant. Dino didn't like that about them either. *He* was the real mute with scales.

'And what inspired this lad to call you all of these things he couldn't pronounce?' Da asked.

'Nothing!' they both exclaimed, and Ronan continued, 'It was just because we didn't feel bad that the stupid game his uncle sent him won't work here and because he thinks we should have great clattering halls full of fake stuff for him to play with. I can't tell you what he called Petaybee but it had to do with shite and it wasn't nice.'

Da nodded, but whether he ever did anything about it, they didn't know. Whatever he did, it didn't work very well. After that, Dino only hit Ronan when he was sure Murel wasn't around. The gang still said horrible, if garbled, things about them and the few other kids actually from Kilcoole, but they said it out of range of Murel's fists, feet, and fingernails.

If their teacher thought the twins were withdrawn, the track cats, Coaxtl, and the curly coats had the opposite opinion of them.

It was everything the helpful creatures could do to keep the pair out of trouble. They were insatiably curious, absolutely fearless, and downright dangerous to be around sometimes.

'They keep leaving their outer coats lying around on the riverbank where anyone can find them,' Nanook complained. The intrepid track cat was getting a little tired of playing nanny. Nevertheless, she dutifully turned around and used her hind paws to spray powdery snow over the snow pants and parkas the twins had carelessly left lying near their latest ice hole in the river before taking an afternoon dip in seal form.

'It's a very good thing for Sean and Yana that they aren't exactly like the seal people in the old stories,' Coaxtl said, settling her white fluffy belly into the snow. She placed her huge paws with their tufts of fur between the toes on either side of the ice hole and watched with flicking fringe-tipped ears for fish swimming across the exposed circle of running water. The water was so deep and cold it looked black at this time of the year.

'Do you recall the song sung at the naming latchkay?' Nanook asked.

'Many songs were sung,' Coaxtl replied. 'It was very tiring.'

'I mean the one about the seal people who shed their coats when they became human, not the other way around. If any other human found the sealskin and kept it, then the selkie had to stay on land with that person.'

'One recalls something of the sort, yes.'

'I fancy Sean and Yana must sometimes wish it were true of the twins so they would have to stay in the nest until they could be safely supervised,' Nanook mused. 'Of course, humans are a bit silly about that. Their young are sooo fragile and they have only one or two at a time.'

'There is no room for those two in any enclosed space,' Coaxtl said, and turned her head to lick her shoulder.

At that moment water geysered out of the hole and drenched the snow leopard, who somersaulted backward in surprise.

She twisted and sat up facing the hole. A gray seal slapped front flippers on the edge and pulled its sleek body after it. The eyes were big and blue and the mouth was grinning.

As soon as the seal was out of the water, it flipped water all over both Nanook and Coaxtl. A childish human laugh pealed from the midst of the spray and a small bare boy stood before the cats. 'Gotcha!' he laughed.

Coaxtl gave the boy a withering look and walked two paces forward until she sat on top of the buried snowsuit. *Cold, youngling?* she asked, purring.

'You took my snowsuit! You big fur ball!'

Nanook walked forward and touched a cold nose to the child's bare rump, nudging him back to the ice hole. *If I were you, I'd be a seal again. At least you're dressed for the weather when you're in seal form.*

Ronan resisted smacking at, though not on, the black-and-white track cat's icy nose. 'Don't get cat snot on me, Nanook. I'm cold enough. I don't want to swim anymore.'

Then I suggest you show submission to Coaxtl and beg her to return the property with which you so carelessly littered the landscape. Honestly, child, you never find us *leaving our pelts lying around.*

'Oh yes we do. During breakup you shed your fuzzy body all over everything.'

We remain attractively clad in fur at all times, Coaxtl said. She allowed a sleeve of the snowsuit to poke out from beneath her belly. *You, on the other hand, cover yourself in small bumps, which do nothing that we can see to warm you.*

'I'm going to freeze to death and it will be on your head!' he proclaimed with something of his father's Irish lilt. It was good for dramatic pronouncements.

From the ice beside the hole came a sharp smack and a swoosh, and Murel rose, flashed pink skin, and then ran to the bank and pulled her buried snowsuit and blanket from under a log. She wrapped the blanket around her as she tugged on the suit, then tossed the blanket to her brother.

'Don't tease him, 'Nook,' she said. 'Can you not see he's about to perish of the cold?'

Perish? It's only minus twenty! Nanook said, but shot a look at Coaxtl, who decamped from atop the clothing while the blanket-clad boy scrambled for it. *Downright sultry weather, I'd call it. It's a wonder the ice is holding. Younglings Petaybean born and bred should be able to withstand this without getting all hissy and breaking out in bumps.*

Murel bullied her twin often enough when he wasn't bullying her instead, but she didn't want anyone else to do it. 'Come on, Ronan, don't give the cats the satisfaction next time. I told you to hide your snowsuit. What if one of the offplanet people was to find it? They'd think you'd drowned and would have set up a huge hue and cry and everyone would have to pretend to find you without letting the off-p's see you as a selkie.'

'Oh, would they? If you're that worried about it, you could have hid mine too. Where would you be during all of this hueing and crying and searching?'

Murel gave a deep and put-upon sigh and strode as purposefully toward the village as her seven-year-old legs would carry her. 'Really, Ronan, you are such an infant sometimes! I can scarcely believe we have the same birthday. You make any pup in Bunny's new litter look downright mature by comparison. You just don't *think*, laddie.'

But Ronan had pulled his mittens on and was bouncing the finger pad off the thumb one. 'See? This is your mouth! You just don't *shut up*, do you, lassie?'

He caught up with her and tried to race past her but

she ran even faster when she saw what he was trying to do.

Kits! Nanook said.

The track cat had meant to bring up the snowsuit issue with Sean and Yana, but her humans were always so busy these days, it took actual claws to get their attention. The company and the offplanet people simply would not leave them in peace. They were always trying to settle some new group on Petaybee or bring in some kind of improvements for the good of everyone, as they said, and they kept Sean and Yana hopping night and day just to field all of their chatter. Some of the offplanet people who were settlers were nice enough. Some even settled into Petaybean ways. But most of them came to Petaybee for peace, healing, a clean and simple life, and then wanted to clutter it up with all manner of things they were used to from their noisy, unpeaceful, unhealthy, dirty, and complicated lives somewhere else. That was what Nanook had heard the villagers say anyway. As long as the newcomers didn't bring with them anything that preyed on track cats, she did not concern herself with them.

'What those younglings need is something that can keep up with them swimming,' Coaxtl said finally. 'They swim farther and farther up the river every time and I'm afraid sometime they'll get in trouble and we won't know because we won't be close enough to catch their cries for help.'

At the same time, Murel and Ronan, having captured their mother in one of her rare moments of leisure, were expounding on the situation to her. 'If Da could come with us, it would be fine. We are really too old for babysitters now, but if we have to have one, it should be another selkie, or at least someone who can swim with us,' Ronan said.

Murel nodded her head, the red tints in her black hair flashing with the firelight from the window in the woodstove. 'Coaxtl can swim and doesn't mind it in the summer but she's really a big wusspuss about swimming under the ice. All she does is hide Ronan's snowsuit.'

'Does she?' Yana asked. 'Why doesn't Ronan hide his own snowsuit? I believe both your father and I have tried to impress upon you—'

'The thing is, Mum, it just isn't practical to have to hide them,' Ronan said. 'Sometimes we'd like to go explore someplace out of the water but we can't because we don't have a kit to put on when we get out of the water. We need a way to take them with us.'

'I suppose we could rig up some sort of harness and a waterproof pack,' Yana said, thinking of diving equipment she had used while still in the Company Corps. 'It would slow you down a bit but that's hardly a bad thing. I'm not so sure I want you exploring outside the water so far from where you got in.'

'Nothing would happen to us, Mum!' Murel said. 'Petaybee wouldn't let it. You know that.'

'I know nothing of the sort. Petaybee has a good many other functions than providing divine intervention for you when you do something foolish and get yourselves into trouble. And once you're away from the village and our summer campsites on the river, there are all manner of things that could indeed hurt you.'

'Not any worse than freezing to death while a snow leopard squats on your protective gear and lectures you,' Ronan said with some residual bitterness at the unfairness of those who didn't let him do as he liked, unchecked.

Murel rolled her eyes at her mother and said, 'Yes, Mummy, please make Coaxtl stop teasing Ronan. He is just so endlessly tiresome about it, and I'm the one who has to hear it all the time.'

'Okay, here's what I can do, kids. I'll see if Marmion can send us some high-tech lightweight snowsuits and waterproof packs and harnesses for you from off world. One of her companies develops that kind of thing, I think. But meanwhile, you don't go anywhere without hiding your suits and letting Coaxtl and Nanook know where you're going. Meanwhile, I'll talk to your father about finding you a swimming companion. It will pain him, you know. He'd like nothing better than to join you, and the three of you could be off sealing around while I fend off would-be settlers and contractors and answer the wretched com unit.'

'Thanks, Mummy, you're the best!' Ronan said, giving her an enthusiastic hug that almost knocked her off her stool.

Murel planted a kiss on her cheek. 'We'll look for a swim friend too,' she said.

'Someone your father and I approve of, mind you!' Yana said, but she was calling out after their heels as they flashed out the door and down the snowy track between the village's shacks, log cabins, and the incongruous but inconspicuous white Nakatira cubes, which blended into the snow.

Sean promised the twins he'd go with them and they could swim as far as the ice floe, farther than they'd ever been before, and look for a friend with flippers or fins who could chaperone them.

The twins were unusually excited when the next ship landed, as it bore the imprint of Marmion's company. Surely she had sent the gear Mother asked for, along with all of these strangers disembarking.

Murel and Ronan hung around until the pilot appeared in the hatchway. 'Johnny!' they both cried, and ran to hug Captain Green, one of their family's oldest friends. 'Did you bring us anything?' Ronan asked, looking around the pilot for something besides his usual flight duffel.

'I brought you all of those exciting new friends, did I not? What more could you possibly be wanting?' he teased, ruffling Ronan's hair.

'But Marmie promised to send us something,' Murel said, hanging on to his belt. 'For our birthdays, you know. We're eight today, aren't we, Ronan?'

'We are. And she did say so, Marmie did, said she was sending us this particular item.'

'Funny, I don't recall a thing about it,' Johnny said with a look of what he intended to resemble wide-eyed bewilderment.

'Maybe you didn't see it get loaded, Johnny. Could you look, *please*?'

Don't overdo it, sis, Ronan told her. *I'm sure he can see through you as well as I can when you bat your eyes at him like that.*

That shows how much you know. If you have any brains, you'll start batting too. He might have to go to a lot of trouble to find it. We'd best be scoring all of the points for adorable that we can.

'Hmm,' Johnny said, scratching his chin, although both twins were quite sure it wasn't itchy. 'Let me think. You know, there was a lot going on at the time, what with all these folks getting ready to board, but I do seem to remember Marmion mentioning something about you.'

'She promised Mum she'd send us something. And you know Marmie would never break a promise to Mum,' Ronan said in a sober, man-to-man tone.

'No, no, of course not. But I can't think of anything at all unless it would be those wee ration packets.'

'Ration packets?' both twins asked at once.

'Yes, now that I think of it, she handed me the little foil packets and said your mum needed them for you.'

'They weren't ration packets, Johnny,' Murel said. 'You did bring them, didn't you?'

'Oh, aye. Though I hardly thought it worth the trouble. There's plenty of ration packets still left over from when Intergal ran the Space Base. What did I do with them? Gave them to the cook, probably. You'd keep things like that in the galley, you know.'

'No, no, they're not ration packets and they were *ours*,' Ronan told him.

'We'll go search the galley, Johnny,' Murel said. 'You needn't bother. How big were they and did the foil have writing on it? We can read that sort of thing now, you know.'

'Ah well, I guess they were about as big as . . .' He reached into the pockets on the thighs of his pants and pulled out two packets bright as fish. 'And the writing says – this one says, "for Murel," and this one says, "for Ronan."'

The twins snatched them and Ronan began trying to open his. Murel looked up at Johnny's grin and said, 'Thank you very much, Johnny, for bringing them. But Deirdre Angalook is quite right. You're a terrible tease.'

'Deirdre said something to you about me, did she?'

'Aye,' Murel said, pretending to scratch her own chin. 'But I can't quite recall what else it was she said except for the bit about the teasing.'

Johnny stabbed a finger to her middle as if to tickle her, but at that moment Ronan figured out the packet and it unfolded, flower-like, blooming into a metallic-looking suit with what seemed to be very light quilting.

'It's very small and thin,' Ronan said, a little disappointed as he felt the cloth.

'Oh, there's directions,' Johnny said. 'It gets bigger and puffier, I'm told.'

'How's that?' Ronan asked.

'See there, that fine print? It says, "Just add water."'

Both of them jumped him and there was a lot of rolling in the snow before he finally admitted defeat and said he had to go report in to their parents.

'You two coming along?'

'No,' Ronan said. 'We need to try these on, test them. So we can show our folks.'

5

When Johnny had gone, the twins headed directly to the river. It connected the former Space Base with the village. In the winter, its frozen surface served as a road where people drove dogs and snocles back and forth from their ice fishing holes or to go after water.

Ronan compressed his suit again and returned it to packet form, then began removing his snowsuit.

'You're not supposed to take off your clothes where there are people around, or change either!' his sister chided him.

'Well, we have to test them.'

'We can go to the spring. And besides, we need to find 'Nook and Co' first anyway.'

'No we don't. With these suits, we don't have to worry about getting caught without our clothes anywhere, and that's all the cats really do. Otherwise they just hang around the water hole. I want to test these, Murel. Let's go somewhere fun. Maybe we can find a new chaperone.'

'Da said—'

'Didn't you see that load of offworlders? Da will be

busy processing and orienting them for days and days. If we can find someone Mum and he like to swim with us, we can go *everywhere*. We won't have to hang around boring old Kilcoole with our skins itching for wet while Mum and Da entertain strangers.'

Murel was not above temptation. She wanted to see what was beyond Kilcoole and the familiar waters too. And she knew what Ronan said was true. It seemed like with their parents, what everybody else wanted always came before what they wanted – or even needed. It was very unfair. If they could be a little more independent, or at least not have to wait on their folks or those land-bound cats, maybe they could even help with the work Mum and Da did for Petaybee. After all, they were eight now. That was pretty old.

'Okay,' she said. 'But not here. That place where they put in the fish wheel in the summer. Nobody is there now and we can strip off and plunge in without getting caught.'

They raced through town without drawing much attention since everyone was busy meeting and greeting the new people. Even though a lot of Petaybeans didn't want the offworlders there, Clodagh and the other leaders reminded folk that they had all been from elsewhere originally and these people, like themselves, were just looking for a home to settle down in. Petaybee would either accept or reject them before long. No need meanwhile for Petaybeans to be inhospitable.

But the twins had had entirely too much of that. While they were in town making nice with the refugees, they weren't swimming and playing and teasing their feline nannies.

The stretch of river on the other side of town had another big advantage besides being less public. The hot springs fed into it, so areas of water stayed open year round, and much of the water that did freeze had a far thinner crust than that between the old Space Base and Kilcoole.

The twins found a good, big open place to enter the water, but first took off their clothes and carefully concealed them under some brush on the bank. Then, having located the little straps to their tiny packs, they fixed them over their shoulders so the packs were in the middle of their backs. Then each took a running jump into the water. It was icy at the top but much warmer underneath, and felt warmer still as their transformation took place. By the time they were completely submerged, they were no longer lanky pale children but shorter, fatter, furrier gray seals.

They played hide-and-seek with each other in the patchy ice, then dove deep, as the hot spring's current was diluted by colder streams. They swam for the joy of it, loving the feeling of being in a cave made of river ice, with the bumpy riverbed below and the bumpy ice sheets above. This time of the year there was little sun, but their eyes were excellent in the dark and underwater. They raced each other downstream, stopping once in a while to claw open a breathing hole in the ice with the talons at the ends of their flippers. When they grew hungry, they snacked on fish. They caught the smaller ones just by opening their mouths. The larger ones they had to take to the surface to eat.

When they had swum farther than they'd ever gone before, another hot spring entered the river, making a large area where they could surface and slide up onto the ice and over to the bank. The wind had come up, and it was pretty cold business getting themselves into their new suits. Had they not been native Petaybeans with the special adaptations to supercold temperatures the planet had engendered in its inhabitants, they would have frozen to death long before they got their suits on. However, since they *were* native Petaybeans, they put on their suits very very quickly. Once the shiny thin fabric covered their bodies, including their hands, feet, heads, and all of their faces but their eyes, they found they were quite toasty.

This stuff is amazing! Ronan thought-spoke to his sister, both because that was how they usually communicated with each other and because the fabric covering their mouths made it difficult to speak or to hear someone else speaking through it. *I bet it's what they make ship suits out of.*

Yeah, Murel said, twirling a little in hers, which was fun because the boots were as slippery as her flippers on the ice. *And we could go skating even in human form while we're wearing these.*

Ronan yawned. *What I'd rather do is take a nap. I'm pretty sleepy.*

Me too. Then we probably ought to start back before 'Nook and Co' start stalking us.

So they found a sheltered place among the spindly trees that grew along the bank and lay down beside them. The snow felt soft through their suits, and not the least bit cold. They had barely closed their eyes when Murel sat up. *Did you hear that?*

What?

That chirpy noise. It isn't a bird. I know it's not a bird.

'Hah!' something said, very close to them.

It's coming from the river, Murel said.

'Hah!' it said again, followed by more of the nervous-sounding chirping, like a mother bird missing her chicks.

Almost sounds like a dog driver coming up the trail, Ronan said.

Only not quite. It's coming from under the water.

Yeah?

Listen!

You're right, it is.

They fumbled removing their suits. Ronan left his on the bank and started to slide into the water but Murel stopped him. *No! Strap it on. It's shiny. A bird might take it. Besides, that's what we wanted them for.*

He grumbled but struggled into it while she, with her pack already strapped over her shoulders, slid into the water and transformed. She dove under the ice before her brother hit the water.

It occurred to her to wonder why they heard the sound as a voice if it was underwater. It was a distinct sound that she'd heard, not a thought.

Swimming deeper under, she saw something struggling in the ice. From time to time it made the noises they had heard, but she felt it tiring and sensed it was frightened.

What's wrong? she asked, approaching to see a body with a short thick tail and four furry paws, the back two webbed, struggling in the water. The body ended at the ice.

Caught. Crack opened up and dumped me in then ice trapped my head. Caught. 'Hah!'

I see. And your paws are all too far below the ice to be able to help you. We'll see what we can do.

Ronan joined her, and the two of them used their clawed flippers and noses to push the ice away from the other creature.

A chunk broke off in Ronan's claws, and abruptly the little animal dropped down into the water with a flourish of bubbles that, when they reached the surface, contained the word 'Hah!'

But what the creature was thinking was, *Seals? River seals? I never heard of river seals before. Did you free me so you could eat me?*

Of course not, Murel answered.

Why? Ronan asked. *Are you scrumptious?*

No, no, no, the creature answered, its little brain whirling with ideas and images. *Actually, my kind are poisonous to seals. That's why I asked, you see. You two seem like very good sorts for seals and I wouldn't want to make you sick if you tried to eat me, or even* kill *you.*

What kind are *your kind?* Murel asked. *Other than poisonous to seals, that is?*

The otter kind, the creature answered, swimming away from them a certain distance. It wanted to escape but its curiosity kept it paddling in the water just under what looked like another hole in the ice. *What kind of seals are you to swim in rivers? You're just pups, I can see that. Did you get lost from your mother?*

How do you know we're seals if you live in the river and seals never swim here? Murel asked.

Otters get around, the little fellow said. He had a

round head with a short black nose and very little neck. His eyes were large and shiny, and his mouth curved up into what looked like a smile regardless of what he seemed to be feeling or thinking. *I've been to the coast to visit my cousins. Well, once. But they told me about seals and how they eat – well, I saw some at a distance. But they all lived on the beach or the little islands right around. None have ever come into the river before.*

We are called Petaybean shepherd seals or selkies, Murel told him, remembering their father's earlier teachings. *We eat fish when we're in the water, but no other creatures. Shepherd seals* protect *other creatures and help maintain the harmony of the water life on our world.*

Thank you very much, I'm sure, the otter replied. *I'm feeling extremely harmonious, now that I think of it, and very glad not to have my head stuck in the ice anymore. So if you're sure you will not try to eat me – and make your good selves very ill if not dead, of course – I'll just be on my way now.*

The little creature was afraid of them, they could see that, but he was also uncontrollably inquisitive. *Unless, of course, you'd like to play?*

We should be getting back to our vil— to our mother, Murel said.

But we could play for a little while, I guess, Ronan answered, and in an aside to his twin said, *It's only polite not to just run away. Besides, he looks like the sort of chap who could get himself right back into trouble if we don't keep an eye on him.*

You should know all about that, Murel said, as if she were the oldest and didn't get into plenty of trouble herself.

All right then, the otter said. *Hide-and-seek? You two be it and I'll go hide.*

Wait a minute, Murel said before he darted off. *There's only one it. You and I can go hide and Ronan can be it.*

Why don't I go hide with the otter and you be it? Ronan argued.

Don't be such a baby, she told him. *It's just till you find one of us. Then we'll switch. Now close your eyes and count to ten.*

The otter had been about to zip away again, but now, once more, curiosity held him. *What's count?* he wanted to know.

It's how to measure things, she told him. *Like how many of them there are.*

Oh, like how many otters there are in my den? There are many, you know. What count is many?

I don't know. Ten? Forty-seven? A hundred?

What's the most many?

A hundred?

That's it then, that's how many otters are here, all with big sharp teeth to defend themselves against the bad *otter-eating seals. A hundred otters in my family.*

That's a very large family, Murel told him. *Caribou have families that large, but I didn't know otters did.*

My parents were very much in love, he told her. *Besides, we need large families with very big sharp teeth to fend off the bad otter-eating seals.*

I thought you lived in this river and we were the only seals you'd ever seen in a river? she asked.

He swam a couple of strokes and pulled himself up through a hole in the ice, onto more ice.

Look, she said. *We really really don't eat otters, even if they weren't poisonous and if there weren't a hundred with big sharp teeth. If we're going to play together, that makes us friends. Friends don't eat friends.*

Ninety-nine, a hundred! Ready or not, here I come! Ronan called.

'Hah!' the otter said from somewhere she couldn't see. *The other seal knows how many are in my family. He said it.*

No, that's just part of how we play the game. The hole in the ice wasn't quite large enough for a full-grown seal but Murel could just pull herself up through it with only a tiny clawed modification around the edges. She found herself in a low tunnel – good height for an otter and not bad for a seal if she slid on her stomach and just used her flippers to propel her slide forward.

The otter slipped and slid ahead of her, weaving in and out of tunnels as she followed behind. He didn't seem to be hiding exactly, though, so she did. One of the otter's tunnels led to a den dug deep into the thick river ice lining the bank. None of the hundred otters with the big sharp teeth seemed to be using the den, so she hid there waiting for Ronan.

If he found the otter first and the otter got to be it and came looking for them, maybe it would set the little guy's mind at ease about their intentions.

Instead, Ronan came sliding right up to her. 'You're it!' he cried aloud.

How?

'Read your mind, silly. Didn't see our friend anywhere.'

Otter otter in free! The otter's sending was from way up the river.

You have kind of an unfair advantage in this game, Murel said. *You know where you are and we don't.*

Okay. Let's go sliding then. I've gathered my family. They have agreed not to use their big sharp teeth on you unless you try something funny.

Are you sure? Murel asked, joking. *We know you now, but are your relatives maybe those seal-eating otters?*

Of course not. Come on! It'll be fun! We can play over the waterfall!

Sounds kinda dangerous.

Not now. It's a seasonal game.

It took Murel and Ronan a long time to find their way back out of the maze of otter tunnels to the hole under the ice.

Then they had to swim back upstream to where the ice was thinner and open another hole so they could surface again without tearing up the otter's home.

They popped their heads out of the water. As long as the rest of their bodies stayed submerged and their heads were wet, they could stay seals.

If we get out now to go play with the otters, we won't be seals anymore, Ronan said.

Oh, bother. Then he'll think we're otter-eating people and we'll have to go all through it again or else those hundred relatives he's trying to scare us with will sink their big sharp teeth into us.

Yeah. As if. But I really want to play with them and I don't want to scare them.

I think we ought to go home now anyway. Let's just send

a goodbye to our little buddy and say we were called away by our own family.

Yeah, but, Murel, we needed a swimming buddy and he could be it. If he went swimming with us, we could go all the time maybe.

True. I guess if he agreed to do that he'd find out about us being people part of the time anyway. Let's see what he says. Oh, Otter!

Come, Murel! Come slide with us. You can slide waaaaay down! It's long and steep but when you get to the bottom you just keep going and going until you slide halfway out to the coast where my cousins live.

We want to come and play, Otter, but we need to talk to you by yourself first. Please. It's a secret.

6

A secret? Otters love *secrets! Hey, everybody, I'll be right back. My new friends the seals I was telling you about want to tell me a secret! Maybe they know a secret place where the fish are especially nice.*

They had to wait a long time because he had already taken his first slide and had to climb back up the hill again. When he finally reached them, he dove into the hole they had made.

What is it? What's the secret?

First we want to tell you why you should know about this, Murel said.

Our parents want us to have a friend to swim with, Ronan continued. *Someone who knows the waters and won't get lost and could go for help if something went wrong.*

I can do that. Nobody knows the water like an otter. Your parents don't eat otters either, do they?

No. In fact, our mother isn't like us at all. Our father is like us, but you'd only know it if you saw him in the water. See, Otter, it's kind of hard to explain but our mother is human and our father is, like us, a seal only when he's in the water. On the land he's a human and, uh, so are we.

'Hah!' the otter said. *That's interesting. Show me.*

You won't be scared? Murel asked. *We don't want to scare you. We really want to be your friends.*

Otters don't scare that easy, he said, chittering a bit nervously. *Some of my coastal cousins can turn into people too if they want to. They can even get human beings who aren't like them to turn into otters if they want. Oh, I shouldn't have told you about that. It's a secret too. No, not a secret. It was a lie. I was lying so you wouldn't think otters don't know about turning into humans and—*

It's okay, Murel said. *Just so you're not scared. Come on, Ronan.*

They both jumped out of the water, slid to the bank, and shook themselves off.

'Hah!' the otter said and 'Hah!' again. He pushed himself out of the water and slid over to inspect them and said 'Hah!' several more times as he circled their legs, which were getting goose bumps. *I don't know why you want to be human. You are all pale and too thin to be warm. You should jump back in and be seals again before you freeze. Being seals isn't as good as being otters, but it's much more practical on the river than being human.*

Good idea, Ronan said, running for the water hole.

Murel turned to show the otter the pack with her shiny suit in it. *If we were going to stay human, we'd put on these suits that are stored on our backs but we—*

'Hah! Hah!' other otters called loudly from down toward the waterfall slide.

'Hah!' their new friend answered. *Wolves!* he told the children. *Wolves have come. Otter-eating wolves. And our den is up here, uphill from where my family is.*

But your family has their big sharp teeth, right? Ronan asked.

Not as big and sharp as wolves', he said, chittering, chirping, and growling aloud in answer to the distress calls from below. *The wolves will eat them all!*

Is there a hole in the ice near the falls? Ronan asked as he teetered on the edge of the ice hole.

Yes, near our slide.

Let's go then! he said, diving in. Murel followed him, and the otter right after her.

Wolves probably eat seals too.

Yes, but we can scare them away when we turn into people, Murel said. But she didn't think that through. She just knew that wolves never bothered her father or her aunt Sinead while they were in the woods. Most sled dogs were part wolf anyway, and she wasn't afraid of them.

It didn't occur to her that nothing had threatened Ronan and her because since they were babies they had been escorted everywhere by a snow leopard and a very large track cat.

A long long dive into the ice cave running beneath the otter tunnels and then, at last, open water. First Ronan surfaced, then the otter, then Murel.

There. There's the slide. Right there. Slide down. Be quick.

Below, the wolves were howling while the otters chittered, chirruped, and hahed as they tried to scramble away. Then one screamed.

Without shaking himself dry, Ronan slid down the long frozen cataract in seal form, Murel and the otter close behind him.

At the bottom he saw a wolf with an otter in its mouth. The little beast was still alive and snapping its teeth for all it was worth.

The wolves lined the riverbank and blocked the ice downstream. The cataract prevented the otters from climbing back up.

Before she shook herself off, Murel dug a hole in the ice with her claws and told the otter, *Get the others into the water, quickly.*

But that's my mother!

We'll try to save her.

Ronan shook himself dry and instantly was a naked boy. No time to put on the silver suit. *Get your teeth out of that otter right this minute*, he snapped at the wolf, trying to look as menacing as he could, which wasn't very.

Mine, the wolf snarled back.

Look at that, he's already defurred! another pack member, this one about a year-old pup, said. *Can I have him, sire? Can I?*

I don't know, son, the alpha male growled uncertainly. *There's something fishy about those two big ones. They were seals just a minute ago. Now they look like men. Men have firesticks, and besides, you never know what they've been into. They might be bad for you.*

Just let the otter go and be on your way and nobody gets hurt, Ronan told the wolves. *Besides, wolves don't normally eat otters. And we have it on good authority that these ones are poisonous.*

She doesn't smell *poisonous*, the wolf holding the otter argued, slitting her eyes suspiciously.

Neither does he, the young wolf said, slinking closer to

Ronan with hindquarters tensed to spring. *He smells delicious.*

By then the last of the otters had popped into Murel's hole and she had changed. While the wolves circled, she put on her silver suit and looked around for a weapon. Ronan's skin was covered with goose bumps. With her entire body protected by the suit, she was better able to defend herself than he.

The female wolf shook the furious snapping otter mother trying to break her neck. Without thinking, Murel took a long slide forward, bowling into the wolf, and smacked her hard on the muzzle with the side of her mitten, making her drop the otter.

Run! she told the smaller creature, but there was no need. The otter hit the water before Murel had formed the thought.

Now there was a new problem. A circle of hungry wolves tightened around Murel and Ronan, so close the twins could smell their breath, which was doggy and rotten at the same time. The wolf who'd had the otter leapt to her feet and with both front feet stiff brought them down sharply in front of Murel, snarling, *Thief!*

Ronan had used the distraction to seal himself into his own silver suit.

Now what is he, sire? The yearling who'd asked permission to hunt Ronan sounded bewildered. *A fish? These creatures can't make up their minds what they are. But they still smell like prey to me.*

And so they are, son, and so they are. Those flimsy shiny hides won't protect them if we all jump them at once. Ready . . . The female wolf waggled her hindquarters, poised to spring. Murel lost her nerve and backed into her twin, who hugged her, and they clung together.

Set . . . the wolf's mate said.

Murel squeezed her eyes tight and hoped she wouldn't be more than one bite to them so it wouldn't hurt so much. There were no weapons. No fire.

Ronan buried his face in her shoulder, and she did likewise with her twin.

Attack! This order was followed by yipping, snarling, snapping, and growling, but no biting.

The twins were braced, ready to be knocked down by the wolves, but nothing touched them. Instead, they heard familiar voices using feline profanity never before uttered in their presence.

Murel opened one eye in time to see Coaxtl pounce on yet another wolf and ride it like a horse while Nanook sat on her hindquarters, swatting wolf bodies right and left.

The wolves were already on the run when the first shot rang out.

'Go on, you mangy critters, get outta here! Those kids are too fraggin' spoiled rotten for you to eat anyway.' Their aunt Sinead's voice sounded so good to them, she might have been promising presents instead of punishment by the time she braked her sled and ran past her spitting track cats to scoop up the children.

She bundled them into the sled and told them, as if talking to one of her team, 'Stay.'

They tried to tell her about the otters, but she didn't pay any attention to them. Her mouth was compressed in a thin line. The only sounds for several hours were the shushing of the runners and the patter of paws against the snow, the occasional dog stopping to relieve itself, and Aunt Sinead's barked commands. Not even Nanook or Coaxtl spoke. Ronan and Murel were too miserable to communicate with each other. After what seemed like a week but must have been sometime during the night, though it was hard to tell in the winter, the lead dog stopped in front of their house. Sinead stamped on the brake to set it, and ripped off her mittens to release the bindings holding the twins on the sled and under the furs. Her hands were shaking, which was funny since next to their mother, Aunt Sinead was the bravest lady they knew. Silently, she pointed to the door.

When they left the sled, Coaxtl and Nanook stalked them all the way there.

7

Only Mum was there, and to the twins' relief, she did not seem upset.

'Where's Da?' Ronan asked innocently.

'Still out hunting for you. I imagine he's on his way home now, though.' Mum's voice was smooth and calm, conversational, her face unreadable. But then, her thoughts had never been easily readable to the twins. 'Suppose before he gets here you explain to me without benefit of telepathy where you've been and what you were doing that required you to do it so far from home for so long and without the company of Coaxtl and Nanook.'

'Well . . . we— There were these otters, weren't there?' Ronan began.

'No, first off, Johnny brought us these suits from Marmie, for our birthday, see—'

'Your birthdays are not until tomorrow,' Mum said, lifting one of her raven wing eyebrows. 'I should remember. I was definitely there.'

'Yeah, well, but we figured it was close enough and we'd be busy on the day and we wanted to try the suits out, that was all,' Murel said, feeling it was best to start at the beginning. 'Co' and 'Nook weren't around, but we just got excited and wanted to see what the suits were like so we decided to swim for a ways and put them on. They're brilliant, Mum. They kept us as warm and dry as a parka, snow pants, boots, mittens, and a hood with a good ruff, and they're no heavier than long johns.'

Their mother sat with her arms crossed under her breasts, and gave a slight nod that they should continue.

'Well, we were just getting ready to come home when we heard this poor little otter crying for help from inside the river. Of course we had to help him. Petaybee would want us to, right?'

Their mother's expression did not change.

'He had his head caught so we got him loose,' Ronan said. 'Then he wanted to play. Well, you know, we were thinking, here's the new swimming buddy we could have to show us around, like you said we could. So we thought we should get to know him better, didn't we? So we thought just a little longer would be okay. Only the hide-and-seek took a long time in all those tunnels the otters dug, and then he wanted us to slide down the waterfall with his family.'

'But before we started down, the wolves came and grabbed his mummy. The otter's, I mean. It was terrible, Mum, the poor little thing chittering and hahing – both our otter friend and his mummy, I mean. We slid down there and there was this big circle of wolves all around them. Ronan was ever so brave.'

'I was, rather. I stood there and tried to reason with

the wolves while sis dug the otters a bolt hole with her flippers and put on her suit. Then she attacked the wolf with the otter in her mouth while I got on my suit.'

'And that held them off until Co' and 'Nook could wade in and scare off the rest of them,' Murel concluded. 'Auntie Sinead fired a shot over their heads too, and that convinced them to look elsewhere for prey.' Mum still wasn't saying anything, just looking at them. Murel decided to press her luck a little. 'So you see, Mum, we were doing a good thing.'

'You visited otters and then reasoned with wolves before you attacked them, is that about right?' Mum asked again in that calm voice that wasn't just cool – it was downright cold. This must have been how she sounded when she was an officer for the Company Corps.

They looked at each other, trying to think if they'd left anything out, decided they hadn't, shrugged and faced her again. 'Well, yeah.'

Ronan added, 'It will make a brilliant latchkay song, Mum. We could do harmony.'

'Oh yes, I can see that,' their mother nodded reasonably. 'All about how you almost got eaten one day short of your eighth birthday. Perhaps we could have some wolves howling to accompany the drums? You'd best be quick about writing it, then. Your father and I have discussed this with Clodagh and the village elders and there will be a special secret latchkay held tomorrow in the Night Chant grotto. You are the guests of honor.' Her voice was grim now, and tight, as if there were much more she wished to say but would not or could not.

Murel put out a hand, tentatively touching her mother's. 'Mum, it's fine. We're fine. We're very sorry we worried you and Da and Auntie and the cats, but we waited and waited and Da never had the time, and really, the suits are all we need to be off by ourselves—'

'Unless there are wolves,' her mother said, grasping her hand and squeezing her fingers so tightly it hurt. 'Or bears, or even people who don't know we never hunt seals here. I told you already, you are too young to even imagine the dangers in which your actions placed yourselves, us, the village, and even Petaybee. I love you. Your father loves you. Everybody who knows you loves you, and if they don't know you very well, they love you even better. But, my little ones, despite your lineage from your father, despite your shape-shifting and your ability to talk with all of Petaybee's creatures, you are my children, not wild animals. And you must learn that side of your nature too. I want you to think about that and know that whatever happens, happens for your good. Now off to bed with you. Your father will look in on you when he comes in.'

Murel thought that in her sleep she felt her father's kiss on her forehead and a sudden drop of water, warm as it fell into her hair.

Ronan dreamed of wolves and did not realize that the touch brushing his face as lightly as a warm breeze was his father's kiss until it was gone. Then, half awake, he became aware of a strange sound from the other room. It was his mother, so stony-faced earlier in the night, sobbing as if her heart were broken.

* * *

Most of the day was suspiciously normal – even better than normal. Father made them a delicious breakfast of blueberry pancakes made with berries stored from the previous summer, caribou sausage, and rose hip tea. Mother was not much of a cook, but after they cleaned up the dishes, she gave them identical presents.

Murel examined the outside of the little hard-bound journal when her mother handed it to her. A diary? It was not very special-looking. But when she opened it, she saw that it was already filled with her mother's writing, including some odd charts and symbols.

'What's this, Mum?' Ronan asked.

'I thought you were old enough for it now. It's everything I know about my side of the family, including the stories about the origin of your middle names and what they were called in my mother's language.' She turned to one of the charts. 'This is a family tree – two branches, my mother's and my father's. My mother's people consider all of the children and all of the houses and land to belong to the women. Also, everybody belonged to one clan or the other. In the old days, people didn't like to give their proper names because your own personal name is like your arm or your hair or anything else of your person that an enemy could grab onto and hold you with. So they introduced themselves to each other by giving their lineage – who their mother's clan was and who their father's clan was. The way they put it, you were born "to" your mother's people, as you were most directly tied to your mother. You were born "for" your father's people because the mother brought her children into the world for the father. Since my father was of Irish descent, I don't have a clan on his side – no "born for" clan, only a "born to" clan, that of my mother's relations, the Far Walking Diné. So this is the same clan you have. If you ever meet someone else who is of my mother's people and they know that your mother is half Diné – or Navajo, as our people were known to others – they may ask you about your clans and tell you theirs. What would you tell them?'

'That our mother was born to the Far Walking Diné and born for our Irish grandpa?' Murel answered.

'This is pretty cool!' Ronan said, thumbing through the book before laying it back on the table.

Murel was puzzled. 'Why did you write this stuff all down, Mum? We can't even read some of the words yet. I like it when you tell us stories about when you were a little girl and your family and everything. If we meet someone from your mother's people, we would just bring them home to meet you.'

Mother's smile faded, and Murel said, 'But it's a really great gift. I didn't mean that. It was really nice of you to do this. I just don't understand why is all.'

Mother nodded once. 'Surely you remember what day it is, pet? It's your birthday, yours and Ronan's. Today you are eight years old. Eight is two times four, which is the number of the four directions, the four elements, and a very special number to my mother's people. It is time for you to know these things.'

Their journals lay forgotten at home, however, when Da proposed the most wonderful part of the day. He wanted to go swim with them and have them show him where they'd met the otters and seen the wolves.

Wow, we picked a good time to get born, Ronan told his

sister. *I thought they'd punish us for going too far yesterday, and instead, I guess they have decided we're old enough to do what we want to because all of a sudden we're getting everything we've been wanting.*

Yeah, funny, isn't it? And a special latchkay tonight too. Even on our birthday, you'd think they'd make us take naps instead of Da going swimming with us.

The trip downriver to the otter den was much faster now. Not only did they know where they were going, they could predict, more or less, where the ice widened and narrowed, and that helped. Also, during the wide-open stretches, Da raced with them or used the straps holding their suits on their backs to tow them, while his sleek and powerful body carried them so fast, the water streamed through their teeth and left a bubbly wake behind them.

They showed their father the maze of tunnels the otter had led them through the day before, but it was all messed up. The ceiling was caved in the length of the central tunnel and the whole area smelled funny. Not like otters.

Ronan sent out a mental call anyway. *Hey, Otter. It's us, the seals who save otters from otter-eating wolves. We brought our father to meet you. He doesn't eat otters either.*

But there was no answer. Da swam around back and forth, sliding up onto the ice where he could and looking at the entire complex. He sniffed and turned his head to scan the trees on the horizon. But he was also looking at the snow, which was trampled with what looked like human footprints.

Da slid out of the maze back into the water.

Murel ventured a guess. She was pretty sure she was

wrong, but maybe it would get Da to tell them what he thought. *The wolves know where they were living,* she said. *So I think they moved.*

These wolves each had two legs and wore military-issue snow boots, Da said. *See there?* He turned his head toward a glint in the trees.

What's that? she asked.

Surveillance equipment of some kind. Did you kids change on the way here at all?

Yes, but only a couple of times, and not for very long.

They know about you, Da said seriously. *Someone told them the circumstances of your birth, and they've been watching ever since, off and on. That's why we've always had the cats go with you. Come on, let's get out of here.*

What did they do to the otters? Ronan asked.

I don't know. Maybe nothing. Maybe they just scared them off when they came tramping around looking for you two. But we need to go now. If they're still watching this spot, they'll be here with dope darts in a moment. Dive below the ice and swim as long as you can. We'll make new breathing holes on the way upriver too. Don't want them tracking us with the old ones.

But before they made their first breathing hole, they heard a familiar mind-voice.

Hah! Ronan, Murel! Hah! It's me, the otter who is friend to brave wolf-scaring river seals who are sometimes human. Wait! Wait! I have a thing to tell you. Hah!

Murel somersaulted in the water and swam back to meet the otter.

We brought our da to meet you, Otter, but your lovely tunnels are all messed up. What happened to them? Where are the hundred otters with the big sharp teeth?

Gone, all gone, Murel who attacks wolves. When the sled woman took you away, we hurried to our dens in case the wolves decided to return. But then came men with big feet and big nets and guns that shot sharp things bringing sleep. Hah! I cried out to warn the others and dove deep but other otters did not. My mother was taken and my siblings and cousins and grandparents and aunts and uncles on both sides of the family. At first they bit and scratched, but the men shot them with sharp things and they no longer moved. The men took them, all of my family. Ruined our house and took my family.

All one hundred otters? Murel asked.

All the otters except me. Otters need families, and mine is all gone now. I tried to follow, but the men had those noise-sleds that are fast as an avalanche. Otters are very fast, but I could not catch them.

Da? Ronan turned to his father. *You and Mum are the governors. Make those men bring the otters back, huh?*

I can try, son, but not while you two are with me. Who do you think they really wanted to catch anyway? Probably as soon as they find out that the otters remain otters all the time, they'll let them go. They do, don't they?

What?

Remain otters all the time?

Otter said, '*Oh yes, Father River Seal, my family remain otters at all times. They are always otters. There have been stories about my cousins on the coast, but river otters are different. We are always otters.*

I'll do what I can, Otter. But those men are not acting under my authority. They had no legal right to take your family. I will have to come back later with more men and if possible make them let your family go.

I will go with you then and come back to show you where the men went, Otter told them.

There's no need, Da said. *We'll find you again tomorrow.*

Maybe you will and maybe not, Otter said. *But meanwhile I am alone and have no one to play with. Otters are not supposed to be alone. Otters need to be with others, even if the others are river seals.*

You might not like our part of the river, Da said. He seemed to want to get rid of the otter.

Oh, let him come, Da. He's our friend. We'll take care of him, Murel said.

He can sleep with me, Ronan said. *I'll make a den for him under my covers.*

He's not a pet, Da said. *Your mother—*

Mother will love him, and we know he's not a pet. He's our friend. We have to help him.

I'll help him but he isn't going all the way home with us. He can stay in the river, as he said, and return with my party to find the poachers. Then he'll be with his own family again.

Ronan started to protest. Da was being uncommonly firm and unyielding, and there was something very grim and sad in his thoughts, but it skittered away before Ronan could read it.

That will be good, Murel and Ronan. You can come and play again and I can be your swimming guide, as you asked. And all of my family will guide you too if you bring them back. We will go see my cousins on the coast and they will show you the sea.

Oh, Da, can *we*? the twins asked, but Da swam hard upstream and did not answer.

Otter raced the twins back up the river, and even though they were swimming against the current, they got home only a little after suppertime. Since they'd all snacked on fish throughout the day, none of them were hungry. Outside of town, Da climbed out of the water, shook himself dry, and put on the human clothes he'd hidden in a tree by the riverbank, while Ronan and Murel put on their shiny suits from Marmie. Otter dove down to inspect the riverbank.

Thin ice and many holes in the bank, he reported when he popped his head up again. *Good holes for otter dens. Not as good as the home ones, but good enough for now.*

Good night, Otter, Murel and Ronan said. They turned and waved, and Otter looked at them with large eyes that once more seemed a bit sad. Then he leapt in the air, did a somersault, and dove underwater again.

8

One last surprise before the latchkay was that Marmie herself had arrived while they were gone. The tall, elegant woman with the curling dark hair and the impish smile greeted them with hugs.

'The suits fit you beautifully! I was just sure they'd be far too big,' she said.

'They work a treat too,' Ronan told her. 'We didn't get a bit cold after we put them on.'

'That was the general idea,' she said, laughing.

'I think maybe even wolves can't bite through them,' Murel told her, knowing that someone as important as Marmie would like to have useful information about her gift.

'Now, how did you get a chance to learn that, I shudder to wonder?' Marmie asked.

'We were saving otters,' Murel said. 'But then after we left they were otter-napped by some men. Da's going to make the men bring the otters back, though, probably tomorrow.'

'Otter-napping? My goodness, I have *missed* Petaybee. I forgot how exciting it can be here. Well, we don't have any otter-nappings where I live but I bet you'd find it exciting too.'

'Do you really live on a space station, Marmie?' Murel asked.

'Yes, a very nice space station. You'd like it. I just had a lovely pool installed at my home. It runs all through and around my house, and there's a big deep part for diving. I had it all landscaped so it looks like a natural stream flowing through the woods.'

'That sounds nice,' Murel said politely. But she thought it was sort of odd to live on a space station and try to make it look like the woods. Why not just live in the real woods?

Ronan was thinking the same thing. 'We can take you to the woods while you're here, Marmie, anytime you want.'

She gave him a hug. 'You are doing just that. I'm going to the latchkay with you.'

'Ronan, Murel, come get dressed,' their mother called. 'I've things for you to carry.'

I wish we could just swim to the springs and go into the latchkay in seal form, Murel said. *We could bring the otter. He's probably lonely out there in the river all by himself without the hundred relatives.*

He might come anyway, if he sees us going. Otters are pretty curious, I think.

They dressed in the furs and fancy bead-embroidered parkas made for them by Aisling, Auntie Sinead's partner, who was the finest sewer in the entire village. The embroidery on both parkas had wiggly blue lines for water and fish of all colors – even purple ones and green ones – swimming around the cuffs, hem, front closure, and ruff of the hood. The matching mittens had fishes swimming in a circle around the wrists.

Mother's parka was blue-green with little pairs of flowers embroidered for trim. She said the pairs stood for the twins. It was a pretty parka, but that didn't mean Ronan thought he looked like a flower.

Most latchkays were held in the longhouse in the center of the village, and that was usually where the food was served, most of the speeches were made, and the dancing took place. Tonight everybody carried food and gifts with them to the hot springs cave. Usually there was a procession to the cave, but tonight everyone just came out of their houses and started walking.

I wonder why they're doing it this way? Murel said as they walked in the dark, slightly ahead of their parents. Their night vision was very good, and if it hadn't been, the cats walked right in front of them. Besides, they'd been to the latchkay cave many times and knew the path so well they could walk it backward, which Ronan decided to try.

The cats caught his thought and stopped to watch. He stepped back onto Nanook's tail. 'Nook hissed and spat, something she never did around the twins, and Ronan was so startled he slipped and fell, dropping the case he'd been carrying.

Oh boy, Mum will be mad, Murel said, and stooped to help him pick it up. The latch had been jarred open by being dropped, and she opened the lid to put back whatever was in there.

Why did she give you this case with all your stuff to carry? Murel asked.

Don't know. What's in yours?

'Hurry, children. We still have quite a ways to go.' The drums began pounding, telling them that other people had already reached the cave.

'Mum, why is Ronan carrying his clothes and schoolbooks?' Murel asked.

Mum shook her head impatiently and pointed ahead. Murel was pretty sure that whatever the answer was, they weren't going to like it.

The path to the cave was well trod by the time they slipped behind the steaming falls and found seats on the ledge.

The space behind the waterfall was not a cave exactly, because it didn't go back very far. It was more of a room up above the hot springs, and it was the closest place to Kilcoole where people could go to talk to the planet.

Usually when everyone was packed in it felt cozy and snug, with the smell of the smoked salmon and soup floating around the people who had feasted at the latchkay mingling with the sulfury smell of the hot springs. The warmth of everyone's body heated the grotto so that after a while they removed their furs.

Even in the winter when everything was iced over there was a strong sense of grasses and brambles, berries, and flowering weeds pushing up through the frigid soil, just waiting for the ice to break. Like the ghost of last summer, Murel thought, or the summers before that.

But tonight for the first time ever the twins felt restless and ill at ease in the grotto. The stalactites protruding from the ceiling seemed in danger of falling and stabbing someone, and the stone seat under their bottoms was very hard and very chilly.

Something bad is going to happen, Ronan said. *And it's going to happen to us.*

I feel that way too but how could it with Mum and Da here – and Clodagh, Johnny, and Marmie, besides? They'll probably give out to us for running off from everyone yesterday – well, swimming off, that's all. I wonder if Da was always getting in trouble like this when he was our age?

Young Desi Sivatkaluk was the lead drummer tonight. Desi was the same age as Aoifa, but his father, Old Desi, had been the lead drummer at the last latchkay. Old Desi and his entire team fell through the ice and drowned while out on a hunting trip only a few weeks before, so now his son played his drum. He must have been practicing a lot because he never missed a beat.

Nanook and Coaxtl stood guard at the edge of the spring, just beyond the watery veil concealing the grotto. Someone uncovered a platter piled high with strips of salty-sweet, pink smoked salmon and started passing it around. When the plate got to Da, he got up and tossed some of the strips to the cats.

When everyone had eaten, Clodagh stood and said, 'We have a troubling thing to tell our world tonight. Who will sing the first song?'

Auntie Sinead stood up. She had good songs and usually sang them Irish-style, to old tunes that went with lots of other words. She was the best dog driver, hunter, fisher, and trapper in Kilcoole, and her songs were full of action and adventure. This one she started by saying, 'The tune is "Wild Colonial Boy" and I call it' – she smiled at Ronan and Murel for the first time since their rescue— '"The Wild Shongili Twins." I've had only a day to find the words, and some of this I heard from others, but for those of you who did not know of my niece and nephew's recent adventure, I made this song.'

She sang, her voice clear and strong:

'When I was young I ran my traps. My brother Sean he swam
As a selkie he could swim much more than human men
Now he has two children and as selkies they too swim
But now Sean's moored to desk work. No more seal swimming for him.

Without their Da to roam with them, these children swam away
To roam the fields of river ice with otters they did play
But wolves find otters tasty and the children almost died
Still our Murel she digs a hole, "Dive, otters, now!" she cried.

My dogs and I we heard them cry, the big cats made all speed
The children now were crying, the wolves poised to do the deed
That would have broken my poor heart, Petaybee's heart as well
And Sean and his brave wife would find a private bit of hell.

The cats they leapt, and me I swept the children to
my sled
But had we not been looking, our twins would now
be dead.
So I ask you, my neighbors, what will happen
when again
The selkie twins go swimming with no one to
shepherd them?'

'It was only the once,' Ronan said when she'd finished and everyone was making appreciative noises. 'We were trying out the warm suits Marmie sent us.'

'We didn't mean to be gone so long,' Murel said, looking into the faces of her neighbors, who were regarding them as if they were the tracks of some strange animals they had never seen before.

Sing them my song, Otter said from somewhere nearby.

Otters make songs? the twins asked together.

Of course otters make songs. Otters like fun, and music is fun. The waters are music to otters, and otters sing songs to its melody. But I cannot speak to the other two-leggeds and make myself understood. I will sing to you and you sing to them.

Okay, fine. Sing.

Announce us first! the otter said.

Ronan told the other people, 'Our otter friend has a song to share he wants to sing through us.'

'You wouldn't be pullin' our legs now, would you, young Shongili?' Kaiaitok Carnahan asked. Kaiaitok had the short stocky build and tilted eyes of his Inuit ancestors, but his sparse beard and mustache were bright red and his eyes green. His hair was red too, but nobody saw it anymore since he always wore a stocking cap in winter, a billed cap in summer. He had taken over the com shed after Uncle Adak retired. Adak said that what with all the new machines Petaybee had now, communications was getting way too complicated for his liking. Kaiaitok had gone offplanet to train when he was only a bit older than the twins were now.

If you were going to leave Petaybee, you had to do it when you were a kid. As you got older, your body was so adapted to Petaybee's extreme temperatures and other special properties that you could die if you were offplanet very long. Kaiaitok had left plenty young enough to survive, but he had returned much changed, folk said. He thought the rest of them backward when he first came home, and himself full of learning. All of his learning still didn't keep the machinery and electronic gizmos working when it was minus 150 degrees Fahrenheit. He had to take a snocle or a sled to give people their messages, just like Adak had done before him, only now there were more messages and people on the offworld end expected faster results. Kaiaitok got over himself pretty fast after the first couple of winters and a few latchkays. But however much he communicated with humans, he was not on social terms with four-legged, winged, or finned creatures. Ronan was hazy on whether Kaiaitok had communed with animals before he left the planet. His skepticism about Otter's song didn't seem to trouble the rest of the villagers.

Da relieved any doubts they might have had by saying, 'Good. I'm glad the otter could compose on such short notice. I've not been able to do as much myself. Go on, you kids.'

Otter's song did not rhyme like an Irish song and did not go with a drumbeat like the songs in the more traditional Inuit style. It had to be danced as well as sung. So the twins acted out their meeting with the otters, and the slide and the wolves and then the coming of the men and the taking of the otters. The words were sung very fast and the dance had to be done fluidly to go with the way the otter was singing it. There were some otter concepts that were difficult to put into human words, and these the twins tried to act out or skip over.

When they finished, Ronan said, 'The otter who made this song is staying in the river near the village now, so he can guide us to the men who took his family. So nobody bother him, okay? He's got enough on his mind right now.'

Da, Auntie Sinead, Mum, and Clodagh all exchanged looks. The twins couldn't read them, and wondered what it was all about. But they could tell the adults were impressed.

'Anyone else got any songs?' Clodagh asked. When no one spoke, she rose and walked deeper into the cavern. The rest of the village followed her until they reached the central communion room. Behind them, Ronan and Murel slapped hands and practically skipped forward.

We really showed them. We are the first people ever to sing for otters. Or any other four-legged, I'll bet, Ronan said.

Murel could hardly disagree. Life was looking up.

Ever since the suits arrived, it had been much more interesting around here. And tomorrow there would be another adventure with Da when he went to get back the otter's family.

Nobody seemed to be mad at them after all, or inclined to scold, and it was past the time when they would.

The singing and talking were over. Now Petaybee would respond. Ronan and Murel always liked this part. It was a little like dreaming, except that the dream wasn't yours exactly, it was Petaybee's. It was also a bit like the way it felt when they became seals and seemed to be part of the water.

But when they got to the entrance of the larger cavern, they were stopped.

As if giant hands were pushing them back from the communion cave, they could not go forward. Murel put a foot out and brought it back right away.

Mum and Da sat down beside Clodagh without noticing the twins weren't with them until Da looked up and called softly to them, 'Aren't you coming, kids?'

'Can't,' Murel said. 'Something's wrong.'

Ronan had big tears in his eyes already. 'It's like there's a big invisible door, Da.'

Clodagh was the one who answered. 'There is a purpose in this that you will learn soon. Go to the outer cave but don't go into the water. We will speak again when the planet has spoken.'

Bewildered, the twins retraced their steps.

It's not fair. We did good. Is it Petaybee that's mad at us and doesn't want to talk to us?

No, can't be. I mean, it can't be mad at us. We're not

offworlders. We're part of the planet just like the rocks are. It can't get mad at itself, can it? Can it?

They fell silent and sat in the outer cave looking longingly at the waterfall. They had never before realized how long the communions took, but it seemed like hours passed. Any moment they expected to hear the footsteps and the very low conversation that sometimes followed communions, but there was nothing.

They're sure taking their time, Ronan said. *I wish Clodagh hadn't said we're not to swim. I would like to go down to the water and talk to Otter a little more. I think we forgot to thank him for his song.*

We don't have to swim to do that. Remember, otters are not afraid of seals who turn into humans. Clodagh didn't say we couldn't go to the water's edge. Just that we shouldn't swim.

They started calling as they took the path out of the cave and down the hill, enveloped in the sulfury and spicy mist from the springs.

But although their new friend had seemed very near when he sang them his song, when he finally answered, it was from far away, with a muffled, *Sleeping. Otters need to sleep.*

Ronan sat down and felt through the snow for rocks to skip across the water, but found nothing. The longer they waited, the more worried and miserable Murel became. Something was really wrong. She knew it but she couldn't think what it was.

Hush, younglings, Nanook's voice, purring and kind, said, as she insinuated her soft furry self between them and lay down with her head cradled on her paws. *No harm will come to you while we're here. We may not be the best swimmers but we are your guardians.*

Sleep. One prefers you when you sleep, Coaxtl said, plopping down behind them to make a plush backrest.

These sometimes grumpy friends had been with the twins since they were babies. Their familiar presence was so comforting that the children fell asleep almost at once, Ronan leaning back against Coaxtl while Murel snuggled with Nanook, her arms around the cat's body and her hands buried in the dense fur.

They awoke to the murmur of voices and looked up from sleepy eyes to see the villagers appear from the mist. The murmurs were not the kind that normally followed a Night Chant. Clodagh's face, and their parents' faces were very grave indeed. Only Marmion seemed to be smiling.

'Slainté,' Ronan said in greeting, sitting up and rubbing his eyes.

Murel stood up and tucked her hands into Clodagh's and Marmie's. Her parents still looked grim.

'So, Clodagh, why couldn't we come into the communion cave this time? Is Petaybee mad at us?'

'I don't know, pet,' Clodagh told her. 'I don't think so. Perhaps it just wanted to talk to grownups tonight.'

'Oh.' Murel thought that over. 'But it's always let us come before. And it is our birthday.'

Over her head, Marmie exchanged glances with Mum and Da. '*I* have something I'd like to talk to you about, Murel, Ronan.'

Ronan arose, giving Coaxtl a pat as he did, and stretched. 'What, Marmie?'

'We've been discussing this for some time, your parents and I, and of course, this is only if you'd like to, but I was hoping now that you're old enough to go off-world, you might come and visit me for a while on my space station.'

'You mean *now*?' Ronan asked. His eyes were wide open. She had his full attention.

'Yes, well, since you've got your things with you already I don't see why not. I'm sure, as you know from your biology lessons, that the older you get, the harder it will be for you to leave Petaybee for any length of time. And I just had that lovely waterway built at home, so I was so hoping you'd come. I know some other children your age I think you'd enjoy very much, and we have rather a nice school on the station.'

'School!' Murel said. 'How long a visit are we talking about, Marmie?'

'Well—'

'The thing is, kids, it may be your only chance to see other places,' Mum said. 'And frankly, your Da and I would like you to get some exposure to human culture on a more sophisticated level than we can provide here.'

'Our schools are okay,' Murel said.

'Yes, but Marmie's are excellent.' Her mother squatted down so that her face was on a level with theirs. 'And one day we're going to need your help with managing things here. I don't know how aware of it you are, but your father has been keeping tabs on some midsea volcanoes. They're building up under the sea floor, preparing a new landmass, a warm island, islands, a continent. Lots of people from offworld will want to move here, and perhaps there'll be room for a great many of them. We may need – *Petaybee* may need

– your help sorting through them. You need to know something about the offworld universe to be able to cope.'

'Right,' Ronan said. That sounded good, but if Petaybee needed them to help with something, you'd think it would have let them into the communion cave one last time at least. Mum was just trying to make them feel better. He looked his father full in the face. 'This is really about keeping us away from the otter rustlers, isn't it?'

'Among other things, yes, but your mother's reasons are very great concerns as well.'

'But we're still going with you tomorrow to get the otters back, right?'

'Son, it's just too dangerous. I think I told you that I'm afraid it was really you those men were interested in when they took the otters. I don't want to give them any more chances to get any closer than they've been to you two already. By the time you're back from Marmie's, we'll have them sorted out and galaxies away, possibly in prison. But I promise you, we will get the otters back if at all possible, and I will send word to you when we do.'

Marmie wasn't really asking us, she was telling us, Murel told her twin.

It might be fun except I really wanted to stay here and get to know the otters better, her brother replied.

I don't think we're supposed to. If those men went after the otters because of us, then we just brought them trouble. Besides, Petaybee doesn't want us here anymore. That's why we couldn't get into the communion room. Not just because we're kids.

If Petaybee doesn't want you, it makes you feel worse than that! Ronan argued. *It drives the offworlders crazy and turns their hair white and stuff.*

But they're offworlders. And maybe it's not mad at us, it just wants us to do this now, like Mum and Da and Marmie and Clodagh said.

That's weird. Planets don't take sides, do they?

Petaybee does. I don't think we get to pick this time, Ronan.

'Okay,' Ronan said, 'we'll go. But as soon as those men are gone, you'll send for us, right? Right?'

Nobody answered, and then Da laid his hands on his son's shoulders and said, 'I can't promise anything right now, but we will send for you as soon as it's time for you to return. Meanwhile, you'll probably be having so much fun with Marmie, you'll be mad at us for making you come home.'

9

A few hours later, the twins watched Petaybee diminish into a blue and white ball and then just another distant dot in the cosmos.

This must be what it's like to swim in the sea, Murel said. Through the fantastic transparent hull of the view deck, they watched as the ship wove through a beaded curtain of star systems, suns with their planets, planets with their moons, all against the deepest blackness.

Yeah, the ship is kind of like a star seal. It's the only thing out here that moves wherever it wants to. Everything else is anchored to an orbit – well, except meteors, I guess. They're kind of wild.

Marmion stood behind them, a hand on each small shoulder. For the time being, the children seemed to have forgotten to be sad at what they saw as their banishment from Petaybee and abandonment by their parents.

Ronan turned suddenly and looked up into her face. 'Marmie, do meteors decide where they want to go, do you think, or are they just falling all the time?'

'I don't know that they have a plan exactly – I don't think every random bit of rock is as aware as Petaybee

– but they do seem to wander about randomly, getting bits knocked off them here and there.'

'But asteroids have orbits, right?' he asked. 'And belts. They have belts.'

'They travel in belts with lots of other asteroids.'

'So the belts are like flocks of asteroids or herds,' Murel said.

'Only in the sense that a belt is composed of many asteroids. They aren't animals.'

'I know that,' Murel said.

The trip was not a long one. Marmie's ship was very powerful and very fast. Meanwhile, when she wasn't on the com unit conducting business, she did her best to entertain them.

When they grew a little dizzy on the view deck, she took them to a large quiet room with a lot of cabinets and a big screen. 'This is the ship's library,' she told them. 'My crew and I pick from the main library on the space station the various media we wish to take on our travels. I pulled some things I thought you two might be interested in before I left.'

'Marmie?'

'Yes, Murel?'

'You sent our suits with Johnny and we were gone for a night, but the next day when we came home after swimming with Father, you were there. We've already been on this ship two nights and we aren't at your house yet. When did you leave?'

'About a week ago. I had business to conduct along the way. I think I understand what you're getting at. You think I came to take you away because you got into trouble, don't you?'

The twins exchanged knowing looks, then nodded.

'That's not correct. I have, as I said, been hoping you would come and visit me for some time. As we explained at the hot spring, if you are going to travel, now is the time you must do it. Later you will be so completely adapted to Petaybee that you won't be able to leave safely. Your parents have been worried since you were born that people such as the men who took your otter friend's family might try to kidnap you for study to see what makes you able to change into seals and back again. When your mother contacted me about the suits, I sent them on the next ship, but both she and I realized that the time was coming when your natural wish to explore your environment might lead you into harm.'

'You could have come with Johnny, couldn't you?'

'Captain Green's ship was conducting other business for me in other places along the way than what I needed to do myself. Besides, his is a transport vessel and mine is a luxury liner. Much nicer, don't you think?'

They shrugged. 'I guess so,' Ronan said. The ship had less people and was more spacious while not being much bigger, but he felt like they all sort of rattled around in it. 'Any word from Da about the otters?'

'No, but when there is, I'll let you know right away,' she promised. She showed them how to use the vid screen, earphones, and other apparatus. 'I have a bit more business to conduct and then I'll be back to tuck you in. Enjoy yourselves.'

* * *

Sean Shongili waved goodbye as his children marched sleepily onto Marmion's luxury spaceship, the *Piaf*. Yana turned away as he did and marched straight back to the snocle. He knew she didn't want him to see her crying – again – which was fine with him. She wouldn't see his tears either that way, which would help them both keep control of their emotions in the days to come. Sinead had brought the team up to collect Sean, and the red dogs were straining against their harnesses, ready to be off for a good run.

His sister didn't say anything as he climbed aboard her sled and she shouted at Dinah, the lead dog, to go. Sinead wasn't happy to see her niece and nephew vanish into space either, but she understood the necessity.

Back in Kilcoole they met with Liam Maloney, the borough sheriff. Sinead herself was now Game Warden and Environmental Control Officer. Two of her rangers and two of Liam's deputies brought their teams along as well. Dierdre Angalook, a student of Clodagh's who studied animal healing, rode a curly coat and brought saddlebags full of items for otter first aid.

'Are you all armed?' Sean asked.

'Yes, Guv,' Liam answered.

'Can't be too careful with otter rustlers, can we?' Sinead asked.

Sean nodded his head gravely in agreement. 'Okay, otter posse, I'll meet you by the shack.'

He had an ice fishing shack on the river he used for removing his clothing before dropping through the hole and changing into seal form. Marmion had provided him with a suit similar to the ones she'd given the children. She said she was glad to find something useful to give him for his birthday. Once he transformed, he swam over to the otter's den. *Are you ready, Otter? My friends are on their way.*

Yes, Father River Seal, but where are Murel and Ronan? Otters like brave children. Otters find them very reassuring.

They had to leave, Otter. They are indeed brave children and their mother and I are very proud of them, but they aren't always very wise. I believe the people who took your family did so because they were curious about Murel and Ronan. They must have seen them changing.

'Hah!' the otter said. *When we get my family back, will you send the men away and let Murel and Ronan return?*

As soon as possible, Otter, Sean said.

The dog teams pulled up alongside the bank near the ice fishing shack. Sean surfaced, but the otter stayed under the ice. 'The otter tunnels are just before the Chatanika Falls. We'll stop before we reach the tunnels. Keep as silent as possible and be alert for any signs of surveillance from the woods or elsewhere. We'll meet you there.'

He and the otter swam on, their noses and eyes barely above the water. They dived under the ice whenever possible. On the banks, the sleds shushed along beside and slightly behind them. Otters and seals were both very fast swimmers, while dogs had to stop to sniff things and take turns yellowing the snow and making their deposits.

Nanook and Coaxtl ranged along with the others, leaving a scallop of tracks along the river as they ran half circles around the dogsleds. Nanook ran along the side of the river where the mushers were, Coaxtl took the opposite side. Away they'd race to the surrounding woods, sniff a few rocks and bits of vegetation, and then return to the river. A half a klick before Sean and the otter reached the ruined tunnels, Nanook spoke to Sean.

There. They are back there. I smell them. I smell otters too. Frightened, angry otters. Now the men will smell like them.

Does the scent grow stronger or weaker the farther down-river we go? Sean asked.

Nanook sniffed for a moment longer, then replied, *Weaker.*

Can you pick up the trail at that point?

I can. I am standing on it now.

Otter, did you understand Nanook?

Cats do not speak as clearly in the mind as otters or river seals, but the cat's meaning was clear. Do we leave the river now?

I will, at least. You may stay here if you wish.

No, my family will feel better if I am near to reassure them. Also, other otters may speak to me when we are closer and I can speak to you.

Fair enough, Sean said. He dived, leapt, and landed on the ice, then slid across to the bank, where he shook off the water and donned Marmie's silver warm suit.

It felt almost too warm to Sean but he was glad of the cover and admired the way it kept out the wind that stirred the light dusting of new snow across the ice.

Something low and brown streaked past him. The otter. *Hah! Come, Father River Seal, I'll race you to the cat,* he called.

Nobody races anybody, Otter, Sean told him. *We must go quietly and carefully, stalk these men as if they are prey.*

Fish? the otter asked.

Very slippery fish.

Slippery fish who steal otters.

Keep trying to talk to the other otters. Let me know when you get a response, if they can tell us anything about where they're being held, what kind of condition they're in, how many men there are. How many? A hundred, Father River Seal. A hundred otter-stealing men all with big tight nets.

I can see this might be a problem, Sean said. Murel had told him about the otter and counting. *Can you get them to say, 'the man with the torn coat' or 'the man with the beard,' and tell us who each of them is that way? Then we'll have a better idea how many there actually are.*

Otters can do that. Otters have good eyes.

And try to stay back here near us, Otter. If you run ahead of us too far, the men might capture you too.

Otters can be very fast, but otters can also be sloooow, like men and dogs and cats.

Carrreful who you call slow, little beast. This cat can run down a caribou herd, Coaxtl grumbled.

The woods were still, as if holding their breath, when the rescue party, dog teams, and the curly coat slipped into the forest almost as silently as falling snowflakes.

The otter chirped and gibbered seemingly to himself, but Sean realized these were the outward manifestations of the little creature's attempts to link minds with his family members.

My mother! She is alive! the otter declared at last. *She did not want me to come because she feared I would be captured too, but at the same time she was thinking that, she was thinking, 'Get me out out out.' And she did not know until I told her that the father of river seals and his hundred friends with their sharp-toothed dogs and their longclawed cats are with me. She was afraid of you too until I told her that you are the father of Murel and Ronan River Seal, the friends who attack wolves who try to eat otters.*

I trust she was reassured by the news?

Oh, yes.

Did she give you any idea of how far away the men took her and the others?

Otter didn't answer for a moment, then said, *Not far. Otters had no time to bite through nets before they were put in dens with heavy bars on them.*

Sean considered. Apparently, while he could converse with the otter who was with him, he was not sufficiently attuned to the species to share long-distance inter-otter telepathic communications.

And how many men – can she say what each man there is like?

After another pause, the otter said, *There is man with wind like dead things, man with chin fur, man with wet nose, man with longer chin fur, man with lip fur but no chin fur, young female and old female.*

Is that all?

Mother says yes. Hah! Mother is growling. Man puts hands on her.

Can't have that, now can we? Sean said, and made a sweeping gesture with his arm ending with a point in the direction the track cats were following. The dog teams and the curly coat swung in behind.

Sean took several more strides forward and saw

Nanook's tail whipping back and forth across the trail in front of him.

Here, Sean. Otters are here, Nanook told him.

That was immediately evident, as from beyond Nanook came otter chirpings and jabberings and explosive 'Hah!' 'Hah!' sounds in the voices of, if not a hundred otters, at least fifteen.

And human voices called out suddenly too. 'What's with these specimens all of a sudden? They sound like someone stuck a pin in them and let the air out.'

'Omigod, I see what the problem is. They see that big old house cat there. Here kitty kitty . . . kitty like otter meat?'

Nanook growled low in his throat, but Coaxtl let out a roar that sounded as if it came from deep inside a cave instead of a snow leopard's chest.

Sean caught up with the cat. 'Slainté. What are you doing with these otters?'

'Uh, studying them.'

'Yes, we have seen some unusual creatures on this planet and we want to make sure these otters are the ordinary kind and not some strange Petaybean hybrid.'

'What if they are a Petaybean hybrid?' Sean asked. 'I don't believe we've met. I'm Dr. Sean Shongili. My grandfather collected and adapted the creatures here on Petaybee. I don't think he'd appreciate it if you attempt to reverse-engineer his otters.'

Sinead stepped into the clearing as well. The men kept the otter cages in the open but they had puff tents for themselves. The puff tents were first cousin to the Nakatira cubes. You set them up, opened a valve, and they inflated themselves with a foot of air in walls, floor, and ceiling. Furthermore, they were totally fireproof, so a heating device or even cooking equipment could be used inside them if the occupants were very careful about how they moved. Four of these tents were set up among the spindly trees that were part of the landscape on this part of the planet. Because of the deep ice, even very mature trees reached no great girth. The otter cages were on a table in the center of the clearing, where they would be in full view of the occupants of each puff tent.

'I am Sinead Shongili, and I'm the game warden for this area. I don't recall issuing you an otter-molesting permit, folks. If our creatures need taking care of or keeping track of, my rangers and I see to it. I'll thank you to release the creatures you have in custody. If any of them have been injured or killed while in your care, you must turn them over to me in the name of the Kilcoole Wildlife Council.'

'What is it with you Shongilis, coming out here to throw your weight around?'

Liam Maloney stepped forward now. 'Dr. Sean and his wife are the co-governors of Petaybee. I am Sheriff Maloney, and you are in violation of ever so many serious statutes. Do as Warden Sinead says and release the otters or we'll be lockin' yourselves up instead.'

'I believe I can clear this up, sirs and madam,' said the small wizened woman with the dark brown skin and heavily chiseled broad features of an aboriginal New Adelaidian. 'I am Dr. Marie Mabo of IGISI, the Inter Galactic Institute of Species Identification. My team and I are here by their authority, so naturally I assumed that our presence and mission were known to and approved by local officials as well. We have been observing these creatures in their wild state for some time and two days ago were privileged to see them interacting peaceably with a pair of seals who seemed to be accompanied by a pair of children who fended off a wolf attack.'

'You saw the wolves menacing the children and you did nothing to help?'

'It looked like the wolves were doing fine to me,' said the man the otters had identified as the one with fur on his chin.

'That will do, Eric!' Dr. Mabo said. To the Petaybeans, she said, 'I apologize that my colleague chooses to display his rather sardonic sense of humor at such an inappropriate moment. I do realize the children must have been yours, Warden, since you and your canines and felines came to their rescue. Had you but known it, we were right behind you, ready to intervene ourselves. We hesitated only because we truly had no wish to shoot the beautiful wolves encircling the children and it seemed we had no alternative. You proved us wrong.'

'Did, didn't I?' Sinead said. She stepped forward, her rifle over her arm, and opened an otter cage. There were only three otters in it but they seemed to explode all over the clearing in their haste to get away, and looked like at least ten times their number. No wonder the otter thought he had a hundred family members.

Sinead signaled her rangers to continue opening cages while she opened the puff tents. An anesthetized pregnant female otter lay on a folding table. Her belly was shaved and a needle fed into one of her paws. She was shivering either from shock or hypothermia. Computer equipment in an enclosed thermal shell lined one side of the tent.

Sinead picked her up and folded her inside a special pouch she carried next to her body. She carried the otter in the pouch over to the curly coat where Deirdre Angalook, Clodagh's student, received her, bundling the injured animal to her as if she were a baby. The only other otter to be seen by the time she emerged was the one who had accompanied them from Kilcoole.

'I'm guessin' the only reason you put this little one out was so she wouldn't bite your hand off, right?' she said to Dr. Mabo.

'Actually, we wanted to preserve the specimens as long as possible for more testing,' Eric the Whiskers said.

Dr. Mabo whipped around so fast the hood from her parka fell away from her face. 'Somebody gag him,' she said.

'Nobody will be gaggin' anybody else,' Liam Maloney said. 'But we'll be cuffing all of you and then taking you back to Kilcoole for deportation, at least until your institute sees fit to consult with us before conducting a study on our four-legged friends.'

Deputy Tukaluk walked around the tents and into the forest. 'They got a snocle over here, Sheriff. Big one. I never saw one this big. Musta brought it with them when they landed.'

'How many will it hold exactly?' Sean asked.

'Six and a driver,' Tukaluk said.

'Very well, then. I'll drive and Dr. Mabo can ride in Sinead's sled on the way back.'

'Ought to make them walk, Sean,' Liam said.

'That would slow us down too much,' he replied. 'I've business back in Kilcoole. I must tell my children, for one thing, that the otters have been released and are safe.'

'Those were *your* children, then, Dr. Shongili?' Marie Mabo asked, but not as if she didn't already know.

'They were. And like my sister the Game Warden, they are extremely protective of the other species on this planet.'

'I'd very much like to talk to them and apologize for worrying them,' Dr. Mabo said. 'They're the age of my grandchildren, and we certainly didn't mean to frighten them.'

Sean's heart pounded extra loud for a couple of beats before he said, 'I'm afraid that won't be possible. They've gone to visit a friend offworld. I'll relay your apologies.'

After the cuffed prisoners had been loaded into the snocle, Sean took the helm. Sinead had already strapped Dr. Mabo to her sled. Deirdre and the injured otter took off on the curly coat while the other sleds followed. Nobody remembered the single otter that had not run away.

In moments only tracks remained where the rescue party, the offworld scientists, and the captive otters had been. The lone remaining otter returned to the tunnels where he had played with his family and the river seals, but they were still smashed and still abandoned.

10

At Marmie's instructions, as soon as the communications officer received word from Kilcoole about the capture of the otter rustlers, she reported straight to Ronan and Murel.

'Oh, good,' Murel said absently.

Ronan nodded and said, 'Serves 'em right.'

If the ship's crew was expecting a big reaction from the children about this bit of news that, according to the boss, the Petaybean kids had been waiting for throughout the trip, they were disappointed.

The twins had eyes for nothing but the viewscreen. Through it they watched the space station, its lights in the darkness of space making it look as if it were decorated for the holidays. Larger and larger it grew until it filled up the screen and only a tiny portion of it was visible. Then that portion, the port hatch, opened like a water lily unfolding to receive the ship into its heart.

'Reminds me of the otter's den,' Murel said, smiling to her brother, who grinned back as they raced to their quarters. There, they gathered the few things they'd brought with them, their warm suits and their more conventional parkas, mukluks, snow pants, and mittens for when they went home, plus pouches of Clodagh's remedies and the journals Mum had given them.

When they followed Marmie out of the ship into the docking bay, they looked all around them.

It's huge, Murel said, her neck straining as she looked up and up and up. Flitters, carrying passengers, zipped from a wall to a bit of ceiling to another bit of wall, busy as – well, insects. It didn't matter if they were bees or wasps or mosquitoes.

Yeah, Ronan said. *I bet you could fit all of Kilcoole in just this part.*

His sister nodded mutely.

'Come along, children,' Marmie said. 'We can do the tour after you've settled in a bit.'

A flitter landed in front of them. A very handsome man in a uniform was at the helm.

'Is that your husband come to collect us, Marmie?' Murel asked.

'No, dear, he's one of the chauffeurs, I suppose you might say. There's an entire cadre of them here just to man the flitter fleet.'

'Flitter fleet?' Ronan asked, laughing. And had to say it several times over until Murel said privately, *Stop. It's getting annoying. You don't want Marmie to get cross, do you?*

Marmie's not cross. You're the one being bossy. What do you think? Now that we don't have Nanook and Coaxtl to mind us you get to be in charge? Not likely, my girl!

Now you're being snotty. I just want us to make a good

impression. Marmie is our friend but she's a very important lady.

So? Mum and Da are governors. That makes them just as important.

Yes, but not us. Mum and Da are our parents. They have to love us. Marmie doesn't.

Maybe she'll get mad at us and send us back, Ronan said. *I wouldn't mind.*

You'd mind by the time Mum got done with you, and once she was through, Clodagh would be after us. We'd bring disgrace to all of Petaybee if Marmie sent us back because we were too big a handful for her.

I don't think that will be a problem. If she gets tired of us, she can just hand us over to the cadre of chauffeurs and their fleet of flitters. With this he began shaking again with another fit of the giggles.

You're impossible, you are, Murel said, and tried to keep a straight face, but then couldn't do it with him tee-heeing all over the place. Apparently, the chauffeur asked Marmie what the children were laughing about, so Ro told Marmie and Marmie told him and he started laughing too, then Marmie. By the time the flitter reached the upper level where Marmie's house was, Murel really had to use the outhouse bad.

But even that was forgotten as she took in as much of Marmie's house as she could.

To begin with, it wasn't a house, it was a whole section of the space station, the upper section. As the flitter rose to cross the garden and fountains, the broad pathways, and, oh yes, the beautiful little river running around the living area, it seemed as if the house was right on *top* of the space station, with no hull around it.

Space showed all around them, a night sky made large by proximity to the nearest planet and its moons, which seemed even more huge than moons and the sun on Petaybee.

'Don't you worry that you'll fall off?' she asked Marmie, feeling a little dizzy.

'Cool!' Ronan said, and then thought about it and wondered how the water in the fountains could fall and the river could flow and the flowers grow without atmosphere. How, in fact, were they supposed to breathe?

Marmie dimpled mischievously, then reached forward and touched a button. Instant sunrise. The blackness and the huge planet and moon were eclipsed by a skyscape very much like the one on Petaybee, the sky blue, the sun distant, and everything else had more color too. The flowers became blue and purple, yellow, red, orange, and pink. The grass was green without even a puddle of snow, and the fountains, made of some pretty pink stone, overflowed just enough to cascade into the river.

'How'd you do that?' Ronan wanted to know. He was watching Marmie's hand on the controls instead of looking at the scenery.

'It's just a hologram. What you saw when we came is how it would look with no illusion and no hull. Oh, I do have an observatory – several, in fact, in various strategic locations on different levels. But one feels so closed in living on the station with no real atmosphere or the boundaries of a horizon, so I had the holos created. We can even have weather if you like. Shall I make it snow?'

'Oh, no. Not when it looks like springtime,' Murel said. 'It would kill your flowers. But – could we have a thunderstorm? Once in a while, right around breakup, Petaybee throws tantrums, so Da says, and they're ever so exciting.'

'In that case I suppose we must have one. I like them too, actually. Do you want lightning or just thunder? Rain? Sheet lightning or the cracked forking variety?'

'Can we have it all please?' Ronan asked.

'With that attitude, you should go far, Mr. Shongili,' Marmie said with a smile.

'Could the lightning strike something?'

'Ronan! You want Marmie to burn down her house so you can see how it works?' Murel scolded.

'No need for that. My lightning can only hit virtual trees. We can feel the wind but we will not get wet from the rain or cold from the snow, and once I turn it off, the ground will not be white or wet afterward.'

'Oh,' Murel said, disappointed. 'Then, why do you do it?'

'For a little variety, mood, atmosphere. I can make it rain, you know, by switching the irrigation system from the belowground sprinklers to the overhead ones. And I have a device that will scent the air with that wonderful ozone smell that comes after a rain. So, do you want to see it?'

'Yes,' both children said politely. Marmie's fake weather couldn't compete with Petaybee's extremes.

At least, that was how they felt when they first arrived. Everything seemed very tame. The little river was nothing but an oddly shaped swimming pool, with jets in the rocks creating the illusion of riffles or eddies.

It never iced over, of course, and there were no other creatures to be discovered along its banks. And there were seldom fish. Even someone with Marmie's resources couldn't keep the artificial stream stocked with enough fish to keep the twins happily catching their own meals for as much as a week.

The only excitement came when Marmie had an unexpected visitor and the twins had to hide their dual nature and talk in a silly way about the 'pet' seals they'd brought with them from their home world.

They hadn't known what to expect from Marmie when it came to their education, but as it turned out, they went to classes with the other kids from the space station.

'I could get you tutors, but that would be a bore, don't you think?' Marmie asked. 'You must meet these other children, and more than the teachers will instruct you, you will instruct each other.'

They were highly skeptical. After all, here *they* were the outsiders, an uncomfortable thought. On the other hand, they weren't the offworlders because on a space station nobody was on a world as such, so they signed up. Instead of books, as they had on Petaybee, they were given individual clipboard-sized screens on which they could receive the text or computerized lesson material for each class. They also carried another clipboard-sized computer for note taking and doing their class exercises and homework.

The flitter let them off on the school level of deck three just in time to join a bunch of other kids pouring in from other flitters, lifts, and staircases.

Murel said, *There's the loo. I'm going before we get to class. Meet you there.*

Yeah, sure, Ronan said, but he was already scanning the doors and the diagram on his text pad, looking for the right room. Looking up and to the side instead of straight ahead, he ran right into a wall and both his pads went flying.

'Hey!' the wall said.

It seemed to be slightly domed and wore floral wallpaper right at eye level. Ronan looked up and stared into the piercing dark eyes and black eyebrows of a boy about three times his size. Oh great. He was in for it now. This guy was way bigger than Dino Caparthy. He so did not want to get beaten up on his first day at Marmie's school.

'S-Sorry, I didn't mean anything. I was looking for my class instead of looking where I was going. I, uh, I have some lunch credits if that will—'

The tall boy put his palms out in front of him. 'No, no, little bruthah. I don' want your lunch credits. I hope I didn't hurt you? I was lookin' too and did not look down.' He made a sudden move and Ronan jumped back. This guy was enormous! But he had only stooped to pick up Ronan's pads, which he handed back to him. 'Good thing these are sturdy, yeah? Where you goin'?'

'Professor Freyasdottur's geography class. You?'

'Same place. I am Ke-ola. You?'

'Ronan. Here comes my sister. Murel, hey, this is Ke-ola.'

Murel looked up and then creaked her neck back and looked up a little farther until she met the large boy's friendly grin with one of her own. 'Hey. Ke-ola, slainté.'

'What's that mean?'

'We say it to mean hello and goodbye,' Ronan, now official Petaybean goodwill ambassador, told him.

'Ah, we say "aloha." Means a couple of other things too. Slainté. You guys twins?'

'Yeah, we are. You got any brothers or sisters?'

'Ten sistahs, twelve bruthahs. Four sets twins. I had a twin myself but he died when we were born.'

'Whew, that's a lot of sibs!' Ronan said.

'Your mum must be tired,' Murel said.

'Six sistahs, four bruthahs are half – we got different mamas,' he told them.

'Here's our classroom,' Murel told him, as if saying goodbye. He reached above her and shoved the door open a little farther.

'Mine too,' he said.

As it turned out, the space station school was sort of fun. On Petaybee there were no other kids their own age from the planet. Almost all of the kids in the lower levels were offworlders. Here it was the same, but everyone was in the same boat, or rather, on the same space station. And now Ronan and Murel had journeyed among the stars too, so even though they maybe hadn't seen other worlds like some of the kids had, they had more in common with them than they did with the offworld kids back home.

Also, they weren't the littlest kids here. Many of the others were younger than they were and several were their own age. A couple of them had never been off the space station.

They were friendly too, if a little too curious for comfort sometimes.

'Hey, twins, I heard you brought your pet seals with you,' a younger boy named Dewey said. 'Madame built them a pool up at her house, is what my mom said. Can I come and play with them?'

What shall we say? Murel asked.

We can say we had to send the seals home, Ronan suggested.

Yeah, but then if anyone sees us accidentally in seal form we won't have any way to explain it, Murel said. Finally she told Dewey, 'You know, the reason we brought them with us, Dewey, is that they're really shy – even around our parents. They hide if they know anybody else is around. They're, uh—'

'They're rescue seals,' Ronan said. 'They were going to be killed by offworld fur trappers when they were babies. The trappers already killed their families and everything. It was terrible. Our aunt Sinead is the Game Warden and she gave them to us to raise but they never have wanted to be around any other humans, only us.'

'Oh,' Dewey said. 'Well, maybe when you've been here awhile and they get a little older they'll get used to us too, if you have us up to Madame's a lot.'

'Yeah, maybe so,' Ronan said. But to Murel he said, *Like we're going to be away from Petaybee* that *long*.

They had one teacher overall for each age group, and that teacher supervised all the computer classes that made up the bulk of their studies. But since they had several very prominent scientists on board the station, Marmie had talked some of them into teaching classes in their specialties in the school too.

Dr. Freyasdottur, their geography teacher for this class, was also a sociobiologist and an environmental systems engineer, responsible for the weather system on Marmie's level, among other modifications on the space station. She was a sturdy young-looking blonde woman with a round face, dancing blue eyes, and large teeth that showed a lot because she smiled often. Her hair was cut short and by the end of the class stuck out in all directions because she often grabbed at it, stuck pencils in it, or pulled at it for emphasis.

She employed a lot of holos as models and teaching tools and hopped enthusiastically around each, pointing out the features of systems full of planets that had worlds within worlds. The holos showed people working in fields blooming with crops or picking fruit from trees, manufacturing parts for electronic equipment, or mining minerals. Each planet had a different skyscape, and after they studied one, Dr. Freyasdottur would zip it back into its star system to show them where it fit in the cosmic scheme of things.

'Now then,' she said at the end of class one day, 'for your homework, I want you all to design a holo of your own home world. Yes, yes, I know a few of you are station born and bred and have never been dirtside, so you will need to ask your parents for help locating, gathering information about, and depicting their worlds of origin. If they are from one of the older planets, you may place your focus on the country from which they come, its language, if other than Standard, customs as they deviate from those in station life, imports and exports, and contributions to the

Federation. If you or your parents come from one of the planets terraformed by Intergal to house the inhabitants of Old Earth and some of the other older worlds, then we'd like to know what life is like there.

'Focus on how your world has been developed and what it's like for boys and girls who grow up there. If possible, compare their lives with yours here on the station. You will be sharing your holos with the rest of the class in two weeks. In the meantime, this class period will be devoted to learning to design holos. My assistant, Top Tech Wayans, will be helping you develop the technical end of your projects.'

Murel's hand shot up and Dr. Freyasdottur called on her. 'What if there's two of us from the same planet? Can we do our holo together?'

'Certainly, Murel. In fact, most of you here have other family members in class. Even if you share a holo, you will each have to do a presentation of a different aspect of your planet's culture, environment, or social structure, of course.'

Marmie's eyebrows rose when they told her about the assignment. 'Alors! That should be extremely challenging for children your age, but no doubt you will all learn a lot about each other as well as other places in the universe and how to design a holo.'

The twins were so involved in their own project, they didn't realize how truly Marmie had spoken until the other kids began their presentations.

'This is Wurra-Wurra, where my folks came from,' a boy named Rory said. His skin was very dark, almost black, and his features looked like the ones some of the old men carved with chain saws out of tree stumps. His eyes were a brilliant and startling blue. He opened his program, and a stretch of salmon pink sky and blowing sand that looked like a spray of blood under two glowing suns spun out before them. Tall rusty spires rose in clusters here and there. 'It's got two suns, see, and they dry everything up. So it's desert, right?'

'Are those tall things the buildings of your cities?' Lan Huy, a girl a year or two older than the twins, asked.

Rory laughed, a sharp little yip. 'Not our cities, Lan. They are cities, though. The ants that live there could probably tell you all the best places to get tea or go shopping.'

'So – you're not the dominant species on your planet?' Ke-ola asked curiously and with no hint of humor or mockery. In school he spoke more correctly than he did when he was just messing around with the other kids, Murel noticed.

'We think so. Don't know what the ants think. Stay away from them, my folks said, much as possible.'

'Where's your water?' Murel asked.

'Underground, what there is,' Rory said. 'Mum says you have ter dig for it.'

Murel said, 'Underground water is the *only* water you have? We have underground water too, but we've got regular rivers and seas and such as well.'

'You'll have your turn soon enough, Murel,' Dr. Freyasdottur said. 'Go on, Rory.'

Rory finished up.

Ke-ola was next. He shuffled to the front and tapped in his program, picked up his laser wand. As soon as he started his presentation, Murel and Ronan realized there was even more to their large friend than there appeared to be. Three worlds started spinning.

'I am Ke-ola O'honu-aumakua. On Old Earth my people lived on islands in the warmest of the two great oceans, the Ocean of Peacefulness. Originally we ate what the islands brought us, fish from the sea, fruit from the trees. The climate was mild and warm, and except for volcanoes erupting at times, or monsoon rains, our lives were peaceful. Then other people came to the islands with things and ideas they said would make our lives better. Some things seemed to but others did not. Finally came the day when Intergal came to the few of us who were left and still in possession of some of the islands in our chain. They told us they now owned our island and we could not live there any longer but would be moved to a better place. We did not quite believe them because, although the islands were not as good in many ways as they had been before the new ideas and things came, they were still a very good place to live. The new place was a specially prepared world that much resembled our own. We brought with us the seeds to some of our trees, and the eggs and young of our fish and animals. My family brought the eggs of the sacred Honu, the sea turtle that is our special animal. Our last name means "people of the sea turtle."

'For a time we lived in the new place fairly contentedly, though it was a new place and never home and we still sang to each other of the old islands lost to us. Then the company came and told us that our new place, which they already owned, had been found to have a rare mineral they needed for a vital manufacturing process, but that another place had been prepared for us and we would be moved again.

'This time, the new place was not as well prepared as the other, and though we brought our plants and animals with us again, they do not thrive in this new place. Neither do we. The gravity is greater, the weather is colder and more changeable, and our animals must be kept in artificial pens and tanks, our plants in big houses with artificial sunlight. Once, on the old world, and to a lesser extent on the second one, we were scientists and singers, ranchers and dancers, teachers and creators of beautiful and useful items.'

He paused, pointed the wand to the first globe and drew up a picture of what looked like a hat made of flowered fabric with a pineapple-shaped container strapped to either side of it. Ke-ola suddenly grinned, a warm and funny expression that seemed totally at odds with the serious and even sad look he'd worn throughout the rest of his recitation. 'Well, some of the items were ugly and useless too, but the outsiders seemed to want them so we sold them to them.' Then the grin went away as if it had never been and he continued in the same slightly singsong voice, 'We were healers, lawgivers and musicians, makers of food and purveyors of goods. We have become a people of zookeepers and gardeners.

'The company tells us that we are ungrateful for everything they have done for us and that our people must learn new jobs and new ways to be more productive to repay the kindness of the company. And so I have been sent here to school on a special scholarship to learn more about how to maintain space stations. I cannot tell you of imports or exports – everything my people have they have brought with them or have had provided for them, at a cost, by the company, who may take back whatever they need, including us. Fortunately, even though the heavy gravity is very hard on the mamas when they give birth, our families have become large with little to do but grow food and children. We don't manufacture much anymore or work away from home much either. Mostly the older people tell the younger ones stories and teach us our old songs and dances so we don't forget who we are or what we had a long time ago. That's all good, but as you can tell, we don't always have enough to eat.' He patted his round stomach. 'So probably it is a good thing I am here among you, my classmates, where I don't get so skinny I blow away on the wind. Makes more food for my family at home too.'

As he talked, he spun the worlds and brought up the animals, trees, volcanoes, fish, and turtles of the first world, and showed people like him doing the jobs he described. The second world he showed had less of everything, and the new one had a lot of the same things, only in containers set on stark landmasses.

That's terrible that they just kept taking his people's homes away from them, Murel said. *They're i.p.'s too, just like us – the inconvenient peoples Intergal moved to terraformed worlds from places the company had a better use for.*

Yeah, that's kind of what the older people were afraid of about Petaybee, that once the company realized how good our world was, they'd try to move us off of it. That was before Mum and Da straightened it all out, Ronan replied.

'That was excellent, Ke-ola, and far exceeded the assignment,' Dr. Freyasdottur said. 'Your holos turned out so well I'm afraid you may have raised the grading curve on this assignment.'

The big kid flushed and grinned but to their surprise said, 'Don' do that, teachah. I cheated a little.'

'You did? You mean you didn't make those holos?'

'I did. But I made two of 'em a long time ago, back on three world. Auntie Kimmie Lee, oldest lady living, she learned to make them to sell to visitors back on two world a long time ago. She taught us kids to keep us out of trouble, she says. Also, it shows us what it was like on those two worlds. What we were like. So I just uploaded the old ones I made for fun for the assignment. I did do the last one though, just like you said.'

'Oh well,' Dr. Freyasdottur said. Both twins could see she was trying hard not to giggle. 'I won't raise the curve then if you cheated, but I'll just grade you on the new one. By the way, maybe instead of bothering Top Tech Wayans the next time we do holos, you must share your unfair advantage with the other students and teach them how to make their holos the way you did. Am I clear?'

'Yes'm,' he said, and sat down, trying to look suitably chastised.

Chesney Janko gave her presentation next. She was a year and a half younger than the twins and had grown up on a large industrial planet that was a company headquarters. Her family had moved to the station when her parents left the company's employment to take a job with Marmie. She seemed to list imports and exports for hours. 'Computer chips and antibiotics and guidance systems and butter and laser rifles and . . .' She listed them as they occurred to her and not in any particular order or with any particular interest.

Lan Huy had grown up on the station. Her father was one of Marmie's top engineers. She said that at one time, a very long time ago, her father's people had come from a small client country that paid tribute to a very large one. Some of the animals in the larger country were dragons, horned beasts that sounded a little like the curly coats, and birds called phoenixes that self-destructed and rebuilt themselves from ashes. She had seen evidence of these things, but had never encountered any herself except sometimes in dreams. Her presentation seemed to be mostly made up of imaginary stuff, which she said was legend, because although her people were once the most numerous on Old Earth, a catastrophic plague had all but wiped them out.

By the time it was their turn, the twins were both feeling even luckier than usual to be Petaybeans. They looked forward to showing their new friends what a proper planet should have.

But when they were finished, Rory made a big display of shivering. 'Brrr, sounds cold to me.'

'It is cold, but we don't mind really. Everyone is used to it and our bodies are adapted to it,' Murel told him.

'How'd they do that?' asked Chesney.

'The planet did it,' Ronan said. His sister looked away. She wished he hadn't said that. She didn't think it was a good idea to tell offworlders any more about Petaybee than they might already know.

'How could it do that? It's not like planets think,' Rory scoffed.

'Petaybee does,' Ronan said. 'It's like it's this really big person we all live on.' The holo spun on his computer screen.

'Looks like an ice ball to me,' Chesney said, shaking her head.

'It is an ice ball,' Murel said, her brows lowering and coming together to make a fierce expression, had she been able to see it. 'But it's *our* ice ball and at least it has ground water.'

'Now then, young'uns,' Dr. Freyasdottur said. 'This lesson was to help you learn about one other's home planets, not to criticize them or brag about your own. Please continue, twins.'

They did, but it was hard to give the other kids the right feeling about Petaybee when they couldn't talk about winter swims without at least hinting that they could turn into seals. And they just couldn't do that. They understood that much about what Da and Mum were trying to protect them from.

But at least the assignment let them know more about the other students and gave them some idea of how many different kinds of worlds and peoples there were on them.

By the end of the week they had heard from kids whose planets were desert, jungle, rich farmland, or mostly water.

'Nobody else seems to be able to talk to their world, though, Marmie,' Ronan said when their hostess asked them how their presentation went and how they liked the others. 'Is Petaybee the only one that's – you know – alive?'

Marmie shrugged. 'I very much doubt it, mon petit. Perhaps it is just that Petaybee is more gregarious than the others. More outgoing. Or perhaps your people are simply more in tune with the world they were placed upon than others are elsewhere. It's a great mystery.'

'Yes,' Murel said. 'But I still think it would be cool if sometime some of those other worlds started letting their people know whose surface they were living on, don't you?'

'Very cool, my darling. Very cool indeed,' Marmie agreed, fluffing Murel's hair with her hand. 'Perhaps, given enough time, they will.'

11

For the first few months, the twins were able to talk to their parents often. At first it was every day, and then one of the expensive relays went down and the com systems had to be rerouted, so it was only possible to talk face-to-face every week. Then Petaybee began emitting electromagnetic interference so that half the time neither one could make out what the other was saying, or see the other either.

'How come it's more that way now than when we left?' Murel asked.

'Lots of reasons,' Marmie replied. 'Sunspots, the increased activity from the midsea volcanic region your father mentioned. You remember him saying that on his last recon swim he felt the heat in the water and smelled the sulfur much earlier than he had on previous trips?'

'Yeah,' Ronan said. 'He said it was just a matter of a couple of years now before it surfaces. I hope we can go home by then. I want to see! Besides, if we can't talk to them . . .'

The face-to-face calls finally became impossible, and

the messages had to be routed through a number of different stations. It was hard to say anything important, much less be silly or share a joke, with so many people between you. Petaybee, Kilcoole, the people of their village, and their family began to feel very far away. Fortunately, school was interesting and they liked the other kids and most of their teachers; and of course they had each other, so they could forget to be homesick for long periods of time.

One day toward the end of the first term, Marmie asked them, 'What flavor cake do you two like best?'

'Chocolate,' 'Raspberry,' they answered at the same time.

'Chocolate raspberry it shall be then. Your parents cannot come for your birthday, but they've sent gifts and I've invited all of your classmates here for a party. I thought, if it was all right with you, we could make it a theme party and set it up as if it were a latchkay on Petaybee. How would that be?'

Ronan looked at Murel and Murel looked at Ronan.

Marmie said, 'You do not care for the idea? Would it make you too homesick?'

'Oh, it's a good idea, Marmie,' Murel said. 'It's just – we don't think the other kids are really ready for Petaybee yet. I don't think some of them liked our holo.'

Marmie gave an elegant lift and fall of her shoulders, with her hands outstretched, palms up. What Mum called a 'Gallic shrug.' It said, basically, What is a sensible person supposed to do when other people are being so silly?

'Your holo was very nice,' she said finally. 'Those

who did not care for it were foolish. But a holo and Petaybee are different, yes?'

'Still . . .' Murel said, and let her voice drift off as she looked at Marmie, hoping she'd understand the rest without her actually trying to say it.

'We'd like to keep the Petaybee part of our birthdays private, I guess,' Ronan said finally. 'I'm sorry. It's really nice of you to want to give us a party, Marmie, but we don't have to have one. We could have the cake anyway, couldn't we?' He looked at his sister. 'And presents?'

Marmie laughed, and it sounded like bells jingling on sled dogs' harnesses. 'Yes, yes, we must have cake and presents and a party too. But the Petaybee part, that will be our own little celebration, after the others have left. I know! Everyone must come as a creature from their planet that either swims or flies.'

'Wouldn't we be a little too realistic as seals?' Murel asked, wincing. She hated to keep shooting down Marmie's ideas, but felt their friend got carried away with enthusiasm before thinking about how wrong things could go. Lately, it seemed to the twins that they'd had a lot of experience with how wrong things could go.

'Ah, but you will not be seals!' Marmie said.

'We will be if we go swimming,' Ronan said grimly.

'Only if you swim in the water. I am thinking you will not be swimming in the water, you will be swimming in the air.'

'Yes, but we can't do that,' Murel said.

'You can in zero g,' Marmie told her. While they were thinking that over, she asked, 'So, what will you be? Eagles? Fishes? Whales?'

'Otters,' they said at the same time. 'We'll be otters.'

Even after the humans rescued his family, Otter stayed in the small den in the riverbank, waiting for his friends the river seals to return. But winter ended and the ice melted and still they were gone and did not come home. Finally, Otter went to the dwelling he had seen them enter and sent his thoughts on the matter to the Father River Seal.

Father River Seal, where are your children? Shouldn't they be back by now? Otters have many more games to play with them and things to show them. Marvelous things they will enjoy very much. Otters know lots of good secrets. Where are your river seal children?

What the . . . ? Father River Seal's thought was fragmented and startled.

It's me, Otter, Father River Seal. Do not be afraid, Otter told him.

Laughter came into the Father River Seal's thoughts. *I was not afraid, Otter. Merely thinking of something else.*

Not thinking of your children? Although they are not here?

Always thinking of my children, Otter. Their mother and I both miss them very much, but we sent them somewhere they would be safe from the kind of people who took the other otters.

Those people are gone. The good people took them away. Why have your children not returned? No danger now!

A smile came into Father River Seal's thoughts. *No danger for otters. But for my children, yes, there is still danger and their mother and I have been working hard to see to it that the danger such offworld scientific groups present will never threaten our children again.*

That is good, the otter said, for he could think of nothing else to say. His friends the river seal children were safe, but they were not in the river and so could not play with otters. *I will return to my family now but later I will come back here.*

I'll tell Ronan and Murel you were asking for them, Otter, Father River Seal said, and went back to thinking his deep, unsealy thoughts and doing the unsealy things he did when in human form.

Otter was surprised, when he returned home again where the ice maze was in the winter, that none of his family were at play on the banks or in the river. *Where have all the otters who are not me gone?* he asked. He was asking himself but unexpectedly received an answer from the otters who were not there when he found a scent message.

Scent messages between river otters were quite complex, and in a way that would have astounded humans or river seals. River otters could write entire tomes with one spritz from the proper area or a rub from another. And there were dialects of scents understood only by otters of the same colony, as well as nuances of meaning, idiomatic expressions or slang of particular families, that only otters in the same colony could fully grasp, or smell.

It was fortunate that otters had excellent memories for scent too, because great otter romantic literature had been composed in scent messages, as well as geography texts and adventure stories.

The message that Otter found that day was

somewhat simpler. It said, 'Kinsman Otter who Plays with River Seals, we do not care for this place any longer. Too many wolves and too many men with otter cages. We are moving closer to the sea to seek solidarity with our cousins the sea otters. See you by the sea!' Otters could pun in scent messages too. The language of otters was full of puns. Not the same ones humans used, but otter puns, which were very funny because otters enjoyed laughing. Like humans, however, otters had similar sounds for the big water *sea* and what otters did with their eyes *see*.

It was a long swim to the sea, especially all alone. The message was three days old, which meant the family was probably already at the shore. But it meant swimming with the current, and the weather was pleasant, as most weather was for otters, and so in a single day Otter caught up with part of his family, which had stopped at a particularly tempting mud slide. It was very long, slick, and muddy, and gave them a little 'Whoop!' before they went splashing into the river, cleaned off the mud, and climbed back up the hill to slide again.

They had been playing for some time and were ready to join the rest of the family, so Otter had time for only a few slides – certainly not hundreds – before he resumed swimming again.

At last, after much swimming, with a few games along the way, they were reunited with the rest of the family on the banks of the river at the mouth where it spilled into the sea.

Where are our cousins the sea otters? Otter asked his mother.

You see that island over there? she replied, indicating a large landmass squatting amid the waves rolling onto the shore beyond their river camp. *They live there. It is full of sea otter dens, and you can see them lying on the rocks eating clams. Some have been coming over to show us where the best places to build dens might be here. We do not swim in that salty stuff they call water, but they say that in the winter, when the ice is in, we could walk to their island, though of course we would not do so unless asked. Like us, sea otters protect their homes with great ferocity.*

She bared her teeth in a suitably ferocious way, and Otter backpaddled away from her a little. He knew his mother's teeth and claws very well from times when she had been greatly ferocious about how her offspring should behave.

The river otters moved into their comfortable new dens in the wide river mouth. There were low hills nearby that made passable mud slides, once the otters removed the rocks at the bottom, which they did with great efficiency. These were useful in breaking open the delicious shellfish they found on the shore, which was technically their cousins' territory, though the cousins did not use it much, preferring their island.

Otter loved the new delicacy and hunted on the shore as often as he could, keeping a careful eye on the island, lest ferocious cousins come and attack him for his boldness. Then one day he noticed that there were no longer any sea otters to be seen on the island. Not one. Not anywhere.

'Hah!' he said. *Where have they gone?* He alerted his family, and they all came to the beach to see for themselves. They could see he was right. No sea otters on the island's narrow beach, no sea otters in the water, no sea otters on the shore, no sea otters higher up on the island. No sea otters anywhere.

Later in the day, all of the sea otters returned. To Otter's surprise, three of the cousins swam straight to the shore. Otter was afraid at first, thinking that he'd been caught stealing their shellfish.

'Hah!' he said, greeting them. *Cousins, where did you all go? You disappeared. Otters who live in the river saw no otters who live in the sea all day*. Otter hid the shell of the fish he had just eaten behind him while pushing forward three rocks. *Otters came to the shore to bring you gifts but we did not see you on your island. Here are the gifts. Rocks for shell cracking.*

Sea otters cannot possibly have too many rocks! his cousins said, accepting the rocks as if they were better than shellfish. *Rocks are for preparing food and also for leaving messages.*

Like scent messages? Otter asked.

Scent messages are for river otters. Rock talk is for sea otters. You live in the riverbanks and the water. We live almost always in the water, and scent would wash away. Rocks are better.

To himself, Otter thought that rocks could wash away too and that otters who lived always in the water had to come out of it to pile rocks and leave messages and to find piles of rocks and read the messages. *I would like to see a rock talk message*, he said.

The sea otters had a lot of fun stacking the rocks first one way and then another, adding one kind of rock and then another, going from just a few rocks to – well – probably hundreds! Each time, they made him guess what the message said and translate it into scent for them. Each time, they agreed among themselves that, yes, rocks were definitely better. Otter did not disagree with them. They were the bosses of otters here, and besides, they had rocks.

Instead Otter tried to learn what he could about their rock messages. They were so pleased that they agreed he surely must have some sea otter ancestors.

Shall we tell this smart river otter our secrets? one cousin asked another.

Yes, he is our cousin and gives good gifts. Besides, we were going to tell all our cousins the big secret.

Before Otter knew it, his family surrounded him, all of them waiting to hear the big secret of the sea otters.

The planet is making a new home for us, said the sea otters. *It's a bit hot, but it will be a wonderful home when it is done.*

How will we know when it is done? Otter asked.

It will come up out of the water and cool off and not smoke or make fire anymore, said a cousin. *At least, that is what Senior Sea Otter says, and Senior Sea Otter has lived a long long time and spoken to many creatures who have lived much longer. A few of the oldest have seen this thing happen in other places, long ago. Others have heard of it happening from their grandparents and their grandparents' grandparents. And now it is happening again and sea otters can watch!*

So you go to watch it being made?

And to eat! Everything in the sea is attracted to the new home and many delicious fish already live near it, sheltering in it.

Suddenly, right under his paws, Otter felt the ground

tremble. It did that sometimes but it always startled him. 'Hah!' he said nervously.

Do not be alarmed, cousin. That is what the planet does when it is making the home.

That is an extremely fine secret, Otter said, impressed. *Is there another secret?*

We have found a new branch of the family.

New branch?

Yes, before there were always you river otters and us sea otters. Now there are other otters.

What otters are these? How different are they?

They are deep sea otters. They can live under the water and have a home there. It is too deep for us to dive but they say it is the kind of home deep sea otters like. They sang us wonderful songs of deep sea otters and wanted us to sing them sea otter songs too. We sang of you, little cousin, the River Otter who Plays with River Seals. It is not a sea otter song but it is a very good song. It was the best song we know and we know many good sea otter songs. You will not bite us for singing your song?

'Hah!' *Bite you! You are our cousins and now our neighbors. You share these very fine secrets. You may sing my song to other otters whenever you like.*

Good. But we will all sing it together soon. The deep sea otters say that one day when we come again to see the new home the planet is making, they will swim back with us. They wish to hear your song from you.

All Otter could think of to say to that was, 'Hah!'

12

Holograms were handy things. They could be lessons or environments or costumes, if you needed them to be. It was a little hard to keep them in place in zero g, but everyone seemed to have a good time swimming or flying, depending on what they were supposed to be. Ke-ola was a sea turtle, a big one. Lan Huy was a dragon. Rory was a shark, which was a little scary, especially for Chesney, who was a lake gull. She flapped her arms so hard she ended up hitting Dewey, who came as a monkey, in the nose, which made him cry until Marmie had him come out to help her bring down the cake.

'I thought Marmie had people who did things like baking cakes and carrying them around for her,' Ronan said.

'She does. I think she wants to do this personally because it's, you know, for us. Letting Dewey help instead of one of the people who work for her keeps him from crying. Have you noticed how if one person starts crying, pretty soon everybody else does too?'

Suddenly, Ronan wasn't having any fun anymore.

He faked being an otter sliding but since he didn't go down, no matter what, it didn't look right. By the time he stood back up, he saw that Murel's eyes were glistening, and he felt a lump in his own throat. But then a voice on the intercom said, 'All members of the Shongili birthday party please report immediately to Ms. de Revers Algemeine's deck for cake and ice cream.'

Rory, sharklike, burst through the hatch and fell with a clunk into normal gravity on the deck outside.

Ronan did a halfhearted otter slide and landed on his butt, without his holo-costume. Murel slid down beside him. 'Your costume is still flickering on and off,' Rory told her. 'But you're barely ottered at all!'

Murel just groaned and rolled her eyes, and Ronan pretended he was puking.

Aboard the intrastation transfer flitter, however, they saw someone who lifted their spirits. 'Look!' Murel said aloud, pointing. 'It's Johnny!'

You think he's come to take us home? Maybe as a surprise?

Why else would he be going to Marmie's on our birthday? Murel asked.

They kept it to themselves, though, thinking Marmie meant it to be a big secret, which they didn't want to spoil. Johnny and Marmie ate cake and ice cream off to one side and watched while Ronan and Murel opened their gifts. Rory gave them each a shark's tooth he swore had been dug out of somebody's leg. He didn't say if the leg had still been attached to the person when the teeth were removed. They were strung on thongs for the twins to wear around their necks.

'Do you like it?' the boy from Wurra-Wurra asked.

'It's awesome,' Murel replied.

'Yeah,' Ronan said, almost forgetting to be sad or anxious about what Johnny was doing there. Rory was turning out to be okay after all.

Lan Huy gave them a scroll that turned out to be a blueprint of the space station. 'There's lots of interesting ways to get where we're not supposed to go,' she leaned forward and whispered. 'You just have to study it a bit.'

Chesney gave them free passes to see the new vids the last supply ship had delivered. Her dad was the morale and recreation chairman.

'Gosh, thanks, Chez,' Murel said. 'I've been wanting to see the one about the explorer who finds the ancient civilization filled with the remnants of a highly advanced race.'

'They never find the ruins of ancient civilizations filled with the remnants of a buncha complete eejits, do they?' Rory observed.

'Probably no ruins left because complete eejits wouldn't have figured out how to build an ancient civilization in the first place,' Ke-ola said.

Ke-ola handed them each a saucer-sized flower from the ponics garden then helped Murel stick it behind her ear.

'There's no music at this party so far,' he said. 'What, nobody sings to you on your birthday?'

Under Chesney's direction, the other students dutifully sang a round of 'Happy Birthday.'

Ke-ola groaned. 'That's lame, man. You got to have real music at a party. You twins say on your world you sing at the parties all the time. So okay, I'll tell you what. I'm gonna make you an old-style song, my little bruthah and sistah, the kind we sing at home. You other kids, you can sing with me.'

'That's great, Ke-ola, but we don't know your language.'

'Don't matter. Just do what I do and say what I say after me. You can do the dance and hum the words if you want to.'

'Dance?' Rory made a face. 'That's sissy stuff.'

'Yeah? Okay, you don't have to do it then if it's sissy. I didn't know that. We do sissy stuff at home all the time I guess.'

'No offense, man,' Rory said. He didn't want to make the big guy mad.

'No offense,' Ke-ola said, shrugging. Then he jumped, stomped, bellowed, snapped bent knees back and forth, and chanted in a language that had lots of great rhyming and repetitive sounds that seemed vaguely funny sometimes and beautiful at others. Murel thought he was choosing the words that would be the most fun to say, to get the other kids to say them too, and it worked. Some of the movements he made, which were a kind of sign language, looked like they might be something rude, and others looked like waves or stars twinkling or wind in the trees.

'I don't see how all of that could be about us,' Murel said. 'But thanks.'

'You're right. It's not all about you. You haven't been around long enough for it to be all about you. It's about where you come from, where you are now, and how you managed to land where you get to hang out with such great people like us.'

Then he told them what the gestures meant and some of the words he said the most.

'That's a lot like Petaybee songs,' Ronan told him, 'except we use drums a lot.'

'We use drums too,' he said. 'Come here, Rory, man. Bring your empty head so I can show you all some drumming.'

But Marmie's butler, who'd been watching everything onscreen inside the house, came out bringing a drum that usually acted as a side table in Marmie's main living room. Ke-ola looked at it critically, then started in on a beat that sounded a lot like a heartbeat and went perfectly with the chant he sang in quite a different tone from the last one. Periodically he danced along with his drumming, stomping for emphasis between drumbeats. Pretty soon everybody was doing it, even Rory.

'What's that one about?'

'Oh, it's just a song we do a lot on birthdays at home,' he said vaguely. 'It's the men's part. You do one now.'

So first they sang the otter song, then Murel sang one about mosquitoes.

Ke-ola laughed. 'You want to see what dance my people do about mosquitoes?' he asked, and when they said they did, he did a rhythmic chant that involved slapping himself silly on his thighs and chest, belly and forearms, the back of his neck and his face, even the soles of his feet.

'Wow, you must have bigger mosquitoes than we do even,' Ronan said.

The kids started trying to make up their own dances

then for a while, but they got pretty silly. Ke-ola jumped into the fake river and floated there like a contented island.

And Dewey was in a much better mood. He helped serve the refreshments, and now sat beside the fake river, his pant legs rolled up and his bare feet kicking back and forth in the water. The lights from below lit up his toes so they looked all white and corpsey. Or at least, what Murel thought corpse toes would probably look like.

'Do you guys swim here?'

'Uh, no,' Murel said. 'We, uh, we're afraid of the water.'

'How deep is it?' he asked.

'Oh, it's different in different places,' Murel said casually. Actually, it was a good five feet deep in some places, and more in others.

'How about right here?'

'I dunno. I could get a line to measure it, though, if you really want to know.'

'I got a better idea,' he said, and slid off the edge, and sank. Bubbles blew up from his mouth, but his face looked really white and corpsey now. Murel didn't even think about the secret. She just dove in after him, clothes and all. *Ronan, help! No, don't you come in too. Just stand there and wait*, she said. *Try not to let anybody else see me*. Fortunately, Dewey hadn't realized he was in trouble until it was too late to scream, so maybe nobody else noticed.

She caught the neck of Dewey's ship suit in her mouth, since she now had flippers poking out of her sleeves, and hauled him up to the surface where Ronan began pulling him up onto the 'bank' of ponics-grown turf.

Ronan was not quite alone, though. Ke-ola and Rory helped, Ke-ola pulling Dewey the rest of the way to his feet. Murel flipped the water off her head and hands and turned her back on everyone.

'I thought you were afraid of the water?' Dewey said between chattering teeth.

'I was more afraid you'd drown,' she replied, as soon as her muzzle turned back into a separate mouth and nose again, which fortunately didn't take but a second. 'I mean, I *can* swim, I just don't like to.'

Lan Huy said, 'Wow, you had a whole nother holo, Murel. Cool one! You looked just like a seal carrying Dewey in her mouth!'

'Yeah,' Murel said. 'So now *this* seal is flapping back inside to change into something dry.'

That sort of broke up the party. Marmie directed a flitter to return the other kids to their quarters.

By the time Murel came out, Ronan was staring at the packages Johnny carried and thinking that if these were from home, it meant that he and Murel weren't going to get to go back to Petaybee now.

'I'm sorry,' Murel said, apologizing before she reached the place where their chairs were clustered around a realistic holo of a blazing fireplace. Enough heat came from it to dry her hair into the long wild red-brown Irish curls that distinguished her from Ronan now. His hair was Inuit or maybe Navajo, straight and black. You couldn't tell them apart in the water very easily, though. 'The water's ten feet deep there, and the silly git doesn't know how to swim. Someone should teach him.'

'I'll speak to his parents,' Marmie said. 'That was very brave of you, chérie. No harm done. The others thought you had a good second holo.'

Murel smiled, but it faded as she saw the presents.

'You don't even know what's in them,' Johnny exclaimed. 'Why the long face?'

'We thought maybe you had come to take us home,' Ronan said. 'I know Marmie said not now, but we thought maybe Mum and Da had changed their minds.'

'No, my pets, I'm afraid you're stuck with me for the time being,' Marmie said.

But she didn't say what the time being might be.

That year, their gifts were new journals from Mum. She had kept them all year long to let the twins know what was happening between the rare times when they could talk via the com units. Da sent them carvings he had made of otters, each carving wrapped with a clamshell. Clodagh sent them a big plastic tub of her rose hip preserves and loaves of zucchini bread. Aunt Sinead and Aisling sent them 'Eskimo yo-yos' – moose-hair-stuffed hide sewed into balls, beaded by Aisling and attached to a long thong. You twirled it and then threw it at a bird, to either knock it out of the sky or snag its feet. They didn't have any birds to try them out on and got in trouble if they used the yo-yos on other kids, so finally they each sort of left them somewhere and forgot about them.

13

The following year, when they turned ten, went much faster. They'd made friends, together and separately, and did a lot of visiting away from Marmie's deck, studying in the excellent multimedia library, playing nonwater sports, studying martial-arts moves, and hanging out at the large shopping mall, the holo deck, and the homes of their friends. Marmie also welcomed the other kids to her compound, but the twins were worried that their friends would want to go swimming. Marmie's private waterway was a treat for the others since the station only boasted a single large pool complex, which was packed all the time. The twins made excuses not to go into the water but hated not to join in. It was fine to swim alone on the waterways, though awfully tame after the rivers around Kilcoole, but it would have been fun to play water games with the other kids.

'I wish we could control the change a little more,' Murel said one day, watching the sparkling drops spraying up from the usually still pool as their friends splashed each other. They had said they had sinus infections and weren't supposed to go in.

'Yeah, swim like people sometimes, or be seals on dry land. That might be good once in a while,' her brother agreed.

A well-known geneticist had arrived at the station and would teach the children during the next round of classes. 'It's my granny,' Rory said proudly. 'She's retired now and come to live with us, she says. But she's been all over the universe with her institute, studying all the different species on all the different worlds. She's really interested in the new ones.'

'What new ones?' Ke-ola asked.

'You know, the mutants that form because of conditions on one planet or the other. Seems the worlds terraformed by Intergal to house different races from Old Earth change things.'

'Like how?' Ke-ola asked, trying not to sound too interested.

'Oh, one of them has a special disease that people who work the soil get. It killed off a lot of them, but then they found a drug to help it, and the ones that get it now are okay but they shed their skin every year.'

'Like snakes?' Ke-ola asked.

'No, not all in one piece. They shed it in big flakes or scales, kind of like some trees lose their leaves.'

'Don't their insides fall out then?' Chesney asked.

'No, of course not, 'cause they have new skin underneath,' Rory said, looking at Chesney as if she were a silly little girl, which, actually, she wasn't.

When the twins told Marmie that Rory's granny was a famous scientist and was going to be one of their teachers, she seemed pleased, but was distracted by business. They realized that though she tried to act interested in their school and what they were doing, she was as busy, or maybe even busier, than Mum and Da. Marmie had lots of people working for her and doing things for her, but that gave her even more problems to solve. Often when they talked to her, she nodded and smiled or made appropriate noises, but wasn't really listening. And of course, she didn't personally pick out the teachers or have a lot to do with the school. She was too important for that.

'I think she liked us better when we were little,' Murel said later.

'Nah, she still likes us. She's just used to us now,' Ronan told her. 'She knows she doesn't have to worry about us all the time. Why should she? We know our way around now and who to go to for stuff. We know how to keep people from finding out about us. We're almost adults, when you think about it.'

'True. And it's not as if she's our mother or even a real auntie,' Murel said a little bitterly. She had wanted to tell Marmie about them wanting to ask the new teacher if she could help them learn to control their shape-shifting. But Murel knew she could have said they were going to jump off the station into space without the benefit of suits and Marmie would have probably replied, 'Bon, chérie. Très bon. You are so clever.'

'Really,' Murel told her brother, 'she's sort of a glorified babysitter. Only not as furry as 'Nook and Co'.'

Mentioning the cats' names made her homesick. She longed to bury her face and hands in their fur, feel their raspy tongues on her cheeks and fingers – or flippers as the case might be – hear their thundering purrs or even their disdainful scolding. She missed mind-talking with them, missed talking with other creatures who were not her twin brother.

The first day of class, Rory's gran strode into the room after they were all seated. She was dark-skinned, like Rory, with the same rough-carved features and broad nostrils. Her eyes were not blue like his, but sparkling black, like anthracite at the bottom of a cold and flowing stream.

'So,' she said. 'You are all my grandson's classmates. Do not think, because Rory is my grandson, that I am a daft old woman who will sit here knitting while you throw spitballs at each other.'

They all laughed. Professor Mabo had a great smile, with shiny white teeth and dimples, and when she spoke, her voice had kind of a song to it. It rose and fell and did little tweaks and twirls that made what she had to say more interesting. And it turned out to be plenty interesting already.

She took out some pictures that looked like the ones the twins had seen in Rory's parents' quarters. They were very stylized and looked kind of like X rays of animals, with pictures of other things inside of them. 'Do you know what these are?' she asked.

'Rory's screensaver?' Ke-ola asked.

'Is it?' Professor Mabo asked her grandson.

'Yeah, Gran, I have the wombat design as a screensaver.'

'It will be Professor Mabo to you too, Rory, while class is in session,' Rory's gran told him. 'As for you, young man, you are apparently correct. Rory does have this sort of artwork as a screensaver. So you are familiar with the design, but do you understand what it means?'

Rory raised his hand, but very cautiously. He wasn't looking nearly so pleased to be in a class where his grandmother was the teacher now. Murel thought it would have been nice if the grandmother had told Rory before class started what he was supposed to call her.

'Anyone but you, Rory. This art comes from our culture, so you should know already what it means. But I want to know if anyone else can figure it out.'

'I think I know,' Ronan said at the same time he raised his hand.

'Yes. It's Ronan, is it not?' But she looked as if she knew exactly who he was.

'Yes, ma'am. I think the drawings inside the bigger drawing are the story that explains the bigger creature. Some of the art of our Inuit ancestors is a bit like that.'

'Most perceptive, Ronan. That is indeed part of the reason for the inner drawings. They also serve to depict the essentially dual nature of all creatures.'

'All creatures, Professor?' Murel asked.

'Oh yes. You will always find the remnants in every living thing of the thing it was before it became the thing it is now.'

'But most creatures are only one thing at a time, aren't they? I mean, they used to be something else maybe, but now, in this time, they are what they look like.'

'Most creatures? That is an interesting way to phrase your question, my dear. Most *students* would feel that *all* creatures are as you describe, not merely most.'

'Oh well, we don't know about *all*, do we?' Dewey asked. 'I mean, none of us have seen all the creatures there are to see. That's what Murel meant, right, Murel?'

She nodded slowly, which wasn't exactly a lie.

'I think in the future – Dewey, is it not? – you must allow Murel to clarify her own comments. Yes?'

'Okay, Professor. Sorry.'

'The other interesting feature of this art form is that it demonstrates a certain knowledge of the anatomy of these creatures. It was probably influenced by the earliest dissections, at least insofar as shown by bone structure, organ placement, and the relationship of the parts to each other. Therefore, we will be doing dissections in this class – hands-on ones, not via computer or videotape. Since there is no extraneous animal life aboard this space station, when I learned I was to have a teaching position here, I brought specimens from my last laboratory. We will begin tomorrow. For now, you are to read the first two chapters in your text, and we will discuss them tomorrow.'

She dismissed the class. Murel and Ronan stood up to leave, but Rory stopped them. 'My mum said I should ask you two if you'd care to come for dinner tonight. She's making a special meal in honor of Gran. Can you come?'

'Sure. We'll have to ask Marmie, but I don't think she'll mind,' Ronan said.

Marmie met them at the flitter when they came home that afternoon. She had a small bag in her hand. 'I have been called away on business for a couple days, children. While I am gone, Petronella will look after you. You must not annoy her. She is not as tolerant as I am, and is much better at hand-to-hand combat, so I trust you will behave.' Petronella Chan was Marmie's chief of domestic security, in charge of the mansion, grounds, and in fact the entire deck housing Marmie and her staff. She reported only to Space Station Security Chief Fadeyka Petrovich, but he also reported to her. They worked together to ensure that the station, and especially their employer, was safer than most fortresses. Neither twin had been in an actual fortress, but knew they were supposed to be really safe. Pet was a tough cookie, but she also baked great cookies, and the twins liked her a lot.

'We always do behave, Marmie,' Murel said.

'Rory wants us to come to his place for dinner tonight,' Ronan said. 'Is it okay? Will Pet let us?'

'I shall call her and tell her I authorize it,' Marmie answered, and bent to give them each a double-cheeked kiss before boarding the flitter and buzzing off to the docking area.

Rory's folks were quite nice and had sponsored class events before, though they'd never invited the twins to their quarters.

His mother, Elizabeth, was a scientist, a biologist like her own mother, Professor Mabo. Rory's father was an engineer. Everyone was bustling around like mad when the twins got there. Dinner was cooking, and it smelled delicious, all spicy and vaguely like roasting meat.

Rory's da carried a large chair and set it down in front of Ronan and Murel, emitting a huff as he did so. 'Have a seat, one of you. Or better yet, pick up something and set it on its chalk mark.'

'Is it a game?' Murel asked Rory.

'Nah,' he said. 'They moved us into bigger quarters now that Gran is with us. She has an apartment of her own next door, but there's a connecting door. Our other place wasn't set up that way. They just told my mum today.'

'That's fast,' Ronan said.

He and Murel helped to put things where they were supposed to go. Finally, Rory's mum called out that they should stop and told Rory to go next door and get his grandmother so they could eat.

Professor Mabo was the only one who didn't look overheated and sweaty. Rory's mum and dad rushed around trying to get the food on the table, but the professor took a seat and stayed there. 'Seniority has its privileges,' she told Murel and Ronan, showing her dimples as she smiled at them as if it were a big joke.

'Sure,' Ronan said. 'I bet you had to run around like this to take care of stuff when Rory's mother was little too.'

'Oh no, I had assistants to do these things. Unfortunately, Elizabeth has not attained the stature I had even as young as I was, and so she must raise Rory and entertain his friends with no help except that of poor Bram, who as you can see is not quite up to the task.'

That's a nasty thing to say, Murel told her brother.

At least she isn't being nasty to us, Ronan answered.

'Rory, go back to my apartment and fetch the book on my dresser,' his gran said. 'There are pictures in there I want to show you all.'

Rory had just settled into his chair and was helping himself to the first ladle of food from one of the steaming dishes.

'Can't it wait until after dinner, Mother?' Rory's mum asked. 'The food is hot now.'

Ronan and Murel exchanged nervous looks. Rory's mother sounded as if it took all of her courage to speak up to Professor Mabo.

I think I'm not so sorry we don't have a grandma after all, Ronan said.

They're not all like her. We know lots of nice grandmas in Kilcoole.

But Professor Mabo looked at the two of them and changed her tone. 'I'm sorry. How thoughtless of me. Of course we must eat your lovely meal while it's hot. Rory can get the photos afterward or perhaps we can all go to my quarters to look at them while you and Bram clean up. My rooms are more spacious and comfortable anyway.'

She smiled at the twins and Rory, and everybody dug in. Professor Mabo seemed to relax during the meal and even told some funny stories about collecting species on various planets and her other work with the institute. '"What kind of a rat is that?" the man asked me, and I said, "It's a bear, actually." He said it was no wonder he had sustained so many injuries while trying to catch them with cheese.'

The twins offered to help with the cleanup, as they'd been taught, but Rory's mother seemed relieved to have everyone out from underfoot. 'No, no, you go. It's quite an honor for you that Mother wants to share her work – or at least its history – with you.'

'Yeah,' Rory said, frowning. 'She never showed *me* any of that stuff before.'

By then, Professor Mabo was waiting impatiently by the door, so the three of them caught up with her.

Rory acts like he's mad at us, Ronan told Murel, with a big question mark hanging over the thought.

Well, she's his grandma but she's being nicer to us than she is to him. I wonder why?

'Cause we're so cute? Ronan asked.

Does Professor Mabo seem like the kind of person who cares about cute to you?

No, not exactly. Why, then?

I dunno. Maybe we'll find out pretty soon.

Professor Mabo's place didn't look very grandmotherly at all, or even homey. It was bare of pictures and personal touches. In the center of the living room there was a long white table with chairs around it, as if prepared for a meeting. Her computer was at one end. Instead of knickknacks, she had specimen jars. They seemed to contain small pickled creatures or parts of them.

I don't think I want to see what's in the fridge, Murel said.

'Now then, children, have a seat and I will bring out my album,' Professor Mabo said. When she came back out, she was wearing a shawl over her ship suit and fuzzy slippers, as well as a pair of reading spectacles, an old-fashioned touch.

She sat down with the album in front of her and asked Murel and Ronan to pull up chairs on either side. Rory had to peer over her shoulder.

After showing them a number of creatures that were

variations on lions, tigers, bears, and camels, she displayed a picture of two different sorts of lizard. 'Now this is a Sorrysaurus,' she told them of the first one. 'Guess what this one is?'

'Dunno,' Rory said.

'Me neither,' Ronan said.

Murel shook her head.

'Just guess.'

'Can't,' they all three said.

'It's a Sorrysaurus too.'

'They look really different.'

'It's a chameleon of sorts,' Professor Mabo said. 'It not only changes colors, it actually changes shapes according to its environment.'

'Weird,' Rory said.

'Not at all,' she said. 'It's simply a natural adaptation, quite practical under the circumstances. The world on which the Sorrysaurus lives changes not only its climate, but the complete environment of its landmasses from one season to the next. The first picture, in which the creature is yellow-green, is a warm-season Sorrysaurus. The second picture, in which the creature is white and spiked, is the cold-season version. Not only does the creature survive the entire year, but also, only one creature of its sort inhabits the same territory year round, which limits predation to some degree.'

'If you say so,' Ronan said. 'It sure looks different, though.'

'Many creatures in the universe change their colors or shapes – for some it is a question of time. You are not the same shape you will be when you are a man, for instance, Ronan. Nor is Murel the same shape she will be when she is an adult woman. For others it is a question of season or environmental coloration. The Sorrysaurus is only one of the slightly more extreme versions. There are many others. I find them fascinating, don't you?'

'Oh yeah,' Rory said.

Murel and Ronan both nodded cautiously. 'How can they do that exactly?' Ronan asked.

'It is so simple it's a wonder more things don't change form more often,' the professor said. 'We are all of us made up of various particles. The important thing about this – whatever the theory, whatever the physicists call them – is that all of these particles, relative to their size, are very very far apart. They have great latitude of movement. If they are somehow manipulated, by whatever science or force, to move in certain ways, the nature of the object or being they compose will also alter. Human beings have known this for many years before they knew about science. Always, throughout history, even before it was written down, there are stories of men or beasts who are first one thing and then another. Once, this was thought to be superstition, but I have made a study of the way life forms are altered, particularly on these new, terraformed planets, and I have seen, as you see here with the Sorrysaurus, that such transformation is not only possible but actually occurs.'

There was a knock on the door then. When Rory opened it, Pet Chan stood there.

'Dr. Mabo? The doctors Upfield say that Ronan and Murel are visiting you. It is time for them to return to their compound and go to bed.'

'Very well. Run along now, children, but do come and visit me again.'

'Thanks,' Murel said. 'Maybe Rory could come up and visit us tomorrow. Would you, Rory? We've got a new card game but it takes at least three.'

Rory looked as if he was about to refuse. He was clearly miffed about the preference his grandma showed for his friends, but it wasn't as if Ronan and Murel had tried to *make* her like them. And it didn't really make a lot of sense that Murel could see either.

'Please, Rory,' Ronan added. 'Marmie has some great vids, and we'll ask Pet to make us some of her chocolate fudge bomb cookies.'

'Right you are, mate,' Rory said finally, with a brief version of his usual grin. 'I'll ask the folks.'

'I'm sure it will be fine, Rory,' Professor Mabo said, waving goodbye as the twins hopped into the flitter.

That night before they went to sleep, the twins had a swim and played in seal form, as best they could in such a tame environment.

Did you feel any particles moving around when you changed? Murel asked her brother.

Maybe I do. Maybe hand particles turning into flipper ones or something, but I never really thought about it. It's good she knows about this stuff and that she's our teacher. And I'm glad she likes us because she's not very nice to her own family, and if she didn't like us, she could really make us miserable.

Yeah, but it might be better if she did that than make Rory miserable and think it was all our fault. I'd hate it if Mum or Da acted like they liked some other kid better than they did us.

Not that they've shown any signs that they really do like us recently, Ronan replied. *Can you even remember what they look like, when they're not on the com screen? It's kind of hard. Sort of like their particles keep shifting around in my head.*

He was joking, but it was one of those jokes that was too true to be funny. It was almost three years since they'd seen their parents in person, or been on Petaybee. He felt tears welling up and tried to choke them down.

But hey, who needs all that cold and stuff? Here we can make the weather any kind we want, we get to see all kinds of vids and meet all kinds of people. Important people are our teachers, not somebody we're not supposed to bother. And Marmie has new surprises for us all the time.

Yeah, that's right, Murel agreed. *It's great here. No wolves to worry about when we swim, or otter poachers even. Of course, there's no otters, or track cats, or snow leopards, or curly coats, or even sled dogs or house cats. And the weather isn't exactly real. And Marmie can't change into a seal. But hey, Da can do that, but he stopped doing it with us most of the time, so that doesn't matter, does it?*

No way. We're a lot better off here. Our parents were right. They were doing us a big fat favor sending us here.

Yeah, Murel agreed. *That is all* so *true. Which makes me feel like a real head case because, aw jays, Ronan, I really really miss them.*

Me too. I miss Petaybee. I miss the caves and the rivers and the otters and the other critters and Clodagh and latchkays, and I miss Mum and Da something terrible.

Me too. But they don't want us there right now. Maybe

when we're better prepared for life and can handle ourselves better.

Yeah, like when we're twenty or something really old like that.

I want to go home now. I don't want to wait till I'm twenty.

Me too.

They didn't cry. Murel crawled into her bunk and Ronan into his. Without talking about it, each of them rolled toward the other and held out a hand. They linked fingers and finally fell asleep swapping mind pictures of their favorite things back home. It wasn't much of a swap, since they'd shared everything from the time they were born, but it was the best comfort they had.

14

All I can say is that I certainly hope the planet knows what it's doing,' Yana said to the committee composed of herself, her husband, Dr. Whittaker Fiske – the originator of the terraforming process used on Petaybee – Clodagh, and Dr. Frank Metaxos. Sister Igneous Rock, a geologist and one of the cult of originally misguided religious fanatics who had come to Petaybee thinking to worship it – before the planet declined their worship – was also in attendance.

'Of course Petaybee knows what He or She or possibly They are doing,' Sister Iggierock chided her. 'We should praise Petaybee's name for its compassion for those among us who need a more temperate zone in which to live. A zone where one need not dress like a polar bear and live in darkness most of the year, as we do now. Your children and your children's children will be able to live in a place where they can enjoy greenery year round. The entire planet will have a source of nourishment from gardens and farms growing fresh fruits and vegetables – even a broader range of medicinal plants, Clodagh – than is now possible with our limited growing season.'

'That would be beneficial, yes,' Yana said, '*if* our children and their children were ever able to enjoy it.'

'Oh well, perhaps I should have said descendants,' Iggierock conceded. 'These things do take time, even for a brilliant sentient world like Petaybee. It will be centuries – millennia, actually – before the new landmass extruding from the sea will be stable enough and cool enough for people to live on it.'

Dr. Whittaker Fiske cleared his throat. 'That is not exactly true in Petaybee's case, Sister,' he corrected her. 'The process that accelerates Petaybee's development also accelerates the maturation process. Once the volcanic mass surfaces, it will begin to stabilize. It will probably be ready for habitation within the next twenty years at the latest. Of course, with Petaybee it is always difficult to say. For a couple of generations, we've believed that the terraforming process was completed and that two large polar landmasses would be the extent of the planet's habitable area, and that was stretching the definition of habitable. However, from what I've learned of Petaybee, you are all being more accurate than whimsical to imply that the planet is choosing to present an island, at the very least, at this time. As all of you know, our usual instrumentation is impeded by the electromagnetic fields emanating from Petaybee, from the sunspots currently mucking up our communications equipment, and from the extremes of temperature it is subjected to on this planet. Although we know that at least one volcanic mass is arising from the sea near the equator, we have little idea of its ultimate extent or what we may expect in the way of seismic activity.'

'That's why I'm going to explore underwater,' Sean said. 'It's easier for me than for divers, and besides, all that equipment would need to be imported, as well as the personnel. We haven't trained a lot of human divers here for obvious reasons. And if you all could see the stacks and lists of individuals and groups and whole displaced populations applying for immigration to Petaybee, you'd understand why we wish to know the potential of the new landmass ourselves before letting outsiders have a look at it.'

He began his journey the next morning, leaving poor Yana with the paperwork and such electronic communiqués as were able to reach them these days. They didn't mind so much being cut off from the more sophisticated offworld amenities such as direct audio-visual contact between callers from space to ground or from planet to planet, but they sorely missed being able to talk to the kids. When sending the twins to Marmie's space station, they had not anticipated being unable to have face-to-face, voice-to-voice contact with their children on a weekly if not daily basis, no matter the cost. Marmie had generously agreed to foot most of the bill. Secondhand messages and written notes were simply not the same. Yana was not the type to pine over anything, but she missed the children so badly that her appetite was off, despite all of Clodagh's remedies.

Sean felt as if part of himself was missing, floating off somewhere inaccessible. His thoughts did not all want to stay in his head – they kept wandering off in search of the twins' thoughts, but those were no longer there. No smooth rounded baby arms to hug him, or flippers either for that matter. But with them wanting to swim freely so much that they ran into constant danger, he and Yana simply couldn't risk having them near. They were too precious, too important. He would have to free the planet of all of those outside dangers like the one the otters had faced. He'd have to look into this new development at sea and figure out what to do with those who wanted to exploit it. Best keep the kids clear of that one too. But he missed them.

Well, the sooner started, the sooner finished. He dove into the running river, free of ice but still chilling and powder-gray with glacial runoff.

Of course, he could have easily ridden a curly coat to the coast, but actually, in seal form, he swam faster than a curly coat could navigate the spongy tundra or the swampy banks where the channels branched and rebraided themselves before reaching the sea. Besides, this mission was a confidential one, and the fewer people – even their people – involved, the better.

When he paused for air, he enjoyed the wild lupine and fireweed turning the riverbanks purple and magenta against the background of a thousand greens. The river teemed with fish, so he could have gorged himself if he'd wanted to, but he preferred to take only what he needed to maintain his energy and not get loggy trying to digest too much food.

When he first pulled out of the water to sleep he was grateful for the suit Marmie provided for him. He had small caches of clothing along the riverbank, but this way he could stop where he needed to without worrying about that. Once he was dressed in the suit, he located his clothing downstream from it and wore that until he was ready to dive back into the water. He wanted to look as normal as possible to any people he might meet, and a shiny silver suit didn't help him blend.

On the second day, he pulled himself out of the water and onto land that was part riverbank and part seashore. A small island lay offshore, perhaps two hundred meters away, but otherwise the horizon was coral-red with the setting sun, the water beneath the color of salmon meat.

Tonight he would rest well, because tomorrow's swim would take him too far from shore to sleep.

He found a dry sandy place and curled up to sleep, but as he began nodding off he heard, *Hah! Father River Seal, why are you here? Have you come to tell otters that your children are coming home?*

He opened his eyes and looked into a round brown furry face with bright black eyes and breath that smelled, pleasantly to Sean, like fish.

What is a river otter doing so close to the sea? he asked the otter.

My question first! I asked first! Are the river seal children coming home? Is that why you're here – oh, no, I suppose not since you did not expect to see otters here. You could not be bringing otters a message if you did not know otters would be here to receive it. So why are you here? Not that you are not very welcome. We have told our sea otter cousins all about our brave river seal friends who are the protectors of otters, and they will welcome you also. But why?

I'm exploring, Sean told the otter.

Otters.

At least a dozen more otters had joined the kids' friend, boldly standing right next to his prone body. Another half-dozen pairs of bright eyes focused on him from the water.

He doesn't look so big now, the river seal man, one said.

No, but he is very fierce. You saw him carry away the humans with cages, he and his family. He must like otters very much to have followed us all the way here.

Are you hungry, seal man?

Do you want to play, seal man? There is a nice mud slide just over there.

Their voices chittered and chattered in his head so busily he had trouble focusing.

I came exploring, he said to the colony at large. *I want to bring my children home but I have to make sure conditions here won't bring more dangerous people to harm them and, er, otters too.*

He barely had the thought out, however, before they had plucked an image from his mind. One forgot to guard against that sort of thing when surrounded by otters.

You're going to the New Home! He's going to the New Home! Where the sea otter cousins go. It's very far and rather deep for a river seal.

I should think it would be out of bounds for river otters, Sean replied.

Hah! It is much too far through that salty liquid for river otters. We are not going there. We are staying right here.

Sean had been so absorbed in river otter thoughts that he hadn't noted the arrival from the darkened sea of the other species of otters – the cousins of whom Otter was so proud.

Sea otters go check out the construction of the New Home, one of these said. To the river otters he said, *This looks like a man. You are sure it is the father of river seals from your song?*

'Hah!' Otter said. *Of course we are sure. Father River Seal and his family are close personal friends and protectors of river otters.*

So you sing, the sea otter said. *Does he come to visit you often? Does he need to be fed?*

I am not hungry, thank you, Sea Otter, Sean said. *I did not know river otters were here, or sea otters either, but I'm pleased to see all of you. I came to see the New Home. My people want to know what our world is doing out there in the ocean.*

It is very interesting and rather tasty, the sea otter told him. *We will take you there. It is also a bit dangerous, so we can show you where to go and where not to go. But first we all sleep.*

The river otters chittered among themselves so quickly Sean couldn't read their thoughts. The otter said, *You have no den. We could enlarge one for you. You will be cold out here although it is summer.*

We could offer you our kelp beds to wrap your seal-self in and keep you afloat, as we do when we sleep, the sea otters, not to be outdone in hospitality, quickly counteroffered.

I'll be grand right here, Sean told them all.

Well, if you're sure, the sea otters said, sliding back into the water, their thoughts washing away on the tide.

Good night then, Father River Seal, the river otters said as those on the edge of the group disappeared into the riverbanks.

Sean lay down again murmuring, *Good night* to the river otters.

Hah! Otter said. *This is not right. Father River Seal will be cold and lonely without his family. Otters will keep you warm.* And with that Otter snuggled in next to the back of Sean's neck and at once fell asleep. Others, close family members including six of Otter's brothers and sisters, his mother and grandmother, four aunts and two uncles, also snuggled next to Sean. He lay warmly immobilized in a living furry blanket for the rest of the night. He fell asleep hoping he would not need to get up and relieve himself and disturb his hosts or squash one of them.

The next morning before school, the twins made it snow. Marmie had showed them how to do it, but most of the time they left it up to her. Now, however, Murel typed with one hand while holding her breakfast bar in the other. 'How heavy do we want the snow?' she asked.

'Real heavy. Not a blizzard, but so it stacks up. And wind. Let's have some wind so we can have drifts.'

'What velocity?'

'Doesn't have to be a gale to blow snow,' he said, and scooped a spoonful of cereal from his bowl.

'I wish we could put some river ice on the waterway,' Murel said.

'Yeah, but it's heated all the time. We could make a rink on one of the flitter pads, though. You can adjust ground temperature by pressing Control GT.'

'Cool.'

'Yeah, it will be. We won't even need skates. We can just skate in our shoes. We'll have to shovel the snow first.'

'Good. I want to.'

That was all they had time to do before school, but by the time the flitter picked them up, the sky was white with snow and the flakes fell like broken crystals. You could tell they weren't real flakes, though. They were all the same.

Their class with Professor Mabo was in a lab that had been set up near the school complex for her use. It was small but there were tables with stools and a desk, besides all of the standard lab equipment for biology, chemistry, and general science courses.

Professor Mabo looked up from the desk. She was wearing a lab coat over her silver ship suit. Her teeth flashed pleasantly as she greeted the students, and her large silver hoop earrings matched the ship suit.

Three boxes sat in front of her, two of them open and full of shiny objects, one closed.

'As you come in, please select an item from each box. Box A contains scalpels. The blades are attached but sheathed. Please do not cut yourself, as taking time to clean up your blood will deprive the other students of lab time and possibly contaminate your specimens. Box B contains hemostats. Box C contains your specimens. You may use the synskin gloves beside the box to extract your specimen and conduct your dissection. You will work in pairs, one specimen to each pair of students.'

Ronan, Rory, and Murel were the first students to enter, and each of them did as directed. Then Ronan lifted the cover from the large specimen box and his eyes widened.

'Nothing to be afraid of, boy. They're quite dead. They won't bite,' the professor said.

Dead frogs, Ronan told his sister. *She wants us to cut up dead frogs.*

Murel came to his side and peered into the box. 'Professor, how did the frogs die?' she asked.

'Of old age,' the teacher snapped. 'While waiting for squeamish students to do as they're told.'

'Oh, sorry, I just wondered,' Murel said. 'It's just that on Petaybee, animals come to specific places when they're sick or old so that they can be killed kindly and their bodies used for food or clothing or whatever the hunter needs.'

Rory flinched, and Murel realized he was waiting for his grandmother's wrath to come down on his friends the way it usually did on him.

The professor's face contorted for a moment, as if she were about to turn into something else, but the contortions ended in a wise smile. 'Fascinating, my dear. Thank you for that enlightening explanation. In fact, it ties in nicely with our lesson today. How indeed did these frogs die? How would we learn that sort of thing? By examining their remains. That is how, and that is what we will be doing today. So, as I said, each of you take your instruments and your frogs and find a place at the table so we may begin.'

Murel and Ronan chose spots adjacent to each other, but once everyone had a place, Professor Mabo said, 'Murel, please trade places with Chesney. Neither she nor Ke-ola obtained a frog, and both you and Ronan have one.'

Murel nodded and did as she was told.

She just wants to split us up, Ronan said. *We could have always given Chesney and Ke-ola one of our frogs.*

Of course, the professor had no way of knowing that the two of them could communicate telepathically. Nobody knew that except maybe Marmie, and if she knew, it was only from observation. They had learned early on that their private line into each other's minds was a bigger advantage when nobody around them realized they had it.

Who was she trying to kid? Ronan asked about halfway through the session. *This frog was perfectly healthy until someone killed it.*

She probably didn't think we'd know how to tell, Murel said. *She thought we were just squeamish. She doesn't know about us helping Da do this kind of thing in the lab.*

Professor Mabo had been circling the classroom and stopped to stand behind Ronan. 'Very good work, Ronan. Very precise. I believe your technique is almost as good as mine.'

Ronan ducked his head, as if he were bashful. *She has no idea what Auntie Sinead would have said if we'd spoilt the meat or hide on one of her kills after she showed us how to clean and skin it*, he told Murel.

No, or how Clodagh has always taught us that we're supposed to use every possible piece of the animal as wisely as possible out of respect for the gift of its body for our benefit.

'Murel, what is taking you so long?' Professor Mabo said. 'Give Chesney a turn, or however that frog died, it will have been for nothing.' She had circled behind Murel while Murel was exchanging thoughts with Ronan. Murel jumped, and the knife slipped, slicing her finger, so that blood dripped onto the table, the frog, and the other instruments.

'Ouch!' Murel said, and dropped the scalpel to hold her finger with her other hand.

'You are supposed to dissect the frog, Murel, not your hand,' Professor Mabo scolded. Chesney produced a grubby tissue, but it quickly turned bright red and the blood kept dripping. 'I think you had best seek medical attention. You may finish your dissection tomorrow.'

The professor didn't seem to notice that Ronan had dropped his scalpel and started to hold his hand, then quickly picked up the scalpel again and tried not to look pained as his twin hurried off to the station's infirmary. *He* noticed, however, that the professor, after handing Murel a fresh tissue, pocketed the bloody one before she handed Chesney a towel with which to mop up his sister's blood.

Murel was home when Ronan got there. She hadn't needed stitches but she sported a big plaskin on her index finger, and it leaked once in a while if she put too much pressure on it.

That evening, Pet made some of her cookies and Ronan fixed Murel a cup of the orange spiced tea Clodagh brewed for special occasions. They sat at the window watching it snow until bedtime.

Professor Mabo doesn't seem to like me anymore, Murel

said. *Did you see how she snuck up on me? That's why I cut my finger.*

Yeah, well, having her like me doesn't feel like any great honor either, Ronan said. *There's something really strange about her. I wonder why she stuck your bloody tissue in her pocket. There was a trash chute right next to the table.*

Do you think she was collecting a specimen?

Possibly. I'm not sure what she could tell by it, though. Maybe we should ask Pet how to send a secure message to Da. He'll know if there's anything in our blood that would tell her how different we are.

15

When Marmie returned, though she said nothing about the deep winter into which the twins had plunged her home, the weather changed. When they returned from school, they found Marmie taking a swim in tropical conditions, sunny, warm, and balmy, with a slight breeze scented with exotic flowers.

When it was time for student evaluations, toward the end of the term, Professor Mabo requested a personal interview with Marmie.

'I feel that Ronan and Murel have a great deal of potential,' she said. 'They are extraordinarily quick and bright. But perhaps they impede each other's intellectual growth. I think if they were in separate classes, they might do better.'

'They have an A-plus average,' Marmie pointed out. 'I scarcely see how they can improve on it.'

'For their age group, of course they get high marks. But they are each capable of functioning far beyond their age group.'

'Well, be that as it may, splitting them up is not an option,' Marmie told her firmly. 'For one thing, it would break their hearts, and they have already been through a great deal, being separated from their parents and their home. For another thing, it can hardly have escaped your notice that ours is a small educational facility with only one class for each age group.'

'Yes, yes, I know all that,' Professor Mabo said, barely managing to keep the impatience out of her voice. 'But I have a suggestion. I think Ronan would benefit by doing an extra lab class with me, as my assistant. I have been trying to teach my grandson to do it but he is not an apt student. Initially the twins disliked the dissections, but now they seem to tolerate them well. I believe that with additional exposure, Ronan may turn into a fine little scientist.'

'He's only ten years old, Dr. Mabo,' Marmie said.

'Immaterial.'

Ronan and Murel had been listening, with the collusion of Pet Chan, on the intercom, and now Marmion said into it, 'Pet, would you have the twins join us in the observatory tearoom please?'

The professor was dressed in an elegant long scarlet robe over her ship suit. She seemed to be trying to appear relaxed, but the twins weren't fooled.

'The professor seems to feel you two should study independently of each other for a while and has offered you, Ronan, the opportunity to be her lab assistant. What do you think?'

Careful, Murel said.

I know. I don't trust her any more than you do, but we've got to start learning more about this stuff, Murel, if we're ever going to be able to control our own shapes.

Da could—

We're not with Da, are we? He's too busy to help us figure this out, and besides, if he knew how, he probably would do a better job of it for himself. Remember their story about how he got shot when he was half changed?

Their message to their father for advice about the blood sample so far had gone unanswered. Pet's advice about making the message they sent their father secure was not reassuring. 'There's all kinds of ways to secure information, and there's also all kinds of ways for data thieves to hijack it. The safest way to do this, if it's really important, is to set up a code with the recipient – a personal code, that is – and encrypt your message using that. Even so, data pirates have strange minds that seem to read yours and they've been hijacking passwords and codes for centuries. Really, the very safest thing is to hand-deliver the message by a courier both you and the recipient know and trust. If it was really imperative that the message not fall into enemy hands or be hijacked, that's what I'd do. Of course, I have been accused of being overly paranoid, but this is the same advice I give to Madame and the procedures we follow in extreme circumstances. Of course, you understand that my duties include only her personal communications. Corporate and station security are the responsibility of other personnel.'

Since they had set up no code in advance, they wrote out the message. When Johnny stopped by prior to his supply run to Petaybee, Murel tucked it into his hand. 'It's top secret, Johnny, but really urgent. Ask Da to give you the answer before you leave.'

'I'll do my best to corner him, Murel.'

'*Really* important,' she stressed.

Johnny had several other stops to make, however, and hadn't returned as yet, nor had Da answered in any other way.

I'm going to do it, Murel, Ronan said. *She's snoopy and cranky, but she is still an expert in what we need to know about. Maybe we'll even get to be friends and I can ask her directly sometime.*

Don't! Murel warned.

I'll talk to you before I do, don't worry, he promised. Aloud, he said, 'I think I'd like to be your lab assistant, Professor, but except for that, Murel and I don't like being split up. Can we stay together in class if I work for you alone afterward?'

'I suppose so,' she said. 'But in my professional opinion – for your own good, mind you – you two need to work on developing some independence of thought and opinion. I realize the bond between twins is supposed to be quite close, but too much interdependence is unhealthy, particularly when they are of different genders, as you two are. You are entering puberty now, after all.'

Marmie frowned but said only, 'Very well. Ronan, I'll place a flitter at your disposal for you to return here after you finish working with Dr. Mabo each day.'

'That won't be necessary,' the professor told her. 'You have kindly placed a flitter at my disposal as well. The least I can do is to give Ronan a ride.' She turned and regarded him with clinical interest that made Murel shudder.

I bet she asks you to climb up on a slide and scoot under a giant microscope lens right away, Murel said.

She's not going to try anything when Marmie knows right where I am. Besides, station security wouldn't let her do anything to me.

I still have a really bad feeling about this, Ronan.

Sean swam with the sea otters, one large gray seal among their smaller forms, gliding through the water with ease for many kilometers.

He had no trouble telling when they began swimming across the volcanic ridge since a very warm column of water bubbled to the surface. Anticipation bubbled through the otters at the same time, and suddenly they all dived at once. Sean followed.

Look at them! the senior otter exclaimed, his thought filled with blissful anticipation. *Such clams! Petaybee must really love otters to give them this food.*

Although the seal in Sean could certainly have eaten something, the clams were not so interesting by themselves as they were as part of the underseascape.

They had to dive quite deeply, but Sean was somewhat surprised to find it was not as deep as he would have thought. Normally, seals and otters would not be able to dive to the most extreme depths of the ocean, but it was comparatively shallow here. The volcanic activity had built up the ocean floor, forming a sort of mountain range that would build the farther south it went. Sean had observed this from a distance on other swims, but he hadn't realized the planet was in such a hurry to produce its new landmass.

The water around them was milky blue, the color, as

Sean knew, coming from the minerals and bacteria in which volcanic areas were rich.

Tall black rocky chimneys rose up from the ocean floor, which was paved with flowing billows and pillows of black lava rock. Each crevice and crack of the lava was stuffed with the foot-long clams. White crabs scuttled along over the blackness, going about their business. Like little gardens of animals, each of these communities had as its centerpiece huge clusters of exceptionally long tube worms, bursting like enormous red flowers among the other creatures.

Surfacing for air again, Sean told himself he had to return with a scientific team sometime and see what was down there. He was certain there were all manner of life forms that Intergal, the company that had ordered the planet terraformed, had no idea were there. He just wanted a quick look in seal form. All around him sea otters surfaced carrying large clams, though not the largest.

Are they good? he asked the nearest otter conversationally.

Delectable. Bright red meat and lots of it. But opening them is tricky. They're not of a size you can crack open on your chest without cracking otters as well as clams.

When we get back, I'll change into man form and get a heavy rock to open them for you, he promised.

You will? The sea otter's round eyes got, if anything, rounder in his round face. *Did you otters hear that? Go for the big ones! The river seal will help us open them and there will be feasting for us all!*

The surface thrashed with otter bodies diving down and popping up with clams bigger than their heads.

Each otter could carry only one clam. Soon, Sean knew, they'd be ready to return. *I'll just swim ahead a little and circle back and catch up with you*, he told them. *I want to see the New Home where it is building the quickest.*

There's not as much food there, an otter told him. *Too hot, too busy. Hey! No fair slipping out of otter paws! Come back you!* And his sleek rump surfaced for a moment before it smoothly vanished under the waves. For the first time Sean noticed that off in the distance what had seemed to be low cloud cover was actually rolling smoke. Petaybee surely was cooking with gas now.

He swam swiftly forward. The bubbly warm spots grew more frequent, until the entire ocean seemed to be warmer by many degrees. He caught fish simply because he had to swim through so many of them to proceed and it was easier to catch some than to go around them.

The water grew warmer and warmer, like bathwater and not unpleasant. The seawater cooled the molten lava almost at once, though that would not be the case once the volcano grew until it erupted on the surface. He wondered how close that was. He'd been feeling a bit foolish for deciding to reconnoiter by swimming over the site, but with the smoke and ash piling up on the horizon, aircraft would be in danger of getting their motors and other sensitive parts clogged.

Soon he realized that he'd left the otters far behind. He could see the bottom of the ocean beneath him now simply by looking down. The piping black smokers and the gentle lava pillows stuffed with clams and other sealife had long ago given way to some true volcanic mounds with vents in the middle. Diving down, he could see a long way into them, into the heart of Petaybee.

He got so busy looking down and diving to swim around the vents and examine the life forms there that he forgot to look up and ahead until the entire ocean shook like jelly, sloshing him about. He was startled to see that a real mountain loomed ahead of him, the summit just below the ocean's surface.

It was brilliant! What a wonderful opportunity. He wondered why he had seen no larger animal life so far, whales or dolphins. They would all love the fish and other animal and plant life as much as the otters. But he did not hear them or sense them. Perhaps the change in the depth and temperature of the water had caused them to shy away. The mineral content was much different around the vents too, some of it toxic. He trusted his seal nose to keep him away from the dangerous parts. The otters, with their curiosity, seemed to be the only mammals venturing close enough to be harmed. But they had been very clever about diving, snatching up what they wanted, and surfacing again.

The sight of the billowing smoke sobered him. It had been foolish to come out here as a seal, he thought. Better to come with machinery and instruments. Petaybee giving birth was not likely to be tolerant. For that matter, Yana, who loved him, hadn't been in the best of moods while in labor. One more dive and then he'd call it quits and follow the otters back to shore.

His dive took him to the base of the underwater mountain. Quake after quake, at first small and then larger, shook the water and sent rocks tumbling down from above.

The water was murky here from all of the sediment. Circling the mountain's base, he tried to gain some idea of its size and shape. Then, in a deep rift below the mountain's base, he spotted something curiously angular and shining, despite the sediment and rock. He surfaced, caught his breath, and dived again. It could hardly be a shipwreck since Petaybee had never had large ships on her waters. The ports were all icebound too much of the year to make it feasible. It could have been a space vessel or even the wreck of a station, but there had been no report he could recall of such a crash. And it would have been noticed. The impression he had was of something as vast as a city.

He forced himself to dive deeper than he had done so far on this journey. The area in question was indeed filled with what seemed to be manufactured structures – angular, architectural, though indistinct because of the opacity of the water. Lying in the rift as it was, it could even be the ruins of some ancient Petaybean civilization, from the look of it.

But before Intergal had terraformed the planet, it had been little more than a ball of ice and rock, and for all anyone could tell, had never been inhabited by sentient life prior to its colonization.

Of course, as his people knew, the planet was itself a sentient being, but still, it didn't build cities, or at least had never been known to do so.

But maybe eons ago there had been other life here and they built this city and perhaps others, still buried under the sediment on the ocean's floor. Although the mountain above him rumbled and shook and showered more rocks and debris so they shot into the water like deadly missiles, Sean dived a little deeper.

Yes, it could be a ruin, although everything looked remarkably intact and – there seemed to be lights. Perhaps it was just molten lava glowing up from beneath, in which case this ruin would be ruined once more in very short order. But it didn't have the red glow of lava, or the green or blue iridescence Petaybee often displayed. No, this light was brighter, whiter, less natural-looking.

He could go no farther without another breath. He shot for the surface, thinking of the lights and what appeared to be buildings where none should be. Though his mind was occupied, his eyes saw the boulder crashing toward him from the murk, and his seal reflexes responded. Those reflexes were fast, and sent him into a dive, but they were not fast enough to evade the impact. A single boulder avalanche smashed into his body, and the pain of it was the last thing he knew.

16

How's it going? Murel asked from class, as Ronan pushed a broom around the laboratory.

So far all I'm doing is housework, he told her. *She won't even let me ask any questions. I think we were worried about nothing. She's like every other scientist we've ever met, so wrapped up in what she's doing when she's working that she doesn't even think about other people.*

Yeah, that sounds familiar. She loaded us down with homework too. But so did the others.

After a while Murel stopped checking in with him, which gave Ronan a lonely feeling. Professor Mabo kept him for a couple of hours every afternoon after classes mostly picking up after her and tidying the lab.

During the first week Ronan worked for Professor Mabo, Murel had the feeling she'd forgotten or had lost something. She wasn't used to being alone, even in her own thoughts, and it felt weird.

She went back to Marmie's alone the first couple of

afternoons, but it was just too lonesome with nothing to do but try to get Ro to tell her what *he* was doing. She knew how lame that was. Other kids could spend five minutes without their brothers around. What did *they* do?

She made the mistake of whining about it to Pet Chan, who said, 'For pity's sake, Murel! Here you are on a space station with a computer that holds the knowledge of the universe in its databanks, holo decks to play on where you could be anything and do anything, and you're *bored* because your brother has to work after school? Give me a break!'

She made a mental note that security personnel, even those who made great cookies, were disinclined to be sympathetic about catastrophes that didn't actually involve explosions, break-ins, beatings, or murders. But she had one more whine coming. 'Yes, but I don't know how to use half this stuff. Remember us, the hick kids from the low-tech world? How do you turn on a holo deck anyway?'

She thought she had shamed Pet into feeling sorry for her. Maybe the security woman, who did after all sometimes make those great cookies, would see how mean she was being to a poor twinless girl and would put aside what she was doing and take her down and make up some story to play with her on the holo deck. People did that, Murel knew. She just didn't know how they did it exactly.

Pet did turn aside from the security cameras, and for a moment Murel thought she was going to get her way, but then Pet said in a tone worthy of Nanook or Coaxtl, 'Not my problem, child. I understand there's a whiz kid student aide on call, so call, already, and let me get my work done.'

Murel scrubbed tears from her eyes as she climbed into the flitter that took her to the holo deck. She'd do that. She'd show Pet and Ro and all the rest of them. She'd make up some holo where they were all getting chased down by polar bears and if they screamed loudly, she might decide to rescue them. Maybe. Maybe not. She was pretty sure the bear would probably eat Dr. Mabo before she could be rescued. Of course, that wasn't a very good thing to do to the bear. Probably break its teeth on the stringy old bat.

She flounced in, not paying much attention. Most of the time the holo lab was a big blue grid, but now there was a sandy beach and huge blue waves breaking off it. Ke-ola sat on the beach playing some kind of a little guitar while people danced a swaying dance with a lot of hand motions and sang beautiful songs and ate roast pig. Everybody had flowers around their necks. It looked like a lot of fun, but Ke-ola was sitting apart from everybody else, his fingers barely touching the instrument, staring out to sea. He wasn't in a good mood either, for the first time since she'd met him. Maybe it was something in the ventilation system that day. Big tears were rolling down his broad brown cheeks.

'Hey, Ke-ola, can I come to your party?' she asked.

'Better you go away, little sistah,' he said. 'This luau is just for us ghosts.'

'Ghosts? You're not a ghost.' He really *was* in a bad mood.

'Oh yes, I am,' he said. He clapped his hands, and

now they were standing on a dirty street between two tall buildings. The sea was still out there but it rolled in a sluggish way and it was a muddy brown color. Where they had been before, with all the happy people, was an island clearly visible from where they stood now.

'You know what happened there, to that place? That second place where we lived?'

'You said there was something there the company wanted so they made you move,' she said.

'No. This,' he said. And suddenly a blinding light flashed. When she could see again, the island was bare of people and palms, and the sea and sand were slimy with bits of dead fish and seaweed. 'What our new home had that they wanted so much we had to go? It was far from other places. So they set off bombs there to see how much damage they did. Better to blow it up than to let us live there.'

'That freezes,' she said.

'We have this kinda luau now,' he told her, and flipped a couple of buttons on the little guitar, which was actually the remote for the holo suite. It changed into a pokey little room with no color, no sea, no sand, and a bunch of ragged, discouraged-looking people tending some anemic plants.

He switched it off and they sat in the blue-gridded room she remembered.

'I'm sorry, Ke-ola. But that's all past, isn't it?'

'Is it? That's no place for us. Only place good for us is too good for us, the company says. Madame brought me here, but so what? Where my family lives now, they're gonna die. They live in little boxes and little fake ecobubbles. We are people of the sea bubbles, not ecobubbles. I miss my family, Murel. I love them. But I got no place with them. One more mouth, one more breather, one more kid to hear the ghost stories about what all of us used to be.'

He never sobbed, but the tears kept rolling until they didn't. Murel patted him on the shoulder, feeling helpless. His questions didn't have any good answers that she could think of. The funny thing was, he was mourning a place he'd never been as much as he he mourned the family that was too big to hold him now. She felt that way about being away from Petaybee sometimes, except she knew she and Ro would be going back sometime soon. Wouldn't they?

Working with Dr. Mabo was frustrating. Ronan thought that once she got used to him, she'd be ready to teach him the things she hinted that only she knew. But usually, even after several weeks of working together, when he tried to ask her a question, she'd grunt impatiently and wave him aside.

Boredom was what finally forced him to confront her. He couldn't take much more beaker washing, computer dusting, or floor sweeping. 'Professor Mabo?'

'Um?'

'I have a really important question to ask you. It's the reason I wanted to work with you, so I'd appreciate it if you'd be kind enough to give me your attention for a few moments.'

'I'm very busy, Ronan. Can this not wait?'

'It cannot, Professor. Well, I mean, I suppose it

could, but you are always very busy, Professor, and if I'm to give up my free time to help you, the answer to this question is what I would like in return.'

She sighed and pushed back from the worktable. 'Go on,' she said, with a grimace that he thought was supposed to pass for a smile.

'It's about your research, Professor. I – well, Murel and I both – are really interested in shape-shifters. We have some species on Petaybee that shift shapes, and we were wondering – do they ever get to control when they turn from one thing to another or is it strictly environmental or what?'

'Gracious, boy, I don't know how to answer that. For one thing, it surely varies from species to species. But as far as I know now, the change is always triggered by something environmental. A full moon is a classic example, although how susceptible species who live on planets that have more than one moon respond to that is not something we've had much chance to study. Tidal or seasonal differences are another influence. But I have not been able to document much of this material – a lot of what has been written about shape-shifters is more folklore or myth than science. Probably, back on Old Terra, the stories were exaggerated or untrue. Sometimes they were about an illness that afflicted certain people. The only creatures it's ever been said that totally control their own shape-shifting are vampires. Which is, of course, a totally silly and romantic notion that is a combination of a misunderstanding of the nature of certain flying mammals and a high incidence of live burials during epidemics way back in the ancient history of European Terra. None of these things have conscious control, Ronan. None of them are capable of such complex thought.'

'But how about the ones that change from human to something else – some animal maybe?'

'Human to animal? Like a werewolf? Oh, child, these things don't occur with humans. We are far too complex in our physiology and too complicated in our mental and emotional makeup to translate easily into some other beast of lesser intelligence. Why, if a human were to transform into a beast, most likely the person would stay the beast because it would not know what to do to change back again, unless by accident. I thought your question was a serious one, Ronan.' She waved him away with an air of dismissal. 'Now, finish your sweeping while I finish this entry, and I will call the flitter so I can take you home.'

Ronan was only too happy to oblige, and that night he confided in Murel that at least they didn't have to worry about the professor suspecting their own shape-shifting abilities since she didn't believe it ever happened to humans.

'She was really scornful about it,' he said.

'It could be just an act,' Murel said.

'Well, if it is, she did a good one,' he answered. 'She thinks it only happens to what she calls lesser beasts. She's not so bad, really. I know she doesn't seem to like *you* anymore, but she was decent to me. It was boring, but when I came right out and asked her, she gave me a straight answer right away.'

'Don't trust her,' Murel said. 'You're not as good at figuring people out as you think.'

'Well, neither are you. You always think you're

cleverer than I am, and you're just jealous because I got picked instead of you.'

'I'm not either. I certainly don't want to spend all of my free time slaving away for a teacher I don't even *like*. And you do realize, don't you, that she had promised before she came that Rory could be her assistant, then gave the job to you?'

'Not my fault. Rory isn't that keen on the subject anyway, and I am.'

'Yeah, now that she's chosen you as her favorite.'

'Look, let's not fight about this, okay? I'm finding out stuff we need to find out, and that's the only reason I'm doing it. It's for both of us, and Da too. I wish we'd hear from him soon.'

'Me too. Marmie said Johnny had been delayed on Petaybee but he's due back in a couple of days. He ought to be bringing us an answer then.'

Professor Mabo was unusually nice to everyone in class the next day, and when she met Ronan in the lab, she wore a rueful smile. 'My boy, I realize I was unfair to you yesterday. You had every right to ask the very intelligent questions you asked, and I – what is the expression? – blew you off. One of the reasons I chose you as my assistant is that I noticed you displayed an interest in these mutant shape-shifting or bimorphic life forms. I had a headache yesterday and was in pain, and therefore in an unreceptive mood.'

Ronan wondered if she had a headache every day then, since she hadn't seemed any more grumpy yesterday than every time he'd seen her since she arrived. Even if she was nice to him, she was always cutting to someone – usually Rory, although lately she'd been picking on Murel too.

'As a matter of fact, your questions anticipated our experiments for today. I was vague on the subject of the shape-shifters, or bimorphs as we call them. Today we will be working with one.'

'Live?' he asked.

'Certainly. I could not very well expect it to alter its shape if it is already dead.'

Ronan perked up. 'What is it, then?'

'A Honokuan sea turtle is its common name. Or one of them.'

'What other names does it have?' Ronan asked. Did she mean scientific names or something like Seymour the Sea Turtle? He was afraid to ask. Although Dr. Mabo seemed to be in what, for her, passed for a talkative and friendly mood, she definitely believed there was such a thing as a stupid question.

However, she continued explaining. 'That is what we shall discover today,' she said. 'I have it on good authority that this creature is able to alter its shape into quite another species altogether. Once we properly stimulate it to perform its metamorphosis, then we will know what other names would best describe it.'

'Like what?'

'For instance, if we discover that the turtle turns itself into one species of – oh, bear, for instance, we would naturally name it 'chelonia mydas trans ursidae Mabo,' to indicate me as the first to identify it.'

Ronan thought about that for a moment. That would make him and Murel what? Pinnipedia;

Phocidae Sheperdus trans homo sapiens Shongili? Since Da was a scientist too and the first selkie on Petaybee, so the first to 'discover' their species. Whatever. Just so they never had to be named after Dr. Mabo. 'What if it just stays a turtle?' he asked before he could stop himself.

She snorted a snort that clearly accused him of lacking the proper attitude.

'Well, where is it?' he asked.

She pointed to a long metal tank he had mistaken for a covered sink before. He wondered why the tank wasn't glass if she wanted to observe the creature. 'Please fetch the turtle for me. You will have to open the front of the tank by sliding the panel upward and encouraging the creature to emerge. Careful, it is rather large and heavy, although it is relatively young. A fully mature adult may weigh as much as 115 kilograms, or 253 pounds, but this one only weighs roughly eleven kilograms, or about twenty-five pounds. A sturdy lad like you should have no problem managing that much. Still, it has a nasty beak. If it bites you, nothing will make it let go short of death.'

Ronan wanted to ask if she meant the death of the turtle or his own death but figured he shouldn't push his luck. Instead he said, 'I thought they just pulled back into their shells when they're scared. I never heard of attack turtles before.'

'These turtles do not have the ability to retreat into their shells,' she told him.

'So they turn into something else?' he asked.

'Apparently so. I have witnessed the phenomenon briefly, but it was all rather a blur and unfortunately my photographic equipment was not yet unpacked at the time.'

'Before I open the tank, I'd like to know what it changes into,' Ronan said, hanging back. 'If it's really a bear or maybe a crocodile or something, I don't think I want to see it very much.'

'Of course it's not a crocodile, you silly boy. I would not have a crocodile on a space station. And I postulated an ursine transformation only as an example. If it were to change into anything aggressive, it probably would have done so previously. It is a vegetarian and not dangerous, except, as I said, for the beak. Mostly it is like others of its kind, torpid and lazy. The tank is kept at fifty-five degrees Fahrenheit, so the cold-blooded creature is quite lethargic now.'

'Okay then,' he said, and lifted the panel by the handle at its top. From inside he heard a slight scrabbling, then, inside his head, a plea. *Help me.*

It's okay, he told the creature. *I'm a friend.*

You understand! Oh, joy! I thought I would never again know communication. Are you a Honu also?

No, I'm a human. Mostly.

Mostly?

I change shapes. The professor says you do too.

So you are also a captive?

No, I'm her assistant. She doesn't know about me and my sister. At least, I don't think she does. Anyway, she told me she wants you alive. She just wants to see you change.

Oh, yes, I'm aware of that. Please don't let her torture me. I may have a hard shell but I'm not very good at withstanding pain.

I don't think she wants to hurt you.

'Is it coming out, Ronan?' the professor asked.

Are you coming out?

You will protect me?

Yes. I will. And my sister will too. And Marmie. You'll be safe. All you have to do is change and she'll probably want you to go right back into the tank.

You speak as if it were a small matter for me to transform before her, and yet you say she does not know that you also transform. So, if I understand you correctly, you are wishing me to do something you yourself are afraid to do?

I'm not afraid. It's just that our changing is a secret, not just ours. It belongs to the place where we live.

You do not live here?

Well, yeah, we do right now, but— Never mind. Are you coming? You won't bite me, will you?

Only if you provoke me.

The turtle crawled very slowly from the sandstrewn floor of the tank, struggling out onto the metal table on which the container rested. *U-hoh! Owww, oooh, my aching flippers! Oh, my shell and scales, I think I've broken something. Oh, mercy! I'm sorry, boy, but I can go no farther.* Far more quickly than it had emerged, the turtle backpedaled into the sandy-bottomed tank.

Ronan felt sympathy pangs in his own arms and legs. He did not weigh as much in proportion to the size of his flippers, when in seal form, as the turtle did, but dry surfaces that didn't slide or give were more difficult for seals to navigate too. Of course, for him and Murel, it posed no problem since they could quickly morph to their human form so flippers were no longer an issue.

'What is the matter with the wretched creature?' the professor asked.

'Looks like maybe he's too heavy to take all his weight on his flippers where there's no give to the surface,' Ronan told her, thinking that if she was such a hotshot biologist she ought to know stuff like that. 'I'll go find some more sand or dirt or something in the 'ponics garden.'

'You will do no such thing,' his teacher said. 'We'll flip the thing over onto its shell and examine its underside. If its flippers are a problem for it, then perhaps on encountering a situation where the flippers are of no use, it will take its alternate form, which is presumably one that does not have flippers.'

Oh, cruel! Oh, pain and agony! Oh, anguish! The turtle groaned, and big tears rolled down its face. *Please don't let her put me on my shell. It's humiliating and I'm so helpless.*

She doesn't listen to me real well, but maybe when she grabs you, you should bite her. Not me, mind you, her.

I abhor violence.

Why? Ronan asked. He didn't underestimate creatures who were not human, but he didn't ascribe codes of morality to them either.

I'm not fast enough to get away when it starts, usually, the turtle replied.

Yeah, I can see where that makes sense. But if you could lower your standards long enough to just bite her and hang on, then you won't have to be fast enough to get away from violence because you'll be the one being violent. And besides, she sort of expects you to.

No, no. If I bite her, she will retaliate when I finally have to let go. But if I don't come out at all, she'll have no choice but to go away and pick on someone else. I hope. Saying this, the turtle retreated all the way back into the box.

'Never send a boy to do a scientist's job,' Professor Mabo said. She shoved Ronan aside, shoved the metal tank to the end of the metal table, kept shoving it until half of it was suspended over the floor, then upended it.

Uh-uh-uh-oh! the turtle cried as it slid out and tumbled, flippers and feet over shell, onto the floor. *Now I'm done for. Don't let her torture me too long, boy.*

Ronan stooped down, picked up the shell in both hands and gently righted the turtle. *I'd tell you to run for it but I don't imagine that's a practical suggestion*, he said.

'Now that it's out in the open, we'll immerse it and see if that causes it to change,' Dr. Mabo said. 'Pick it up, Ronan. Come on now, what's the matter with you? Afraid of a little turtle bite?'

He wasn't, actually. He was just trying to pick the poor creature up without harming its flippers or any of its tender bits. The professor slid a wall panel aside to reveal two tanks, each about eight feet deep and just as wide, side by side.

One was clearly freshwater, since it was, well, clear. 'In here first,' the professor said. Ronan climbed a metal ladder up to the top of the tank, not an easy thing to do with his hands full of turtle. 'Release it!' she snapped. Ronan did, and the turtle first sank like a stone then struggled to right itself. To the professor's disgust, however, it remained a turtle. It was a very angry and frightened turtle but that was all. It did not change into anything else. It did demand of Ronan, *What is this stuff? It feels like water but there's no buoyancy.*

Ronan said, 'Professor, if this is a saltwater turtle and people where it comes from claim that it changes, don't you think that it probably does its changing in salt water, since that's where it lives?'

'I suppose so, but we must be thorough in exploring which stimulus is the one that activates the change. Scientific method, my boy, scientific method.' She handed him a sturdy net to fish the turtle out of the freshwater tank, which he did, and directed him to release the creature into the saltwater tank instead.

The turtle, so clumsy on land, was graceful as an otter or a seal in the salt water. Its flippers flowed beside it like wings as they propelled it around the tank. It was in raptures. *Oh, oh, my dear boy, you are a wonder! This is fantastic! Look! Backward roll! Forward roll! Sideways flip!*

By then it was quite late, and the professor said, 'We can leave it there for now. Tomorrow afternoon we'll try electrical stimuli and a few other methods to see if we cannot persuade the specimen to display its alternate form.'

Not if I can help it, Ronan thought, and Murel answered.

Huh?

Professor Mabo locked up the lab with the old-fashioned key, grumbling because she didn't have access to the high-tech facilities of the station guarded with 'proper' retinal scan locks. The flitter waited for them in the corridor outside.

Climbing into the vehicle beside the professor, Ronan sent his sister images of the turtle, telling her, *We have to help it escape.*

Where does a turtle escape to on a space station? she asked.

Eventually back to its home world, if we can manage.

Where's that?

I dunno, but he said something about a place called Honuania.

That's on Ke-ola's world! Murel said. *Remember his holo? I think he even mentioned the turtles, come to think of it. Called them 'the sacred Honu.'*

Great, I wonder if he'd have some idea how we can get the turtle back where it belongs.

Marmie could make Professor Mabo return it, couldn't she?

Maybe, but I'm not sure it would be good to try to make her do anything. She thinks the turtle is her personal property and refers to it as 'the specimen.' She might just kill it if Marmie told her she couldn't have it here. She plans to 'stimulate' it with electric shock tomorrow, Murel. She's trying to make it change into another shape, but the turtle doesn't understand what she's talking about. I have to help it get away.

No, you were right the first time, bro. We *have to help it get away. Just because we're not together all the time anymore doesn't mean I don't still care about the same things you do. I haven't ever met a sea turtle before, but I'm sure I'd like him. And I'd help him escape torture and maybe death even if I didn't. You* used *to know that.*

Aw, sis, I still do. I'm just worried. And the professor is right here next to me in the flitter so I can't think straight.

I can. Has she got the key to the lab on her? Can you nick it?

Yeah, as a matter of fact, I think I can. It's in the pocket of her lab coat. Sometimes you're really quite brilliant, you know. I suppose that's why I keep you around.

Yeah, yeah. Now all you have to do is sneak the keys away from her.

Oh, well, if that's all. His thought was accompanied by an image of him rolling his eyes.

Look, when the flitter lands, Murel said, *I'll create a diversion. I've been watching lots of vids. Creating diversions is how people always manage to swipe things. There's an accomplice or two, and while one person creates a diversion, another one does the actual stealing.*

Mum and Da are going to be really pleased to know they've sent us here so far from home just so you can study how to lead a life of crime.

Do you want to save the sea turtle or not?

As the flitter set down, Murel ran up to it. Her eyes were red as if she'd been crying, though Ronan suspected an onion had more to do with it, and she seemed very upset. 'Professor Mabo,' she whined, poking her head into the flitter and blocking Ronan's exit. The professor leaned forward to hear her over the flitter's motor.

'What is it, Murel?'

'When do I get to be your assistant? Ronan and I always share everything, and now he gets to do all this interesting stuff and— and— you don't let me do anything. It's not fair! I'm just as smart as he is. I'd be just as much help.' Murel reached in and grabbed the professor's hands.

Now, she told Ronan.

The old-fashioned keys were outlined by a bulge in

the lab coat pocket nearest Ronan's fingers. The way Professor Mabo was leaning toward Murel, the pocket was practically in his fingers. He slipped the key from her pocket as easily as he slipped through the water in seal form.

When the professor snatched her hands away from Murel's grasp with a cutting remark, Ronan jumped out of the flitter.

17

Johnny Green knew something was wrong the moment he saw Yana Maddock-Shongili waiting at the dock, her hands folded behind her at parade rest, her eyes first on the ground, then looking up as he climbed off the gantry. Her jaw was set and her eyes were blazing.

'Yana, how good it is to see you. And how is Sean? Busy as always, I imagine.' He always talked too much when something made him nervous, and women wearing that look – especially women with advanced training in sophisticated weaponry – definitely made him nervous.

'He's not here at the moment, Johnny,' she said, her voice as tense as her jaw looked.

'What a shame. I've a message for him from the children.'

'They sent their father a message, but not me? Why? Is it in seal-speak or something?'

'Worse. It's about biology and genetics and such.'

'I know a bit about that too after all these years on Petaybee. And I am their mother.'

'Yes, Yana—'

'Whatever anyone thinks, I *am* their mother. Petaybee may have given them to me, but it's a planet. If it had children, they're – let's not get into that right now, actually. But my kids are mine too, and they're half human. I never meant, in sending them off to Marmie, that they should stay three years. I would never have agreed to that.'

The normally taciturn Yana was babbling like a brook let loose from the winter ice. He knew something else was bothering her too, though. It wasn't just the kids' absence.

'You can send for them at any time, Yana, you know that. Marmie would never keep them from you. She is only trying to help you keep them safe.'

'Well, their father and I have a disagreement about that. I thought, after they'd been attacked by wolves and almost snatched by those otter-napping biologists, that they'd be safer away. But the truth is, Johnny, I can take care of my children better than anyone else. I'm trained to be able to care for the people under my – you should pardon the expression – command. They are safer with me than anywhere else.'

'I'm sure they'll be glad to hear you feel that way. You see, the message I had for Sean concerns their own worries about some security issues. I don't know if you can answer for him, but once the kids are back here, they can ask him themselves.'

'Fine. But we have to find him first.'

'Where is he?' Johnny asked.

'He went for a long swim. Out to the coast, and then to explore a new volcanic mass building up at the equator. He's been gone ten days now and we've heard not a word. That little otter the kids are so fond of seemed to come looking for him, but I am the only member of my family who doesn't speak otter, so I haven't a clue what he wants.'

'I don't speak otter either, Yana, but I do fly helicopters. Has anyone gone out to have a look?'

Yana nodded. 'Scads of people. I've gone out there too. But the ash and steam are so bad out that way you can't see anything. Divers can't get near the place. I don't know why the man thinks that just because he's a man who turns into a seal and vice versa that it makes him superseal or something. He's a mortal man and a mortal seal, and I am mortally afraid he's got himself into more than he can handle.'

'He's been in scrapes before, I'm sure. Superseal he may not be, and mortal man he may, but he is a most resourceful fellow and wise in the ways of this world.'

'Yeah, I know, and too cocky by half about it sometimes. Clodagh has been petitioning the planet for news, and Sinead and her posse have joined up with the coastal folk to patrol the shoreline looking for – in case Sean swims ashore. But so far all they seem to be doing is annoying the local wildlife, including some otters. Possibly that's what the kids' little buddy is here about.' She gave a small smile that bloomed on her anxious face like a flower in the snow. She had a sense of whimsy, did Yana, and a connection with natural things that had come with her to Petaybee despite her offworld life. 'He wants to protest the human invasion of his territory to the Petaybean government officials.'

'Or perhaps he's just looking for his friends.'

'Yes. I can't blame him there. As for fly-bys, Bunny

has tried it in Frank Metaxos's single-engine plane, and Aoifa organized the divers right off. But the bloody volcano is hampering any efforts they have to make a good search.'

'It can't hurt if we go out there again, Yana. You still have a chopper available?'

She shook her head. 'Not until the last one that went out searching returns. I can try to get them on the radio, but the com unit has been fried by the quakes and the electromagnetic waves Petaybee is putting out. I guess I could feed you while we wait.'

Johnny had eaten Yana's cooking in the past. 'Let's just go see if Clodagh has had any luck with the planet, shall we? She could tell us over dinner.'

Clodagh seemed outwardly as imperturbable as ever, large, round as Petaybee, moving about her cabin with a fluid grace that seemed strange in such an enormous woman, as if she were swimming through the air instead of constrained by gravity like the rest of them. Though her eyes lit with welcome when she saw him, Johnny felt she had known all along he'd be showing up at her door. Yana had already told him that she'd been haunting Clodagh when she wasn't haunting everyone else.

Clodagh dished each of them up a huge bowl of rabbit stew and served it with blueberry bread and rosehip jelly. As soon as she served the food, however, she slung her pack onto her shoulder and went to the door. 'You can leave those things and I'll clean them when I get back, Yana.'

'Going to the spring?'

'Yes.'

'Wait and we'll come with you,' Johnny said. 'Unless you'd rather be alone.'

'No, you should come. Petaybee is pretty excited right now. I have a hard time getting any attention. We should have a latchkay, but folks are too busy looking for Sean to get organized. A couple more voices might get heard better than just mine.'

On the way to the spring and the communion cave, Johnny nearly fell twice with the force of the quakes shaking the ground. Petaybee had always been prone to earthquakes and volcanic activity, the legacy of its comparatively recent rebirth by terraforming, but this was quite energetic shaking, even so.

'Is it safe in the cave, Clodagh?' he asked.

She shrugged. 'I guess.'

Johnny was more reassured by that than he would have been were he not a native-born Petaybean. He was a brave man, the veteran of many years of military service in the Company Corps and numerous hazardous missions on behalf of his civilian employer. Still, he found himself reluctant to step into the tunnels leading deeper into the planet's grumbling bowels, which sounded as if Petaybee could use a dose of antacid and a nice cup of tea.

However, though the walls shook and the footing was uncertain, though the water sloshed and rolled in the little hot pool as if it were a miniature ocean, they reached the communion cave without incident. The major pieces of rock all seemed inclined to remain where they were.

Clodagh pulled out a thermos and four cups, as if she'd read its mind about the planet needing tea. 'There now, just you simmer down, love,' she murmured to Petaybee.

Yana smiled and said quietly to Johnny, 'Clodagh's talking to the planet like she did to me when I was going into labor with the twins.'

'Our Sean is still missing,' Clodagh said conversationally, not to Johnny or Yana. 'We'd like him back safe, please.'

After a while other people began filing into the cavernous room, people with drums and other instruments.

They started singing songs. Yana and Johnny sang a couple too, then Yana said, 'I can't sit here. We have to go look. Call Marmie and have her send another chopper if we must, but we have to go back out there. He could be hurt, clinging to a log or something.'

But one of the search copters had returned by then, and the pilot, who had been out since daybreak, was more than willing for Johnny and Yana to take the evening shift. With summer, evening was very long – it lasted until twilight, and somewhere around midnight the sun, which had only taken a slight dip in the sky, began to rise again.

Even so, the weather was hardly bright. Debris in the air almost obscured the sun entirely. Johnny didn't expect to be able to find anything farther away than the copter's nose.

Unfortunately, his expectations were fulfilled. He and Yana ventured as close as they could get to the steaming smoking vent in the ocean, closer than they should have gone, but to no avail. They spent hours circling it, waiting while the quakes grew greater and subsided, backing off as the rumbling grew more intense and edging closer when it stilled, but they couldn't see more than the surface of the water, and even then infrequently. They had to return to refuel twice, and both times he could almost hear Yana fretting that they had missed Sean at the very moment when they might have saved him.

At her insistence, they did the same thing after the next crew went up, and again the following day. They spoke very little the entire time. Yana's focus was total and she could not seem to bear a word to break into her thoughts.

But finally, after the third search shift, Johnny said, 'I think I'd best give you the children's message, Yana, and you pass it on.'

At once her eyes snapped to his like an eagle fixing claws on its prey.

'They want to know if people can tell about their selkie nature from a blood sample. Their new science teacher, Dr. Mabo, was seen to pocket a handkerchief Murel bled into after cutting herself in lab class. They thought it suspicious and figured their father would know.'

They were on their way back to the helicopter, but Yana turned and pointed in the direction of Johnny's ship. 'Go get them now and bring them home, Johnny,' she said, and as an afterthought added, 'Please.'

'I guess the answer would be yes to that question then?'

'I don't know about the blood, but a Dr. Marie Mabo was one of the scientists – the head one, if I remember correctly – Sean and Sinead arrested for, as Sinead put it, 'unlawful detention of river otters.' Mabo and the rest were deported. It may not be the same person, but I don't want to even entertain the possibility that the woman might be anywhere near my children. Losing Sean is bad enough.'

'I'll go then,' he said, his hand on her shoulder squeezing a little, trying to be reassuring. 'But you've not lost him yet. He may have swum to the other pole to get out of the way, for all you know. Communications haven't been the best so we wouldn't necessarily know. But I'll get the kids nonetheless. They'll be glad to be returning.'

18

The twins were tired by the time they reached the laboratory. First they had to convince Marmie that they were too sleepy to stay up and play a game with her, as she suggested, but needed to go straight to bed. Then they had to wait until all was quiet and they were sure she'd retired to her quarters before they crept out of the house.

Marmie had set the weather for fall. Holo leaves fell from holo trees and wind gathered them in breathy gusts into holo piles along the banks of the fake river, from which a holo deer was drinking. Realistic rattling and rustling sounds accompanied the whistle of the wind as if an overly friendly ghost were trying to get their attention.

They made it through the garden without arousing Pet or the security staff, and reached the utility stairs leading to the next level. Stairs and elevators honeycombed the vast station, though most people chose to use the flitter fleet.

The stairs were metal, grated, and zigzagged back and forth in a seemingly endless sawtooth between

Marmie's deck and the next one. Every step the twins took clanked and clattered, but it didn't make a lot of difference since most of the station's nonresidential areas operated continuously, were brightly lit, and had people coming and going at all hours.

The third level, where the school and Professor Mabo's science lab were located, was an exception. The white-tiled hallways that were so brilliantly lit during school hours were now dimly lit tunnels demarcated by strip lighting running the length of the hallway where the floors met the walls.

Each footstep seemed to them to echo as loudly as a blacksmith's hammer on an anvil as they tried to creep forward toward the lab.

When they reached the lab door, Ronan pulled out the keys. *This is it. You keep lookout.*

Out here? By myself? The whites of Murel's eyes seemed very white indeed as she peered down the maze of hallways.

Sure, what are you afraid of? If there are any wolves around here, you can trust Professor Mabo to have them locked up in cages.

Professor Mabo makes the wolves look gentle and friendly as sled pups, Murel said. *I don't mind admitting I'm a bit afraid of her. What if she decides to come back?*

Oh, she won't do that, Ronan said with more certainty than he felt, once he had a moment to think it over. *She doesn't plan to do any more work until tomorrow, when she tortures the turtle.*

Well, go on then. And make it snappy, will you? We have a lot of stairs to carry a turtle up before it's time to get ready for school again.

Ronan fitted the key, gave Murel a thumbs-up sign, opened the door and let it snick gently closed behind him. The lights in the lab immediately flared into brilliance. They did that when anybody walked in. It wasn't so – sudden – during school hours, but now he felt as if a spotlight had been focused on him. He shook himself a little, as if misgivings, like water, could be dispersed that way.

The lab seemed huge now, the tables with the chairs upended over them for the custodian to clean the floors, the racks of beakers and bottles above each table. His footsteps and even his breath sounded unnaturally loud.

He had not pulled the curtain over the front of the water tanks again, but even so, he couldn't see much but the ladder at the top of the tank and the glint of water among the chair legs and beaker racks as the light sparked white from its surface. As he drew nearer, he could see more of the tank walls, and expected to see the turtle by the time he'd drawn close enough to touch the tanks and could see their bottoms. To his surprise, however, both tanks appeared empty.

He couldn't see the turtle at all. True, the saltwater tank did seem a bit murkier than it had before, the sandy bottom stirred into the water making it cloudy, but that shouldn't have kept him from seeing the turtle. He checked the freshwater tank and the tank in which the Honu had been housed to begin with, but both were empty. *Turtle? Honu? You there? Where are you? It's me, Ronan. I came to—*

Heeeelp, a feeble thought reached him. The turtle sounded weak and frightened. *Help me, Ronan. I'm stuck.*

Stuck? Where? Ronan pressed hs face to the glass, cupping his hands around his eyes to try to see into the tank more deeply without interference from the lights in the room. They cast his reflection back at him so that he got in his own way when he tried to see.

Down here. In this cave.

Cave? The tank was glass, not natural landscape. Why would there be a— *Oh, you mean a drain, I bet. How did you get in there?*

Tried . . . escape . . . but . . . I . . . am too big. No air here. Need air.

Sea turtles, like seals, needed to breathe every few minutes, Ronan knew. He and Murel had done a search for the Honu's species in the station's extensive computer databanks. They'd learned some other interesting things about the Honuian sea turtles too, while trying to figure out what they would feed the turtle and where the best place would be to keep him once they rescued him.

Hang on, Ronan said, and began stripping off his clothing. *Murel, the turtle got stuck in the drain. I have to dive in and pull him out. I'm not sure how I'm going to do that, of course, when all I have to use are flippers, so you may have to come into the room and help us.*

Now?

No, wait till I tell you. Keep lookout meantime.

He climbed up the ladder to the top of the tank, poised over the edge for a moment, and dived in. His vision underwater and in the dark was much better as a seal than as a human. Diving to the bottom of the tank, he spotted the back half of the turtle's shell and its tail and rear flippers sticking out of a round hole in the rear wall.

Ronan swam all around the drain and the turtle, wondering why the hole hadn't been covered. He tried the claws on his flippers to tear at the portion of the drainage pipe farthest from the turtle's body. It was made of much sterner stuff than ice and he quickly gave it up.

I'm going to take hold of the edge of your shell and pull, he told the turtle. *Your tail doesn't look sturdy enough to withstand my claws or teeth.*

Oooh, I should say not! The turtle's thought came out with a sort of squeak. *Be careful to bite only the shell. I'm quite tender underneath. And ticklish.*

That was a problem. Ronan couldn't get his teeth to lock tightly enough on the turtle's shell to pull at it. His teeth kept sliding off the slippery carapace. He tried first one side, then the other. Once he thought he felt the turtle slip a little and intensified his efforts, but Honu remained as stuck as ever.

Okay, let's try one more thing. I'm going to ram, er, nudge you from each side and hope to jar you loose. I'll try not to hurt you.

The turtle winced. Ronan felt it, though he neither saw nor heard any physical change in the trapped creature. Backing up as far as the small tank allowed, he swam at the turtle from the left, bumped into the back of the shell and felt it move a little. He did it again. When there was no further movement, he swam up under the trapped creature and butted it from below. Then he attacked from the right and started over again. Gradually, the vibrations his movement set up caused the turtle's shell to separate from the lip of the drain. The turtle felt it too and its tail began to bob like a rotor warming up while its rear flippers started to backpaddle.

Someone's coming! Murel sent a warning thought.

We're allllmost there, Ronan told her. *But you're going to have to come in now. I need you to lift him out and help me out of the tank so I can change back enough to climb down the ladder.*

Before he finished the thought, he heard the clanking of feet knocking the rungs of the ladder against the side of the tank. As he pulled the turtle free, he looked up to see Murel peering down at them.

Come on. Hurry, she urged.

The turtle popped loose of the drain and lay on the bottom of the tank for a moment, the movements of its tail and back flippers twitchy instead of purposeful. One of the front flippers looked like it had a small tear. Ronan hoped he wasn't responsible.

The turtle's thoughts were fainter than ever and disjointed. Ronan carefully picked up the shell and balanced it between his front flippers and his body.

You can make it, Turtle, Murel coaxed. *That's it. The tank's not that deep. Just a bit farther.*

Finally, the water splashed just above Ronan's nose and the weight was lifted from his flippers and neck as Murel said, *Gotcha!*

The turtle's thought was something like the turtle equivalent of *Ahhh*.

Ronan thought he was making a lot of noise, or Murel was, clanking against the tank, when all of a sudden the turtle plummeted back into the tank and Murel fell in after, her body striking Ronan's and driving him downward with the force of her plunge. She changed shapes as she fell so that the fall turned into a less than graceful dive.

Looking down at them, where Murel's face had been a moment before, was the small dark face of Professor Mabo. She wore a gloating expression. 'I do not know what I am going to do with that assistant of mine,' she said. 'I thought I told him to clean the tank, but although it is not growing algae, it seems to have grown two seals since I last looked. Hello, Shongili twins. I trust the water is fine.'

Neither of them could answer her or ask how she had known they'd be there, but she told them anyway. 'You couldn't resist trying to steal my specimen, could you, Ronan? You are too much your father's son. He wouldn't allow me to study the otters either. Perhaps he realized I'd rather be studying you. And here you are. I have my wish. Little Murel has even granted me some immediate gratification by changing shape before my very eyes. I know you thought you were being clever, Ronan, with your questions about the causative factors of transformations. Now you and your sister will have the opportunity to help me answer those questions and more, in earnest.'

Ronan was exhausted from struggling to free the turtle. He had not been able to get a breath himself before Murel and the turtle came back down on top of him. But Murel was angry. He could feel her anger although she said nothing. But the anger spewed her upward like a slippery furry geyser from the bottom of the tank straight up to Dr. Mabo. Ronan saw his sister's sharp seal teeth snap and Dr. Mabo shriek and fall away from the ladder.

Murel dived back down into the tank with a big sealy smile stretched across her muzzle.

Did you bite her? Ronan asked.

No, but I scared her, didn't I?

'Thank you, Ronan or Murel, as the case may be.' Marmion's voice reached the twins from beyond the tank. Actually, her words were a bit garbled by the water, but they also caught her thought. It was clearly projected and easy to pick up, although they could not normally read people other than each other and sometimes their father.

The water in the tank quivered and the glass vibrated with what felt like a herd of moose galloping across the lab floor. Not moose, of course, but people! Help? The ladder clanked and groaned as someone clambered up it again.

'Get away from there!' Dr. Mabo's voice, muted by the water, was still nasty. 'What are you people doing here anyway? Madame, I insist on privacy to conduct my experiments. You students have no business here without my permission.'

Other voices, both male and female, obscured hers until they all sounded like they were speaking through layers of cloth.

Then Johnny Green's friendly face appeared at the top of the tank where Mabo's sneering one had been before Murel scared her off the ladder.

'Okay, kids, come along,' Johnny said, holding out his arms. 'You're safe now.'

The man will lift you out, Ronan told Honu. *He is a friend.*

Honu shot to the surface while Ronan surfaced long enough to watch and catch his breath. Johnny lifted the creature gently and handed him off to someone else standing behind and below him and blurred by the water.

Johnny was not strong enough, however, to lift either twin in slippery seal form. Pulling them out of the water and up over the ladder while they changed would be difficult.

The tank was small for two half-grown seals, and there wasn't much room to swim. Besides which, the turtle, having caught his breath, told them that he wanted to return to the water too. Their rescuers had set the turtle on the floor beside the tank, and the weight on its flippers was more than it could bear. Ronan kept bumping the glass next to the turtle to try to alert Johnny and their other rescuers, whoever they were, of the turtle's needs.

Then Ke-ola, previously hidden by the rungs of the ladder while he stood at its foot, bent over, picked up the turtle and lifted it back up to Johnny.

'The sacred Honu wishes to return to the water,' Ke-ola told him. Johnny grunted and shook his head but set Honu loose again inside the tank.

Ahhh. The turtle once more emitted the turtle equivalent of a sigh.

The people outside the tank looked in as the turtle dived back down toward the seals. Ke-ola had come in answer to the distress broadcast by the Honu. Johnny Green, Marmion, and Pet Chan were there because

Rory alerted them to what his grandmother was doing to the twins.

'So,' Johnny said. 'The turtle is back but the kids aren't out. I don't see how we're going to do this unless we just break this sucker open.' He gave the side of the tank a little kick.

'The children could be injured by fragments, assuming we found something strong enough to break the glass,' Marmie said. 'It is shatterproof, laser proof—'

'Et cetera. I understand. Very well then, what do you suggest? The kids can't stay in there forever.'

'How about a crane?' Pet Chan suggested. 'It could hoist them out of the water with no problem. I'll just call down to the hangar and have them send up a small one with a basket on it, shall I?'

'We don't have to do that, ma'am,' Ke-ola said, kicking off his shoes. 'I can help. If you'll move alongside there, Captain Green, sir, I'll just dive to the bottom and boost the seals up to you.'

'Can you do that?' Marmie asked. 'You have no diving equipment.'

'Excuse me, Madame, but my people have been deep-sea divers for eons. We hold our breath almost as long as the sacred Honu. The water will make the seals light as long as we're submerged.'

'Hmm,' Pet said, 'I believe I'll just get that crane anyway, in case.'

Johnny climbed down and Ke-ola swarmed up the ladder in his bare feet. He wore only a pair of shorts. Like the turtle, he looked heavy and lumbering on dry land, but in the water, even so little water, he was strong and graceful. Blowing a fine stream of bubbles, he dived down to the seals, met their eyes, and jerked his head toward the top of the tank.

Ronan was reassured by Ke-ola's calm presence when he entered the water with them. As his classmate gave the signal, Ronan swam to the surface. Ke-ola boosted him up toward Johnny as effortlessly as an otter might heft a clamshell. Ronan was surprised that Ke-ola was *that* strong. He was also surprised to see Rory's face and his arms reaching for him along with Johnny's from the top rung of the ladder, which Rory now shared.

Johnny had a towel with him and began patting Ronan dry as soon as he was half out of the water. When Ronan's upper half began to change so that his hands were free to help himself, Rory scooted down the ladder. Then with Johnny's support, Ronan held on to the ladder with his hands, pulled his sleek flippered back end free of the water and let Johnny pat that dry until the flippers turned to feet again.

Rory was looking up at Ronan with eyes so wide, white showed around his pupils.

Ronan, human again, grinned down at him, said, 'Thanks, Rory. I can take it now and help Johnny fetch Murel up. Good of you to come to our aid, though.'

Rory nodded but looked a little hurt and a lot puzzled. Pet Chan returned with the crane but it wasn't necessary. Johnny and Ronan repeated the previous procedure with Murel, though she kept the towel closer to her than her brother had.

Rory handed lab coats up to them both, since Murel's clothing was at the bottom of the tank, torn during her transformation after Dr. Mabo pushed her in. Ronan picked up his own discarded clothes and put them on, stealing glances at the others. Marmie, Johnny, Pet, Rory, and Ke-ola were there, he confirmed when, fully dressed, he turned to face them. Dr. Mabo was not.

Murel caught his thought before he spoke and said, 'Hey, where's Mabo?'

'Oops,' Johnny said. 'Guess she slipped away while we were all helping you kids and the turtle. Oh well, she can't have gone far.'

Pet Chan pulled the radio from her belt and spoke into it. 'Chan here. Put out an APB on Dr. Marie Mabo. Arrest and detain her until I can arrive to take custody. Charges of kidnapping and possible child and animal abuse.'

'Sorry, Chan, but she's gone. Her shuttle departed a few minutes ago. You want us to launch a posse?'

Marmie shook her head sadly. 'There is no need to risk our personnel. She will not return to trouble us again.'

'Good,' Rory said when Pet had passed on the order and clicked off the com unit. 'I thought it would be so great to have a grandma, and she just kept Mum upset all the time.'

Marmie turned to the twins. 'You've Rory to thank for alerting us to your danger,' she said.

Rory waved his hand in dismissal, 'Nothing, really. I went to take her something and caught the old cow watching you on the labcam in her quarters as you entered and dived into the tank, Ronan. I backed out before she saw me, but I knew she was up to no good so I called Madame and raced down here to see if I could help you.'

'You're a good pal, Rory.'

'Not so much,' he said, shaking his head and looking as if he'd just opened what he thought was a fresh can of milk and found it had gone sour.

'Rory,' Marmie said, 'you cannot hold yourself to blame for your grandmother's actions. If I had realized the connection between her and the twins, I'd never have allowed her on the station. You are not responsible for who your relatives are. It's how you treat your friends that matters.'

'What connection, Marmie?' Murel asked. 'Mabo said something about Ronan being Da's son like she knew Da or something. She said something about him keeping her from studying the otters and that he knew she'd rather study us.'

'Yes. Of course, we knew a group of scientists had been deported from Petaybee after you left, but no one sent any details, just that the otters were safe and their captors had been dealt with.'

'When I gave your mum your message about Dr. Mabo keeping a sample of Murel's blood, she was horrified,' Johnny told them, speaking carefully. Ronan thought he was measuring his words so he didn't say the wrong thing. What wrong thing could he possibly say now? But Johnny kept talking, as if to ice over the cracks between his words. 'Your folks thought they were sending you to safety. They never figured Mabo would follow you here.'

'Bad luck for the twins, us being here for my lovin' granny to latch on to as cover,' Rory said.

'It's not your fault, Rory. Marmie's right,' Murel said, putting a slightly moist arm around him. 'If you hadn't been here, she'd have come up with some other excuse since she was so determined to trap us.'

'How'd you know to come tonight, Ke-ola?' Murel asked.

'Once I knew the sacred Honu was here, I opened my mind to accept his bidding. He bade me come here double quick and help him, but you got here first,' Ke-ola said, his shoulders rolling in a shrug that was like the tide coming in and going out again.

'So what will happen to him now?' Ronan asked. 'Will you take him home?'

Before Ke-ola could answer, Johnny Green spoke up.

'Speaking of returning to your native habitat,' he said to the twins, 'you two need to pack up your belongings and say goodbye to your friends here. You're coming back to Petaybee with me.'

'We're going home?' Murel asked. 'Just like that?'

'Just like that,' Johnny said, trying to sound cheerful, but again there was a cautious note in his voice that neither of the twins cared for. Something was fishy, and it wasn't the edible kind.

Ke-ola said, 'The sacred Honu and I come with you.'

'Oh, no, Ke-ola,' Murel said. 'It's much too cold on Petaybee for Honu. Probably for you too. Not that we wouldn't like you to visit.'

'The sacred Honu says a home is being prepared for him and his kind. I will send a message to my family. They will find she who is to be the mate of the Honu and bring her to him.'

'You mean on Petaybee?' Johnny asked, looking puzzled. 'How would a turtle from here and parts beyond have any idea what might or might not be happening on Petaybee?'

Ke-ola gave him a pitying look. 'The Honu are not sacred for nothing. They know many things.'

'If he knows about Petaybee and this home he thinks is being built for him, why didn't he know my gran was going to turtle-nap him and experiment on him?'

'I said the sacred Honu and his kind know many things, not all things,' Ke-ola said, and after a sigh, added, 'They are somewhat more likely to know of distant things and future things than what is right under their flippers, perhaps.'

Murel said, 'Well, whatever the reason, I think it's brilliant that he's coming to Petaybee with you! I was just thinking that what Petaybee needs are some sea turtles.'

'Do they really change, Ke-ola?' Ronan asked. '*She* said they were shape-shifters.'

Ke-ola smiled a smile that made him look every inch of his height and girth. It was a very superior kind of smile. 'That is for the sacred Honu to tell if he wishes.'

'Do you know, though?'

'That is for me to tell if I wish, and I do not wish at this time.'

19

Marmie was going with them, which surprised the twins. They were more surprised to see several helicopters andsmall submarines and a lot of diving equipment being loaded ontothe ship.

'That going to Petaybee, is it?' Murel asked Marmie as they boarded.

'Yes, it is.'

'Our folks want all that and us too or did you make them take us back if they wanted all the tech stuff?' Ronan asked, teasing.

They were inside the ship and strapped to chairs in the lounge before Marmie answered. 'It's search and rescue equipment. Remember how everyone was thinking Petaybee was building a new landmass?'

'Yeah, is that what's happening? The volcano is erupting? Cool! But why the need for rescue equipment? Nobody lives anywhere near there,' Ronan said.

'It's probably also for scientists to go study it, isn't it, Marmie? Good ones like Sister Iggierock.'

Marmie started to say something, then closed her mouth again and said, 'Something of the sort.'

'Okay, Marmie, what's going on really?' Murel demanded. 'We haven't had any sleep and a tiring time of it lately. You're holding out on us. Why?'

'I wasn't going to tell you or let Johnny tell you either,' she said, shaking her head regretfully and smoothing her skirt across her knees. Marmie almost never wore ship suits. She usually wore something elegant and flowing. Today it was iridescent blue syn-silk. The rings on her fingers twitched a little, which was unlike her. She was something like an old-time queen, making all sorts of decisions every day. It wasn't like her to act nervous and uncertain. Seeing her that way gave Murel a sick feeling, and she felt the same trepidation from Ronan. 'It seems unkind to make this journey last longer for you than need be, when we can have no news between now and the time we land. But your father has gone missing.'

Neither of them said anything, but each felt the other reeling. They'd never thought, when they left Da on Petaybee, that he might not be there when they returned. Then Ronan said staunchly, 'Good job Mum's sent for us then. We can find him.'

'Non!' Marmie said. 'What I mean is, I don't think your mother will want to risk you two as well. I certainly wouldn't in her place. The volcano is very active. It could completely blow at any moment. Johnny says there's almost no visibility even in Kilcoole.'

'We don't need visibility,' Murel said. 'We can hear our da in our heads.'

'I'm sure you won't be able to go near enough to do it.'

'We hear pretty good,' Ronan said, 'and at least we could tell your searchers how to look – better yet, if you *really* want to find him, we should be leading.'

But Marmie was shaking her head again. She unstrapped herself, rose and left the lounge. After that, when they tried to talk to her, she pretended not to hear them or ignored them or changed the subject.

Ke-ola, who stayed close beside the tank containing Honu, watched one of these encounters with a little twist of his lips. 'That Madame is very stubborn,' he said.

Murel crossed her arms on her chest and glared at nobody in particular. 'She's not the only one,' she said. 'He's our da.'

When at last the ship set down on Petaybee, the twins saw their mother pacing the ground, waiting while they climbed down the gantry to meet her. It was in some ways as if they'd never been away at all, and in some ways as if they were coming here for the first time and didn't know anyone.

She's so little, Ronan told his sister. *She always looked so tall and straight.*

Could be because you're looking down on her from about forty feet, dopey, Murel said. Then relented. *But I know what you mean. And, well, Petaybee isn't as pretty as I remembered it, even in summer, but it feels good to be here.*

Can't tell if it's pretty or not with all that stuff in the air, Ronan replied, swatting at the space in front of his face as if to clear the air of the smog that turned everything gray. *At least our river is still there.*

Murel stopped on the step she'd just set foot upon. *Even if our da is not.* Her throat hurt suddenly, and not just from all the particles in the air. Her heart felt as if it twisted up inside her not to see her father standing there, and Ronan felt it too.

We'll get him back, Mur. You'll see. We will. We'll show them all.

Of course we will, she sniffed, and started down again. Fortunately, she still held firmly to both rails of the gantry because suddenly it and the ship shuddered and jumped, and when it stopped, their Mum and Marmie, who was already down, were picking themselves off the ground and looking anxiously up at the twins.

After that they hurried down. But when she reached the foot of the gantry, Murel waited for Ronan, and the two of them walked over to their mother and let her put her arms around them. After a moment they each put an arm around her too.

Marmie smiled, wiggled her fingers in a 'See you later' gesture, and returned to the dock, where she helped Johnny Green supervise the unloading of some extremely large crates, boxes, and uncrated hunks of equipment. Among the large things was the Honu's tank, with Ke-ola sometimes walking along, sometimes crouching, beside it, apparently soothing the Honu.

'Marmie told you why Da isn't here?' Mum asked them. Left to her own devices, Mum never was one to beat around the bush. The more difficult or distasteful something was to discuss, the sooner she'd bring it up. Da was the one more likely to wait for the proper moment.

'She did,' Murel answered.

'And you're not to worry, Mum. We'll get him back,' Ronan said.

'Yes, we will,' she replied. 'I'll brief you on what we know already on the way back to the village. As soon as you've had a chance to settle in and have been brought up to speed, we'll fly back out again.'

The twins exchanged looks. 'You'll let us help?' they asked incredulously.

'I'm counting on it,' Yana told them. 'Not that you're to take any unnecessary risks, of course, but if anyone who speaks the human tongue can find him, it's you kids.'

Just then Clodagh, surrounded by orange cats, strode up the river road toward them. The twins squealed and raced forward to embrace her. Clodagh smiled and patted them on the heads, said how big they'd grown, and disentangled herself, continuing on to the ship. The Honu's tank was being loaded aboard some sort of a wheeled barge, and Clodagh stopped there, bending over to peer into the tank for a moment before straightening to clasp Ke-ola in a huge hug and even exchange cheek kisses with him.

In spite of their excitement over their own homecoming, the twins couldn't help being distracted by this uncustomarily effusive display on the part of Kilcoole's shanachie. Almost as surprising was the way the often taciturn Ke-ola seemed to be brimming over with things to tell the woman he'd just met.

Well, I guess we don't have to worry about making Ke-ola and the Honu feel welcome, Murel said.

I didn't know Clodagh was so keen on sea turtles, but you'd think she'd been dying to meet one her entire life.

Mum hadn't noticed their lapse of attention. She pointed to where three curly coats, now shedding badly, stood flanked by Nanook on one side, Coaxtl on the other. 'When I told Sinead you were coming home, she sent Chapter and Page here to help you get around on the ground. They were born last year to Book and Novella. Can you tell your aunt has been doing her bit to support the Petaybean literacy program?'

Page, it's them! It's really them! The twins. They've come to be our humans.

Semihumans, old chap.

Close enough for the likes of you younglings, Coaxtl growled at the colt, then stretched and regarded the twins with narrowed eyes. *Grrreetings, Ronan and Murel. One had hoped it would have been more peaceful without you to guard, but this has not been so.*

Nanook was not so droll. She rose from her haunches and rubbed each twin so hard with her body that she nearly knocked them over. Then she rubbed the side of her mouth against each of them, marking them as hers while they stroked her.

Murel almost forgot that she couldn't be entirely happy, what with their father missing. It was good to be home again. She gave Nanook's neck a hug and kissed Coaxtl between the ears before mounting Page.

They rode slowly along the river from what used to be Space Base, the former Intergal toehold on Petaybee, toward Kilcoole.

'You guys are as tall as I am,' Mum said. 'When did you do that?'

It wasn't a question that needed an answer, but they had other questions that did.

'So, I get the impression Da was in seal form when he disappeared?' Murel asked.

'Yes. He wanted to swim out to the volcanic ridge where a landmass has been developing. I can only guess that he may have wished to talk to the ocean creatures and get their impressions of what was happening.'

'That gives us a starting place then,' Murel said. 'We can put the word out and see if anyone knows what happened to Da or where he might be.'

'Johnny thought Sean might have fetched up on the southern continent, but no one there has seen him. He's swum that far before but I know he'd find a way to let me know that he's safe.'

At the river bend just before town, they saw a once-familiar sleek brown form diving into the water.

Otter? Murel asked.

'Hah!' The otter popped almost entirely out of the water. *River seals! You are here now. Before, you were gone. I looked for you hundreds of times, but Father River Seal said you were gone.*

'Mum, it's Otter!' Ronan said, sliding off Chapter and stooping at the edge of the river, reins still in his hands. Murel did the same.

'So I see. I don't suppose I can compete with that. Just make it snappy, will you? I want to make one foray to the volcano with you aboard before we lose any more light, okay?'

Mum looked all tight through the back and military again, so Murel handed the reins to her brother, caught up with her and touched her calf. 'Mum, sorry, we really are glad to see you, but Otter might know something about Da. They talked too, you know.'

Mum's expression warmed a bit and she put her hand on the top of Murel's head. 'I know, sweetie, I know. Visit your friend, gather your intelligence, and come home, okay?'

'Right, Mum. Love you. Can't believe we're home again.'

'Me too, sweetie. Me too.'

Coaxtl and Nanook lay a discreet distance away from Chapter and Page, and Murel turned their way for a moment to give them each a stroke.

But Nanook asked, *What's he doing?* and bounded away.

Ronan had his shoes and shirt off and one foot in the river.

Good question, Murel said. *Ro, wait! No fair turning when we just got here. We can play with Otter later.*

He saw Da, Mur. He swam off with some sea otters. I want to go talk to them.

Swimming to the sea will take too long, she said, shaking her head as she ran to the bank in case her brother decided to jump in before they'd finished talking it over. Otter watched them, first one face and then the other, with a wary eye cast in Nanook's direction. *Otter*, she said, *we are flying out to the sea in a little while. Do otters like to fly?*

Hah! Otters love to fly. Otters always fly when they can.

So you've flown before, then, have you?

I would have flown hundreds of times when I could, but I never could, Otter admitted finally.

Well, river seals have flown hundreds of times too. If an otter flew with river seals, that otter would see things no otters have seen before and we would make sure he was very safe and went home to his hundreds of relatives.

But why fly? River seals can swim. Swimming is fun, and there are mud slides along the way and fish to eat. Are you sky seals as well as river seals?

Nooo, but humans fly all the time. We are sky humans. We fly because flying is very very fast, much faster than swimming, and we want to talk to those other otters about our da, the father river seal.

Hah! Flying, huh? On a smelly man thing?

Smelly and noisy, but we could carry you personally with us so you could just put your nose inside a shirt and not have to smell anything but river seal. And it is very fast, as I said.

You could be the first and only sky otter, Ronan said slyly.

Hah! That would make the other otters of all other kinds very impressed. Yes, this otter will be a sky otter.

'The thing is, Mum, Otter trusts us and maybe his relatives do too, but the sea otters don't know us and they're the ones who were with Da. So we should talk to them ourselves, without you or the copter or anything around. If you drop us off by the river upstream from the shore, we'll swim with Otter to meet the cousins, and maybe they'll even show us where Da went. It's a *lead*,' Ronan said.

'What I'm thinking is that you two have this psychic contact, right?'

The twins looked at each other, shrugged, looked back at their mother and nodded. 'Uh-huh.'

'Well, then, how much distance can there be between you before you lose it, have you any idea?'

'It's pretty strong,' Murel said. 'I could hear him from Marmie's when he was levels and levels away.'

'Yeah,' Ronan said.

'And it works underwater too?'

'Especially there,' Murel said.

'And you've the same thing with your father?'

'Yeah, but maybe not quite as strong because we aren't with him as much as we're with each other,' Murel said after pausing to think about it and trying to remember.

'Well, then, my strategy would be for one of you to go with the otter and get the goods on where your father is, while the other one stays in the copter with me and relays information from below. That way I don't lose contact with you both at once, and if one of you gets in trouble, the other can help us with the finding. If you both got in trouble, I'd have no way of knowing it unless I went with you, and I'm not really a diver.'

'Well, I guess so,' Ronan said. 'I'll go with Otter and Murel can stay with you.'

'I wanted to go with Otter!' his sister protested at once.

'He had dibs,' their mother said, settling it. 'Now let's go collect the otter and get out to the helipad.'

20

Since Ronan was to be the one swimming with Otter, Murel insisted on holding the little creature on the way to the ocean. Otter had other ideas.

Otters do not need to be held. Otters can stand on their own paws, Otter told her as they settled into the helicopter. He ran to the window and put his front paws on the glass.

Then the blades started rotating, *chuck-a, chuck-a, chuck-a*, and in a moment the aircraft lifted up, tipping slightly and spilling Otter onto the floor. He leapt back into Murel's lap and buried his nose in her armpit for a good deal of the rest of the trip.

When they reached the broad river delta, all ice for most of the year but now with braided channels of free flowing water, the copter set down, Mum grabbed Ronan for a quick hug, and he opened the copter door.

You can come out now, Otter. We're going to swim.

Otter disentangled himself from Murel, who combed her fingers through his soft thick fur as he left. *Hah! Yes, swimming is good, though sky otters can also fly.*

Ronan ran to the water, shucked off his outer clothes and, with the suit that Marmie had given him so long ago strapped in place on his back, dived into the water and emerged in seal form. Otter splashed him happily and swam off downstream.

Murel felt aggrieved. *No fair. I haven't even got to swim since we arrived*, she said.

Ronan barked a laugh. *This mission is much too dangerous for a female river seal. Only males and sky otters can do this bit.*

She sent him an image of her sticking out her tongue at him. She supposed she was being silly. This was a serious mission, after all, and the point was to find Da and bring him back safely. It didn't matter which one of them talked to the otters. The other one could hear and ask questions too. She just preferred to be there than up here above everything.

It was even more frustrating that they couldn't even fly out to the volcano where Da had said he was going until Ronan finished interviewing the appropriate otters. It took quite a long time too. Otter etiquette, which seemed to involve a lot of rocks changing paws, had to be observed. Ronan held back during this part of the negotiation, as the river otters all gathered around and declared themselves pleased to see him, though he could tell by their thoughts that some of them hadn't a clue as to who he was. Otters were live-for-the-moment creatures. Their otter friend was exceptional in that respect.

Murel caught all of this from Ronan and Otter's internal conversations and passed it along to her mother, to make the time go faster, if nothing else, since it was hardly the sort of information they'd come for. She liked to think she could have moved things along more quickly had she been in Ronan's place.

The thought escaped somehow, and Otter answered her directly. *Hah! Murel could not make sea otters come. Sea otters come when they wish to come.*

Where are they, do you think, Otter? she asked.

They live on the island – there. She received a slightly distorted otter-generated image of an offshore island and also Ronan's image of the same place. *But sometimes they are gone. They go back to where they lost Father River Seal, back to where they gather the big big clams.*

Big big clams?

Yes, and very large white crabs as well. They are easy to catch if you are a sea otter. They cannot see and they are easy to find against the black rock sea bottom.

I never heard of white crabs and giant clams before, she told him.

The sea otter's song says the crabs and clams live in the folds of the black rock sea floor beneath the tall black rocks that puff hot bubbles.

It took a lot of river otter chatter and a few turns on the mud slide – which made Murel, who thought she'd outgrown such foolishness, feel sharply envious of her brother – but at length Ronan and Otter spotted the sea otters swimming from the offshore island. One of them carried a giant white clamshell. It was almost as big as the sea otter carrying it, Ronan told her.

It made everything easier that the twins were famous

among the otters. *Where is the other river seal?* the sea otters wanted to know. *This river otter—*

Hah! Sky otter, Otter corrected. *Now there is a sky otter. Me.*

Sky otter?

Ronan explained. *My sister, the other river seal, is in a sky machine with our mother, who is not a river seal but a human all the time. The sky otter bravely rode with us to the sea so we could meet you and ask you about our father.*

What sky machine? the sea otters asked, swiveling their heads from side to side, to the back, up, and back down to face Ronan again.

I will call it so you can see, Ronan told them.

Murel told Mum what he'd said, and she spoke to the pilot, who lurched the copter skyward and flew to the shore to hover a little ways away from the otter colony.

Can your sister come and play with us too? We want to hear her song as well.

Hah! Murel said. *I can.* To her mother, she said, 'Excuse me, Mum, but if you'll have the pilot fly a little lower so I can dive in, I have to make an appearance as a river seal for the benefit of my otter public. They know about two river seals, the song is about two river seals, and two river seals are more believable than one.'

'Fine. Meet the otters, but then tell them you have to be a sky seal when Ronan goes to find your father.' Mum let a small smile play at the corners of her lips, though her eyes were still sad and anxious.

Murel didn't like seeing her mother sad, but then again, she didn't mind leaving her in the copter either. After all, Mum had sent them away for three long years without even asking what they wanted, so now her mother could get left when she herself wanted to go. The girl shucked her clothes and dived out the copter door into the sea. No need for her suit since she would be returning to the copter.

The water was cold cold cold after the warm and regulated pool at Marmie's, but it felt wonderful, especially when her skin covered itself with its seal coat. It smelled fresh and exciting and full of life and adventure and – fish! She gobbled three small ones as she swam toward the otters. Delicious! Nothing like Petaybean fish.

Feeling like some sort of a seal celebrity – the kind that never appeared on the vids available on Marmie's station – she joined Ronan and the otters.

Yes, that is right, Otter said, being the official spokes-otter either for them or for his relatives. *Now there are both river seals and that is the right number. Ronan is not enough river seals.*

Gee thanks, she said. Then she and Ronan listened as Otter sang the song he'd made about them again. It was no good for them to sing their own song because it was in the human language and lost a lot in the translation. Otter's version was far more appropriate to the audience at hand, or paw or flipper.

The sea otters then favored them with a song of their own, about finding the great clams and leading the father river seal to the beds. Ending the song, the sea otters sang, *But he swam away. He did not want clams and had no paws to hold them. He swam toward the great smoke and the thing beneath it. He swam to the great mystery and the otters who guard it.*

Otters guard it? Murel asked.

Yes, the sea otter said, sounding a bit nervous.

But is it not a big fiery underwater mountain? Why would it need otters to guard it?

That is a mystery.

Surely not to the otters who guard it. Do you know them? Are they a related clan of sea otters?

We have seen them, we have spoken with them, we have shared food with them, but we do not know them. They are not sea otters like us. They are deep sea otters and live beneath the waves.

Beneath the waves? But otters are – otters need air like seals, don't they? Otters cannot always live beneath the water.

The deep sea otters do, the sea otter told them. *They can stay above the water too but have to go down into it to breathe the same way we have to come up above the water to breathe. It is very strange.*

Are you sure they're otters?

Oh yes. They look just like us only they live beneath the sea.

Weird, Ronan said. *But if they live near the big volcano and that's where you think Da was swimming, then they may have seen him. Will you take us to them?*

We will take you as near as the clam beds and call to them. If the smoky mountain is very busy, they might not hear.

That would be good, Ronan said. *My sister and mother will follow us in the sky machine, okay? That way they can help us if there is trouble.*

Your mother who is not a seal nor any of your human people can know about the deep sea otters, the sea otter said. *They are very shy. They do not want to be taken by scientists for study as the river otters say they were.*

I suppose if they stay below the waves, Mum wouldn't see them. But she and Murel do need to follow. It's entirely possible nobody but Mur and me will be able to tell one sea otter from another. Do they look much like you?

They look almost exactly like us. Maybe larger.

Then nobody will know. Besides, there's no one here now to give any of you sea otters or your larger friends the kind of trouble Dr. Mabo gave the river otters.

'Hah!' Otter said. *Sea otters do not know about that trouble the way river otters do. But river otters cannot swim in the sea, so if sea otters and river seals are in trouble, this otter and his hundreds of relatives cannot help them out of it.*

Murel heard the disappointment in Otter's thought. *A river otter may not swim in the sea but a sky otter could fly over it if he wanted to,* she said. *Then if the kind of help a river or sky otter could give was necessary, that otter would be there.*

'Hah!' Otter said, and at once she knew that although he had no real wish to go up in the copter again, he was now a sky otter, and having said so of himself, his relatives would expect him to want to go into the sky. *That is true. Sky otters could go.*

Of course, they might have better things to do, Murel said, to give him an out.

But Otter said staunchly, *River seals help river otters, and river otters who are also sky otters help river seals.*

The little guy was trembling as Murel carried him back into the copter. At her signal, it had landed once more on the shore. The hundreds of relatives – there were actually probably less than twenty – chittered and chattered anxiously as she and Otter climbed aboard the noisy, smelly, wind-blowing machine and rose into the sky over the ocean. Otter himself kept saying 'Hah!' a lot.

Mother smiled at her and nodded to Otter as if he were a respected acquaintance.

Ready when you are, Murel told Ronan.

Okay then, sea otters, shall we swim?

You realize that we are very tired, having just come from there, the one they'd been speaking to said. *However, some of us did not get clams, and these otters will return to the lava beds with you, river seal, because of your song.*

Without further fanfare, the sea otters knifed into the waves and Ronan followed.

Murel put her earphones on and heard Mum say to the pilot, 'Just keep them in sight. We don't want to frighten the otters. They might be able to lead us to Sean.'

Murel thought her mother was awfully brave. Da had been missing for more than a week now. Where would he go in the middle of the ocean that he might be safe? He was all alone unless those deep sea otters knew where he was. Murel didn't want to think about it where anyone could read her, but she didn't see how Da could still be safe. There was no way, really. And yet, if he were gone for good she was sure she would know, sure that Mum would know, and Ronan too. *Da?* she called experimentally, and imagined her thought sending out ripples in the waves, ripples in the air like a very special kind of father-seeking sonar.

It rippled away into nothingness though, if she didn't

count Ronan's irritated, *You think I haven't been trying that?*

I think you're doing what you show me you're doing, she told him.

We're still not to the place where the sea otters lost him, so you may as well save your energy.

Within another four hours, however, there was a different kind of energy crisis. The pilot's voice boomed and crackled inside Murel's earphones. 'We're going to have to go back to refuel pretty soon, ma'am.'

'Frag,' Mum said, pounding her knee with her fist in frustration. 'How close are we now, Murel?'

It had been a long time since Ronan had sent her pictures of anything but waves rolling around his ears, or diving under ice, or otter hind ends. The sea could be very boring if you weren't actually in it. And it wasn't as if they could see much of anything in the copter. You couldn't even make out the otters swimming right below. The farther they flew, the worse the fog became.

In fact, Murel realized she'd been dozing when the pilot's voice awakened her.

So, Ro, how are we doing down there? she asked her brother.

Good! The water is a lot warmer here and it smells like rotten eggs, which seems about right for a place with volcanic vents, from what we studied in science class. The otters have been getting more and more excited, and making me hungry talking about those delicious red clams.

River otters like those too, Otter said suddenly. He'd been very quiet, and Murel thought he might have been napping.

Ooops, there goes an otter bottoms up, and another. We must be there. I'm diving too.

'Well?' Mum asked impatiently. Murel had almost forgotten about her.

'We're at the clam beds now. The sea otters say this is where Da left them.'

'Tell your brother to steer clear of those vents. They have sulfuric acid coming out of them.'

'We know all that stuff from school, Mum. Besides, we can smell the difference in the water. So can the otters.'

'We have to turn back now, ma'am,' the pilot's voice boomed into their earphones once more. 'Just enough fuel to make it back.'

'Let me get out, Mum. We'll lose Ronan and the otters otherwise.'

'I don't want to risk losing you both. Besides, what about your little friend here? Didn't you say he doesn't do salt water?'

Another voice crackled into the headphones. 'This is Captain Johnny Green aboard the amphibious yacht *Melusine*, registered to Lady Marmion de Revers Algemeine of Versailles Space Station. We are desperately seeking Petaybean Chinook-class helicopter zero-seven-three-niner-penguin-tango-bear, newly renamed the *Flying Otter*. Lady Marmion wants to know, "Is that you, Yana? Have you found him? Do you need fuel because the *Melusine* is equipped with a helipad and a fueling station."'

'Yes, no, and *merde alors*! Marmie, but you think of everything,' Mum replied.

Johnny and their copter's pilot exchanged coordinates

– normally you could see from a copter, but the smog from the volcano kept that from happening. The result was that soon the copter banked to the left, flew for a while, then settled down toward the sea like a bird fluffing down into her nest.

'Hah!' Otter said. *We have left Ronan and the sea otters, Murel. Where are we?*

The Flying Otter *needs fuel,* she told him.

Yes, even flying otters get hungry, but there will be clam meat later.

I didn't mean you. They've renamed the helicopter after you. It's called the Flying Otter *now. And I was thinking. We always think of you, and you refer to yourself, as Otter. But with so many other otters around, and you being our special friend, maybe you would let us call you a special name. How about Sky?*

Hah! Sky! Hah! Of course this otter is called Sky by his friends the river seals. Other otters know each other only by individual scent names, but Sky has friends who are not otters and must make sure it is their friend who hears them. Yes, this otter is Sky. Sky is a good name. A high name for an otter so special that even flying machines are named for Sky the sky otter.

Murel had to smile. Otter – Sky – was obviously well pleased with the distinction he had picked up simply by flying with them. Well, at least things were going well for someone.

Ronan, can you still read me?

Yeah, but I can't hear you anymore. Where did you guys go?

We have to refuel, but Marmie brought her special refueling yacht she packed with her aboard the ship when we came here. So we're not far. Any news of Da yet?

No, mostly just the sound of breaking clamshells and otter bodies diving back down for more goodies. They got a little sidetracked.

21

What is that? Sky asked, as Murel opened her arms to let him leap from the copter to the pad on the deck of Marmie's yacht.

Sky was looking through the puffs of smog and smoke at the Honu's tank, and Ke-ola beside it.

Oh, that's Ke-ola and the sacred Honu. Honu is a sea turtle. We don't have them here on Petaybee but he wanted to come and see it.

Loving greetings, Otter of the Skies, Honu's thought voice said.

Greetings, shelled creature who comes from space and is not for eating by river otters. Or sky otters. What brings you to our world and waters?

My kind love the places where the ocean bed is closest to the heart of the world and this is such a place. Your world is giving you a new land place, and my two-legged family is in much need of such a place. I have come to examine its suitability for us all, and ours for your world. I go now with my grandson Ke-ola to swim. Would you swim with us?

River otters, even when they are also sky otters, do not swim in salt water, Sky said regretfully.

Murel walked over to Ke-ola. 'Ronan is already in the water with some of the sea otters, looking for our father. I'd dive in with you but I can't change in front of so many people. Besides, Mum needs me here to let her know what's going on with Ro.'

'That's okay, sistah. The Honu and I will look. I think we will see more below than we can up here.' He inhaled deeply, throwing his arms out and drawing them back to his chest. 'But, ahhh! The air smells wonderful here.'

Murel wrinkled her nose. 'You're kidding! It smells like rotten eggs!'

Ke-ola just grinned. He liked the smell. Maybe it was some ancestral memory of volcano fart in his bloodlines, she thought.

Marmie's crew had lowered the tank into the hold of the yacht far enough that Ke-ola could simply reach in and lift out the sacred Honu, which he did. He stood on the deck where there was no railing.

'Slainté, Ke-ola,' Murel said softly.

Ke-ola paused. 'You told me slainté meant hello and goodbye.'

'It also means "to your health,"' she said.

'Slainté, Murel,' he said. 'Slainté, Sky.'

In her mind she heard Sky and the Honu echo the sentiment, and then Ke-ola, with Honu under one large arm, held his nose between the fingers of the other hand and happily dived feetfirst into the water.

The sea otters were restless. After each of them dived to get a clam and returned, some empty-pawed, they were ready to swim back to the shore again. Ronan couldn't blame them. He had never been swimming in the ocean before this and wasn't used to tides and waves. He thought it would be way more fun than rivers but this was no fun at all. Even the otters were finding swimming conditions difficult. When they led him to the first of the lava beds, he'd been able to see the tall rock chimneys pumping out their smelly bubbles and smoke, could feel from the warmth of the water where the black smokers lay beneath him.

But now, just a short distance farther, everything had changed.

A hot wind blew out of nowhere, whipping the waves high over his head. He couldn't even see the otters most of the time. Every once in a while the whole ocean would shudder and shake.

Hey, Ronan called out to the sea at large. *We should call those deep sea otters now. I don't think we can go much farther.*

No farther at all, River Seal! the closest sea otter said. Ronan couldn't see him through the smoke. *Going home now. No deep sea otters today.* Then suddenly he saw the crest of a wave bearing three sea otters riding the swell. One was floating on his back and almost sinking from the weight of the clam held to his chest with his front paws. *Water is too rough to play, food too hard to get. Wait for better seas and not so much smoke.*

Good idea, but my da is out here somewhere. You guys promised to help me. Otters were great playmates but except for Sky himself they didn't seem to be very reliable. *Could you just call them, though?*

If they are near enough to feel us calling, they'll already know we're here, the clam bearer called back, finally flipping over and releasing his prize before undulating away into the waters.

Yes, but . . . How did you argue with otters?

No sense trying. He had come all this way to find Da, and he wasn't about to go back after nothing more than a fishing expedition on the part of his trusty native guides. No way was he calling this off on account of waves.

This was as far as the otters had come with Da anyway, and they said he'd swum out to sea a little farther – toward the large and active volcano, which would mean swimming into thicker smoke at the very least.

He started to let Murel know, then thought better of it. He knew this was the right thing to do if he was going to find Da, but Mum might not allow it. Or Mur might try to come with him. She was now on Marmie's yacht, however *that* got here. He gathered it was some distance away, so he'd have to wait for her to catch up. The air quality here was terrible, and he could almost breathe water better than he could breathe the air. He didn't think it was going to improve and he didn't know how much longer he could hold out, so if he was going, he'd better go while the getting was good.

He tried drawing a diving breath but kept choking on the air. Swimming Petaybee's clean rivers, he had never had this problem before, but he thought full-time seals probably did sometimes. He wouldn't be such a baby. He'd do what he'd come to do. Finally, he took in what air he could and dived. He wouldn't be able to stay down long, but though the water was churning with mud, ash, and other debris, it was cleaner than the air.

By repeatedly diving and barely surfacing enough for his nose to suck in air before he dived again, he made some progress. He thought he did anyway. Actually, he didn't even know which direction he was going except he thought the smoke and debris were worse, and the water smelled worse and burned at times, not a hot burn so much as an irritating one. He thought surely he must be drawing nearer to the big volcano.

So, good for him. The only problem was, he could hardly see his own flippers, much less another seal or person in all this muck. He'd dive just a little deeper and then he would have to turn around. Mum and Mur would never forgive him if he got himself killed while trying to help Da.

That was such a grim thought that he dived deeper than he intended, and ended by touching the ocean floor – which was quite a bit closer than he'd supposed it might be.

He glided forward, his belly grazing the smooth lava bottom, where already plants were fringing up from the cracks, tickling his fur and flippers.

This was as far down as he could go. No way could he comb the entire ocean floor looking for – well, for what was left of Da. He didn't like to admit it, but Da could not have survived this for many hours, much less days or weeks.

His air was giving out. Little spots sparkled before his eyes, turning into dazzling stars, blinding after so much darkness. Then, to his surprise, his eyes adjusted – not to hallucinatory spots, but to real light, coming from what looked like real windows. In front of him and towering above him were what seemed like buildings, domes, towers – a gateway.

Murel knew her brother was in trouble right after Ke-ola hit the water. Sky felt it too. *The sea otters have gone. Your river seal brother is alone.*

Usually the twins communicated directly with each other, but Ronan wasn't doing that. Still, Murel felt from the tight constriction of her chest, the heaviness of her limbs, and the stuffiness in her nose that these sensations were Ronan's, not hers.

She found Mum talking to Marmie and tugged at her arm. 'Mum, you need to cover for me. I have to change and go to Ronan. He's become separated from the otters and he's not well.'

'Not well how?' Mum asked.

Quickly, impatiently, Murel described what she was feeling. Marmie whirled around and began gathering items and thrusting them at her.

'Even seals aren't safe in the sea at times like these, dear,' Marmie told her. 'You will need a respirator, a hard hat, probably a line to help you haul your brother to safety, and, oh yes, a homing beacon. And really, you should wear protective clothing and carry a knife as well.'

'I don't know how to break this to you, Marmie, but seals don't have pockets or anything to carry that stuff with, and the little packet my suit fits in won't hold it all. Just cover for me so the others don't see and I'll change *now.*'

'No,' Mum said. 'You will take these things or I will take them and dive with you.'

'Mum, you'd slow me down. Ro's in *trouble*.'

'And if you go without taking the proper precautions you will be too.'

Finally everyone was satisfied – except Sky, who wanted to go too but still didn't think river otters could swim in salt water. Murel put on the protective gear, with straps for the knife, rope, and hat. Then she cut the arms and legs out of the clothing to make room for her flippers, which would need the room once she was in the water. She dove in and made her change under the yacht. The hard hat was slippery on her seal's head and ended by sort of dangling around her neck.

'We'll be right behind you,' Mum called through the earpiece that was the other item they insisted she wear. They'd wanted her to wear a voice mike too, but she pointed out that they probably wouldn't understand her until she was back somewhere where she could speak without barking. The earpiece would probably float out of her ear once she started swimming.

Okay, Ronan, where are you and what kind of a jam are you in? she asked, but received no reply. So she struck out toward the lava beds where the otters and her brother were last seen. She called and called but although she continued to get the sensation that he was in deep trouble, he didn't respond.

Ronan, Ronan Born for Water Maddock-Shongili, where in the water are you? she cried in exasperation.

Come and see for yourself, sis, he replied. *You're not going to believe this!*

What do you see? Keep in contact. I'm on my way and Mum and Marmie and the yacht are following. I've a locator beacon so we'll find you.

It's some kind of an underwater city, Mur. Not too far from the main volcano cone.

Is it a ruin, you think? Maybe from way back before Petaybee needed terraforming.

It's a pretty lively-looking ruin. There are lights and things moving around.

She swam as quickly as she could, undulating toward where she felt him to be. *The moving things could just be sea creatures swimming through it, but the lights? Bioluminescence, do you suppose?* Petaybee exhibited that kind of thing in many places, inside the caves, sometimes along the inner banks of the river, but it hadn't ever gone so far as to light up buildings, not that she knew of. Usually you had to use at least a candle or a lantern or something.

No, no, you'll just have to see.

Don't go in yet unless you have to. Wait for me.

Suddenly the entire ocean gave a violent shudder and she was buffeted back and forth by the swell before she could proceed onward with any speed. On the surface, rocks rained into the water, which told her she was getting closer to the cone. Below her the water was warm, sometimes uncomfortably so. She knew the vents spewed acid, and could only hope it was diluted enough by the water that she wouldn't suffer burns to her exposed flippers and face. She was very glad now to have all the silly equipment Mum and Marmie had insisted on loading onto her.

The respirator especially was coming in handy now when she surfaced, even though it didn't fit a seal's snout very well. Mum forgot her seal daughter didn't have hands to adjust the darn thing.

Funny, with all the smoke it looked like the weather was stormy, but really, back on the boat the sky had been blue where you could see it beyond the smoke.

She dived again and swam on, calling and calling. Behind her she heard the engine of the *Melusine*. She surfaced and looked back. Mum, Marmie, and some of the other people aboard the yacht stood on deck wearing hard hats, protective coats, and respirators. There were human divers on board too, and they were prepared to help, but Murel had asked that they stay aboard the boat until she located Ronan. No sense in muddying the waters any more than they were already muddied, and besides, it would be impossible to keep their secret from all those divers.

Although Ronan looked up to the tops of the towers of the city stretching out before him, the city's base was beneath the place where he stood, sunken into a wide volcanic caldera that glowed cherry red all around the edge of the city.

How could people live there? Well, maybe they didn't. There were lights and shadows, flickering and movement, but he couldn't identify what was causing the movement. After staring at it for a while, he wasn't even convinced it was real. It could be a hologram, he decided, although why anyone would project one in an isolated undersea spot near a volcano was beyond him.

Then he realized the lights were changing colors – that a progression of colors beginning with white turned to yellow, lime, emerald, teal, aqua, brilliant blue, purple, red, orange, and back to yellow. From the bottom of the towers to the top and back down again, from the spires closest to him to those farthest away, the lights ran their rainbows.

Fascinated, he swam forward, thinking to explore the streets that surely ran between the towers, but instead of swimming straight ahead, he found himself swimming to the surface, there to be assaulted by more rock showers. Lightning bounded through the smoke in front of him. Taking as much air as he dared, he dived again, but although he thought he was swimming into the city, he reached the ocean floor pretty much where he had been before.

He surfaced and dived many more times, each time drawing shallower breaths and growing more light-headed. He should turn back, he thought, try to meet Murel, but he didn't want to lose sight of the city for fear that he wouldn't find it again. He half thought it was an illusion. Each time he went up for air, he tried to dive at a different angle, but always he was off to one side of the city. Perhaps it was farther than it looked, though he could feel the heat from the glowing crater beneath it.

It wasn't just that the city had a hypnotic effect on him, he thought. No, he could break away from that if he wanted. It was just that if this were a real place, it was the best hope that Da was still alive and well. Unless, of course, whoever ran the city was evil or something.

Ronan? Ro? Where are you? Murel's mind-voice was very close to him now.

Here, he said, but even to his own mind his thought was not projecting very well. *I'm here, by the city.*

By the – what are you on about anyway? Have you been eating funny seaweed?

He didn't answer. He felt her glide up next to him. More distantly there was a rumbling. He thought it was the volcano again but then felt the churning of the water and heard echoes of other human thoughts.

Oh. I see, Murel said, her body hanging lengthwise in the water beside him as she looked into the city. She looked very funny, wearing a hat on the back of her head and neck and something weird and mechanical over her nose. She also had on some kind of clothing, not becoming to a seal. Though it was comical, he didn't feel like laughing. He just stared at her for a moment then back at the city. *That's incredible. I bet Da is in there somewhere. Have you tried calling to him?*

Uh, not yet, Ronan replied, feeling incredibly stupid. *I was – was waiting for you.*

Let's get some air, then we'll try, she said, but she had begun to sound less direct and certain and more as if she too had been mesmerized by the city and its lights.

This time when they surfaced, he was aware of the yacht, a slightly darker shape through the smoke, with figures moving purposefully about there.

River seals! River seals! Sky called to them. *Have you found the deep sea otters? Have they seen your father?*

No, but Ronan has found something else very strange, Murel said. She was about to suggest that they return to the yacht to tell their mother about the city when there was a splash that sounded more like otter than rock, and presently the sleek brown head of Sky peered at them out of the smoke.

I thought river otters didn't swim in salt water.

Normally we don't but this was just a short swim, just a little ways and besides, if there are deep sea otters here, maybe they only speak to otters. Maybe they don't know that river seals don't eat otters.

What we've found isn't exactly deep sea otters, Murel told him. *Come.*

The three of them dived back down to the city, which was still there.

It's almost like it's not real, Ronan said. *I tried over and over again to swim into it but I couldn't.*

But Sky was not interested in the city as much as he was in contacting its inhabitants. Standing on the ocean floor on his hind paws, he moved the top of his body to the right and then to the left, then back again, inspecting the entire thing. Finally he sent out his message, *Deep sea otters, deep sea otters, it is your cousin Sky the River Otter who is also a sky otter, calling you. Our cousins the sea otters say that you live here. This otter has braved the salt water, which is not the element of river otters, to find you. Please answer. Your cousins have a problem and seek your help.*

From within the city came the first thought any of them had sensed. *Do you think deep sea otters are so easily tricked, little cousin? We know you brought that boat full of scientists to study us. We know there are seals out there with you.*

Hah! That is so. But the boat is full of rescue people and family members, not science people looking for you. The seals are only partly seals. Partly they are two-legged children. Their father, also only partly a seal, is missing and was last seen swimming your way. Did you see him? Do you know what became of him?

Maybe. The thought was cautious. *We don't want boats and seals around our den, though. Those seals, especially the one, have been here staring into our den for a long time.*

Murel said, *It's a pretty exotic-looking den, deep sea otters. We were just wondering how it got there and if our father might have found shelter there.*

If he did, if deep sea otters helped him, then his children wouldn't tell the scientists about our den?

If you don't want us to, we won't, Murel said. *Nobody wants to hurt you or molest you, and we won't let anybody study you if you don't want to be studied. We just want our father.*

You will tell no one else about us? No two-legged people?

No one, she said.

Not even Mum, Ronan promised.

River Otter, you believe these seals? the alleged deep sea otter asked.

These are the seals that save the lives of otters. They do not lie. They do not tattle. But they will keep searching until they find their father, and so will the big boat. There are other men too. Men who can enter the water and swim like otters.

Deep sea otters are very shy, the thought came to them, but to Murel, it sounded more sly than shy. *No men must come and find our den.*

They won't come if we don't tell them to, Murel replied. *But we need to find our father. He is a very important man to this world and none of us will rest until we know where he is and how he is. If we don't find him,* she warned, *there will be more men and women here than any deep sea otter has ever seen before.* It was a safe threat. Since no people had ever seen deep sea otters that she knew of, it stood to reason that deep sea otters had never seen all that many people either.

Above them, through the murky water, she saw two new shadows – a large human-shaped one and a round one, which she recognized as being turtle-shaped. *One of our friends is seeking us now*, she said. *You know what?*

She received an image of otter ears pricking forward as if to say 'What?'

I think you know where our father is. I think you found him and took care of him in your secret den and he is still alive. That would be very good for deep sea otters, you know. It would make my brother and me and the sky otter here and even all the men who don't know about you owe you big-time.

She got the impression of confused inter-otter chittering. *We would be your friends and wish you well and maybe do something for you sometime.*

You must keep us a secret, the thought returned clearly. *If you do this, we may be able to help you with what you seek.*

Great. She looked up and saw the Honu and more of Ke-ola than she had before – hands and upper torso gaining shape. *Oh look! One of the divers is coming now! What do you say? Shall we keep him away? He'll go away if we say so.*

Yes. He must not find our den, the spokes-otter replied quickly, though again she felt there had been some excited consultation before he spoke.

Okay then. We're all going to surface for air now and to

keep our friend up there from finding you. You otters think it over.

She conveyed this, and the three of them lofted themselves toward the surface. It was none too soon, as the ocean floor rolled and fiery liquid belched beneath the city/den. Strangely, the eruption didn't seem to hurt or move the odd collection of lighted towers in any way, but it splashed upward. Had they delayed another moment, they would have been burned.

The three of them rose straight up underneath Ke-ola and the Honu, nudging Ke-ola back up into what could now only loosely be called fresh air.

'Ronan and Murel! River Otter! The Honu felt that you were in danger. We came to help you. We must go back to the boat. The Honu and I would be fine but the boat could sink from the falling rock. It's very hot, you know.'

They couldn't answer him. The waves swelled like angry cats and attacked them, driving them apart and spinning them around with the force of the tormented water.

Hah! River otters are not meant for salt! River otter fur is full of dirty ashen stuff that stinks and stings. Sky was fretting, but neither Murel nor Ronan could see the otter or each other because of the water and the steaming ash.

Only the Honu bobbed on top of the waves, sliding down them and riding back up.

But more than anything they were actually experiencing was the pressurized sensation that something ominous was building very near them, something about to explode.

Why is Petaybee so furious with us? Murel couldn't help but wonder.

Not furious. Spawning, the Honu told her.

Well, as soon as the planet's between contractions we should dive one more—

At that moment something bobbed up beneath her, bumping her underside. Murel rolled off it and down and saw another seal. *Da!* she cried. But the other seal did not answer her. It bounced helplessly with the waves, not moving a flipper to help itself.

Then suddenly the ocean seemed to fly apart as a torrent of water plummeted from high up in the sky, smashing into her body with more force than a speeding snocle.

22

This can't be happening. It's too weird and too unfair. Murel sent the message to all and sundry as a wave slammed her under, the force of it almost driving her back to the ocean's shallow bottom. She choked on dirty ashen water and tried not to breathe until she fought her way to the surface again. Wherever that was!

The whole world rumbled and roared louder than a giant snocle. Clumps of burning rock pelted her and she kept dodging scalding steam. *Da? Ronan? Otter? Sky? Honu?* she called silently.

'Murel! Ronan!' Mum's voice called out to them somewhere very near.

Murel heard the thought as much as the words and struggled toward her mother's voice.

Here you go, little seal, came another thought, and she felt herself snatched clean out of the water and handed up, so that she tumbled onto a hard, knobby surface.

Almost immediately something huge and heavy was dumped on top of her. She tried to roll sideways but there was very little room. Before she could pull herself entirely clear, something else was dumped on top of the other thing. The things wiggled and breathed, and, of course, when her vision cleared, she saw that they weren't things at all. It was Ronan and Da. Mum and Johnny sat at the bow and the stern of a lifeboat with the three of them in the middle. Nobody was rowing, and Murel feared they'd be swamped. But as she dragged herself out from under her relatives, she saw that there were lines attached to the lifeboat tied to the *Melusine.* The boat was being towed back toward the yacht by all hands on deck, fighting the swamping waves and the swell.

Something else, small and wriggling, flopped into the boat. 'Hah!' Sky said, his favorite otter expression mingling indignation and relief in the same puff of breath. 'Hah!'

Finally one more object landed in the boat, clattering on the side. *I could have made it myself, foolish boy*, the sacred Honu said. *I was swimming before you were an egg.*

'Ke-ola, get in!' Mum cried. 'You're exhausted.'

'No room!' he bellowed back up at her. 'Sink . . . you. Hang . . . onto . . . hull.'

A huge wave slid the lifeboat back to the yacht, smashing into it and dumping everyone back into the raging sea. The crewmen were tossed backward, to sprawl on the deck, and the ropes went flying. The lifeboat, its hull splintered, sank beneath them as they scrambled for safety.

Murel saw Mum thrown against the yacht's hull and swam over to break her fall. Ke-ola grabbed Johnny, who, being unhurt, shook him off. Da started to sink with the lifeboat, but Ronan fetched him up again.

Otter clung to the Honu's tail.

The lines were tossed over the side once more. Mum, Johnny, and Ke-ola caught them. Then Ke-ola boosted Murel up on a rising wave so that she practically washed onto the yacht. He did the same thing with Da and Ronan. Mum, who was shaken but didn't seem injured, tried to help, but Ke-ola nodded to her own rope. Seeing that he had matters in hand, she climbed aboard and was helped on deck by Johnny, who had by that time helped Marmie pull Da and Ronan onto the deck. Sky scampered up across Mum's back and hair to safety. Johnny turned to pull Ke-ola aboard but the Kanaka boy rode another wave up and clung to the deck.

Darkness descended on them almost as quickly as the waves. Marmie bundled them all in blankets, which were soaked but not so thoroughly that the seals couldn't change back into Shongilis.

Wanting to stay human for a while, and unsure that they would do so if the waves kept washing over them, the twins tugged on their waterproof suits, pulling up the hoods.

Johnny tried to stuff Da into a waterproof suit too. Da struggled to sit up, saw Mum's face and said, in a voice much the same as the one they'd heard him use when he'd drunk a bit of the blurry at latchkays, 'Jayz, darlin', what are you doing out here? The weather's terrible.'

Mum made a funny half-sobbing noise Murel could barely hear as Da finally managed to sit up and pull on his own suit.

Because of the darkness and the fact that only their

family and closest friends were helping, the selkies' secret was preserved as much as possible. They couldn't be sure, of course, but none of the crew members said, 'Hey look, those seals they hauled up just turned into a couple of kids and their old man!' so it seemed their secret was intact.

But that kind of exposure was the least of their worries. Marmie and Pet Chan helped everyone but Sky and the Honu lash themselves with ropes – lines – to the sturdier and more permanent features of the yacht. Although Murel wondered how sturdy the boat could actually be since apparently it had come off the spaceship in pieces with some assembly required. 'All secured, Captain,' Pet told Johnny.

Johnny in turn shouted to the crew, 'Okay, give her full throttle and get us out of here.'

'Uh, Captain?' the nearest crew member said.

'Yes? Wait a tick. We are supposed to be idling. I know it's noisy here but we're not idling. Why are we not idling?'

'Not actually sure, sir, but the engineer said something about ash clogging the fuel pumps.'

'That's just—' Another huge wave washed over the deck. Murel felt paws wind tightly into her hair. When the water subsided with the yacht miraculously still right side up, she saw Ke-ola leaning over the railing, apparently communing with the Honu, who was in the water. '—brilliant,' Johnny finished.

Sky, you're pulling, Murel told the otter.

Grooming, the otter mumbled through a mouthful of hair.

Da and Mum were hanging on to each other literally

for dear life. Murel felt rather than saw her father staring at her and Ronan as if he could hardly believe they were there. *How long have you been home?* he asked.

Dunno, Ronan replied. *Feels like not very long and nearly forever at the same time.*

What happened to you, Da? Murel asked. *Everyone thought you were a goner.*

Far as I knew, I could have been. The last thing I recall was something falling on me, and then I woke up floating in the water beside you two.

So you don't remember anything about otters, for instance?

Oh, the sea otters were having a grand time bringing up clams from the lava beds when I left them but I finally swam onward. Not all that clever of me, really. It would have been a better job for people with two legs and equipment. It's dangerous around here, in case you haven't noticed.

We noticed.

Who's the big lad being chummy with the turtle? And for that matter, how did the turtle get onto Petaybee? No turtles were authorized that I recall.

That's Ke-ola, one of our classmates from the station. The sacred Honu is the turtle. I believe they're considering immigrating. Ke-ola just saved the lot of us, pulling us out of the water and sticking us in the lifeboat, so I think you might want to give their request special consideration.

Should Petaybee allow us to live through this, I promise to do that very thing, Da said.

The sun, having disappeared for half an hour or so, once more swung around on the horizon until it was over the ocean. Of course, nobody on the boat could actually see it, but they knew that it had because the rays shined through the shroud hanging over the ocean and dyed it brilliant scarlet, fuchsia, and tangerine.

Almost as if the sun's rising soothed the volcano's temper, the rumbling quieted and the seas became comparatively calm. With the yacht's motor out, the loudest noises were the tinkering and swearing that could be heard clearly from the engine room. The twins and their parents loosened their lines enough that the twins could turn around and give their father huge hugs.

'You took that business of being hero twins seriously, didn't you, kids?' he asked aloud. 'Your mum says it was you who came to fetch me from what I can only presume was almost a watery grave.'

'Much as we'd like to take credit for that, Da, it was actually Sky—'

'Sky?'

'Otter. Now that he's ridden to your rescue in a helicopter, he is a sky otter instead of merely a river otter, so we've given him an appropriate name and he likes it.'

'It is more original than Otto or something of the sort,' Da agreed. 'And it was good of him to come along. River otters do not go to sea, as a rule.'

'So he's told us. But in your case he made an exception. And it's a good thing he did,' Murel said. 'He's the one who, uh – found where you were for sure.'

'But you two got me out? How did I survive?'

'There seemed to be air pockets or something – maybe the volcano created a kind of grotto with an air tube to the surface?'

'Which, providentially for me, did not turn into a lava tube? Petaybee was being extremely thoughtful there.'

'Pity that mood didn't continue,' Mum said.

Lookit Ke-ola, Ronan told Murel while their parents were discussing Petaybee's moods.

Ke-ola stood on deck staring straight out at the tip of the cone, becoming slightly visible above the water at times, when the steam wafted up and away from the rim. His expression was thoughtful. A dome bulged in the cone like an egg about to hatch. Although the volcano was quiet for the moment, once more they could feel the pressure building.

'Whatcha think, Ke-ola?' Murel asked.

'I was just thinking about my twenty nieces and twenty-five nephews,' he said.

'Are you worried you will never see them again?' she asked sympathetically. At least she and Ronan were back home with their parents and their friends, even if it only meant they wouldn't die alone. Not a happy thought. Murel choked up in spite of herself. She didn't want to die, but the dome inside the crater was bright red and pulsing.

Sky was puzzled. *Is there not enough water here for you?*

We were thinking of our families, Sky. Ke-ola was remembering his relatives who are not here.

He has many?

Hundreds, like you.

Many Ke-olas. Good. Honu likes Ke-ola. Sky otters like Honu. Sky looked over the side, where Honu was swimming back and forth beside the yacht.

Johnny Green returned from belowdecks and reported to Marmie.

'How long?' she asked.

'Too long, I'm afraid,' he replied, shaking his head. 'They're clogged as bad as if they'd been poured full of concrete. The lads are working as fast as they can but they'll be no match for Herself,' and he nodded to the volcano. He turned to Marmie. 'There's one lifeboat left. You and Pet, Yana and the kids—'

'Not us,' Murel said. 'We're better off as seals now that we're rested, right, Da?'

'Yes, but I'll be alongside the boat where your mother is.'

'Mother isn't going in any lifeboat,' Mum said. 'There's room enough for Marmie, Ke-ola and the crew. Too many people depend on Marmie for her to be lost this way. She's been Petaybee's number one outside ally. You'll need her help.'

'*We'll* need her help, luv.'

'He's right, Yana. I'm the captain, not you. I'll go down with the bloody ship if anyone does,' Johnny said.

'No, Johnny. Marmie needs you too . . . and I outrank you.'

'Not anymore, you ridiculous baggage. Get in that boat, and that's an order.'

'You can't talk to my wife that way, Johnny. I'll do it,' Sean said. 'Get into that boat, Yana, and stop being such ridiculous baggage. You're the mother of our children and *they* need *you*.'

Meanwhile other sailors, more practical and less noble, had lowered the remaining lifeboat over the side and were climbing in. Pet Chan practically forced Marmie in along with the crewmen. Once Pet was seated, there was room for two more passengers.

'Not the way they need you,' Mum argued with their father. 'You understand them. You can all speak without words. I—'

'No time for this nonsense, Yana,' Da said, and tried to lift and manhandle Mum over to the lifeboat. When he proved too weak to do it, Johnny scooped her up but she fought them both off.

'Hey, Mama,' Ke-ola said, padding barefoot over to the three of them and separating the men from the twins' furious mother. 'You don't gotta do it, lady. I'll go now. I know what has to be done. It's in the oldest chants. Your keikis need you, your man, your world.'

'Petaybee does not seem highly attached to any of us just at the moment,' Mum snapped, and turned on Ke-ola, her dark eyes flashing. 'And where is it you think you're going, young man?'

'Ke-ola knows all this old stuff from when his people lived near volcanoes, Mum,' Ronan told her.

'Yeah, I bet they had some really neat way of dealing with eruptions and stuff, didn't they, Ke-ola?' Murel asked.

'Yeah,' he said. 'That's right. Those old ones knew that if you were gonna have life, there had to be death so somebody had to give themselves to Pele – our volcano goddess. I'm not afraid. There's too many people where I come from anyway. I'll do it, then the volcano will quiet and you all can go home.' He turned and walked to the rail, and in another fraction of a nanosecond would have slipped into the waves. Ronan and Murel exchanged looks and ran up beside him, stripping off their dry suits. He gave each of them a chagrined look. 'Little bruthah, little sistah, you should understand!'

'Are you out of your *mind*?' Mum demanded. 'Johnny, Sean, someone brain this child before he does something monumentally stupid.'

'I don't care what your chants said, Ke-ola, if they told you to jump into a volcano, they were wrong,' Murel told him. 'I thought that was a good place you came from to begin with. Why would your volcano want anyone to jump into it?'

'Yeah, it's not hungry, for pity's sake,' Ronan added. 'It's trying to pump stuff out, not take stuff in. You'd just be polluting it. We'd have Ke-ola bits all over the nice new island Petaybee's trying to make. Honestly, I know it looks bad, Ke-ola, but nobody has to die here. If anyone does, it will be an accident, and Petaybee, well, I think Petaybee will be really sorry. You were the one who said the planet wasn't angry, it was just giving birth and a little out of control.'

Murel had a flash of insight. *I think that's what Mum understands, maybe without knowing she does. She sort of knows what Petaybee's going through. It was hard enough for her to have twins. Think what it must be like to try to have an island. Ugh. I don't ever want to have any kids.*

'I honestly think you misunderstood those chants, guy,' Ronan said earnestly.

'That's what you think, do you, little bruthah?' Ke-ola asked with maybe a little of his old twinkle returning.

'It is. You're our friend, you know, partly because you were the one kid at school who kind of understood about Petaybee. I think you're supposed to live here, not die here.'

Murel realized that she thought the same thing, but she didn't see how that was going to happen. The lifeboat had not yet completely detached from the yacht, Mother and Father and Johnny were still arguing, the yacht was still dead in the water, and the waves began slapping ominously against the side of the hull again. *Slap-slap, slap-slap.*

She hoped it was her imagination that made the dome look bigger – and as if it were throbbing steadily.

'Shite on a shingle,' Mum said. 'Here comes another contraction.'

Steam jetted up suddenly from vents around the dome, and the sea started shaking again, rumbling as if it were full of bones. Which it could be pretty soon if they weren't careful.

'A contraction.' Ke-ola smiled and turned to them, asking casually, 'Maybe I got to thinking of the wrong chant at that. You remember that one song I sang at your party – the one I didn't translate?'

'Which one?'

'The one with the stomps. Like this.' He stomped, bringing the opposite leg up sharply, then stomped again so the rhythm was *stomp-stomp, stomp-stomp*, like the *slap-slap* of the ocean against the boat. The stomps shook the whole boat.

'Oh, yeah, that one! I like that,' Ronan said. 'It's fun. Only – maybe not now.'

'Now is a real good time, I think,' Ke-ola replied. 'You do it too. You too, Mama and Papa and Captain,' he called back, continuing the stomp.

'Like a heartbeat!' Murel said.

'That's it, sistah. Because it's a birthing chant. Like I told you, all we got to do on that asteroid where we live now is make babies, and because of the gravity, it ain't easy. So everybody has to help the mamas. The men's part, with the stomping, goes something like, "Swim swim," to the baby, with the stomps being like canoe paddles. To the mama we say "Breathe breathe," until it's time to "Push push," and the verse that just repeats is something like, "Have no fear your men are here. We will protect you," to put it in your language, which is, sorry, really not good for poetry. There's a women's part that goes something like, "Take it slow, sistah, take it easy, be calm, breathe easy, the birth is a beautiful dance, bring your child into the sunshine so he can dance with his relatives." Or something like that. But I think if you just clap, soft, like this,' he showed her, 'in the same time, that will get it across.'

'Okay,' Murel said. 'So, you think we should do this now?'

He shrugged tidally once more. 'Can't hurt. If your world is as willing to listen to you as you say, maybe we can make her hear, before she's making too much noise again.' He kept stomping and shouted again at the twins' parents and Johnny, 'Mama, Papa, Captain, do what we do. You folks in the lifeboat, drum on the side. Paddlers, strike the sea with your oars.'

More fumeroles gushed steam, Petaybee exhaling through her teeth. The sea rocked the yacht, but Murel liked to think that the stomping feet and clapping hands steadied it somehow.

Ke-ola called out the first words of the chant, addressing the laboring volcano not as a goddess, but as he probably already had sung many times to his mother, aunt, or sister. He waved his hand to Murel and Ronan and sang the words to them. They repeated them after him as loud as they could, matching his beat. Then he called out some more. This time he added a little lilt and melody to the words.

The dome swelled and throbbed, the fumeroles spewed and steamed, and the column of steam and ash rose into the coral sky, deepening its hue to bloodiness.

The rumbling got louder, but not as loud as before.

Ke-ola stamped and chanted. Murel and Ronan, and soon their father and mother, stamped and chanted after him, their words finding an unbidden harmony with his, so accustomed were their voices to songs in a mode more familiar to their world. Marmie and most of the people in the lifeboat drummed on its side or with paddles against the sea. Johnny didn't join in, nor did the chief engineer. They chose the more pragmatic path of going below and trying to fix the engine with the time they hoped the chant might be borrowing for them.

Ke-ola looked straight out at the volcano the whole time, his head held high and his body erect as an arrow, shooting his words into the horizon. His bare feet alone shook the entire yacht. Amplified by the stamping of the other feet, the sound gave a heartbeat to the rising waves, measured the rising smoke with its cadence.

The twins stamped and sang until not only their feet, but their knees hurt. The throbbing dome could burst at any moment and send a fountain of lava into the sea and onto the yacht, but it didn't.

But their throats began to burn with the singing and with the little particles of ash that should have made them cough but didn't.

Ke-ola did not cough or falter in his singing either.

They stamped until their hips ached and their soles began to bleed. Their throats longed for water but they could not stop singing.

From the corner of her eye Murel saw Sky dive into the sea. Following him, she watched him swim after the Honu, both of them toward the cone being joined slowly in the middle of the ocean by other cooling lava being spewed by the lesser volcanoes around it.

Honu and Sky swam back and forth, back and forth, and before long it seemed other creatures were swimming as well. Among them were some sea otters and great shoals of fish, dolphins, orcas, and larger whales that came right up under the boat without touching it. Instead of swimming back to the boat, however, these creatures swam to either side of the cone and onward. Only Sky and Honu went back and forth. Soon Murel realized their journeys were in prolonged counterpoint to the stamping.

The dome could have blown, should have blown, all at once, but didn't. It seemed to recede a little, the throbbing developing into a regular pulse. When it opened, the top of the dome didn't blow. Instead its sides opened and pumped rather than spewed the lava into the sea, to be cooled almost at once by the water.

As the volcanoes blew and the islands formed and joined, it seemed to Murel that the sea itself was working with their party, a pathetically puny bunch of humans, occasionally some seals, plus an otter and a sea turtle. Instead of swamping the boat, the waves picked it up and carried it away from the volcano. They had been perhaps a mile away from the throbbing dome to begin with, but soon the swells carried them two miles, then five, then ten miles farther from it. By the time the cone's pumping escalated into the fountain they'd been expecting, they were safely away from it. The lifeboat, still attached to the yacht, was also carried to safety. Honu and Sky ceased swimming back and forth and watched as the other sea creatures paraded past, greeting the new arrival, which would breed food and shelter for them in time to come.

Ke-ola did not stop singing and stamping, however, and neither did the twins or anyone else, though they badly wanted to. Surely it was safe now? But maybe not. There were still those volcanic beds beneath the sea even this far out. Murel thought they would be agitated too.

But she got out only another half-dozen stomps and another line of chanting that she wasn't even sure got from her sandpapered throat to her mouth. Then her legs gave out and she sat down on the deck. To her surprise, she saw that Mum and Da were also both sitting down and no longer chanting. Ronan almost fell on top of her. Still, the rhythm and melody of the chant rolled on toward the volcano, as strongly as ever, and the beat seemed even stronger. Maybe the people in the lifeboat, sitting as they were, could carry on with more force?

But as she glanced back she saw that something different was happening. A line of fishing boats bobbed along on the yacht's port side, and more were fighting the waves to reach them, the paddles keeping time with the chant. No motors were running now. With the ash in the air, they would suffer the same fate as the yacht's engines.

Everyone seemed to be carrying the melody of Ke-ola's chant, which was a good thing, because strong as he was, their classmate was beginning to droop a little.

But reinforcements came just in time. Clodagh climbed over the side of the boat, as always amazingly graceful despite her great size, and, singing and stamping as she went in a kind of a dance, she joined Ke-ola, singing the same words he sang. The first time he faltered, she touched his shoulder to signal him to sit.

She sang only a few lines more before the cherry red of the volcano faded to orange, then yellow. The rumbling quieted, the smoke cleared, and a shallow star of land rose above the ocean's surface, its rays spreading from the central crater, while the sky's bloody fever receded to a rosy blush.

23

Absolutely nothing happened next, because nobody who was at the volcano was able to talk or move around much for the next couple of weeks.

The fishing boats rescued the yacht crew and passengers and relayed them back to shore. The copter, which Johnny had left near the river otter dens when he and Yana finally joined up with Marmie and the yacht, once *its* motor was also cleaned, returned them all to Kilcoole.

But nobody talked, because nobody could. It was even too much trouble to thought-speak for a long time because the chant was burned into their brains. Murel's feet hurt up to her tonsils.

Clodagh's student, Deirdre Angalook, under the drooping eyelids of her teacher, made up salves, tinctures, syrups, and packs for everyone's lungs, throats, and muscles. By the time she had everyone dosed, she needed sleep and the muscle salve herself.

Finally, Murel, Ronan, and their dad were able to walk as far as the river and change to seal form, which was easier because then they wouldn't have to walk and their seal muscles were configured differently. The river was silvery and cool, the slender trees on the banks a hundred shades of green – evergreen, or variegating from silver green to grass – as they flipped back and forth in the wind. Mum put on a wet suit and joined them since even in the summer the water of the Kilcoole River was too cold to brave for long in just human skin. The sky was the blue of a glacier, with fluffy clouds and no hint of smoke or steam, but the light faded far more quickly than it had just two weeks before. Some of the leaves on the deciduous trees were already yellowing where the sun lingered on them the longest.

A little after the twins and their parents entered the river, Clodagh, Dierdre, and Ke-ola ambled down to meet them. Ke-ola actually looked great for a guy who'd done all that stomping around.

'Did Dierdre give you extra salve while you've been staying up at Clodagh's?' Murel asked him when she'd dragged herself out of the river, dried off, and put on the change of clothes she'd brought along. Her voice was still a bit husky, but at least audible now.

'Naw, it's that gravity thing,' he said, sounding almost normal. 'I'm used to being heavier so I'm way stronger than you wimpy Petaybee guys. I could go back out and talk to Pele Petaybee some more right now if I wanted to.'

Ronan was out of the water now too, and said, although he was once more in human form, 'I flash my furry seal butt at you, big fella, and flap my hind flippers in your general direction. I don't want to see anything hotter than a teakettle for the rest of my life.'

Ke-ola laughed and waded in, turned the color of the sky and waded out again.

'We can take you to the hot springs if you fancy a dip,' Murel offered. 'And there's parts of the river warmer than this, but this was the closest place with any privacy.'

He nodded and lay back on the grassy bank with his head cupped in his palms.

Mum used the newcomers' arrival as an excuse to escape the water. She did her best, but she just wasn't a watery person at heart. 'Clodagh, I need to know something.'

Clodagh lifted her eyebrows. She never used words where an expression or action could do the job, and seldom used two words when one would do.

'Why did all of you show up in the fishing boats the way you did, when you did, and how did you learn Ke-ola's chant?'

'Petaybee told us,' she said simply.

It was Mum's turn to raise her eyebrows. 'It did?'

'Sure. We were all down in the caves when the drumming started coming through the walls, and the words. We knew you were out there with that volcano, so that was the only place it could be coming from. Petaybee echoing the words back was a good sign that the planet liked what you were doin', so we joined you.' She shrugged. 'That's all.'

'Well, of course,' Mum said. 'Silly me. Who wouldn't mount a major rescue operation on the basis of an echoed chant heard inside a cave from hundreds of miles away. Why didn't I think of that?'

Clodagh patted her on the shoulder. 'It's okay, Yana.

You're not a cheechako anymore, but you didn't grow up here. You'll get used to our ways one of these days.'

A wistful look spread across Ke-ola's big face, but he said, 'You folks think I could borrow a boat to go check on the Honu?'

Clodagh surprised him. 'Not now. Maybe later. Fall latchkay time now. Lots of people coming and we gotta get ready.'

He nodded but Murel could see he was disappointed.

'But latchkays are wonderful, Ke-ola. You'll like them and – Ke-ola gets to come, doesn't he, Clodagh?'

'Sure. Marmie isn't leaving until after so you can all come.'

I don't like the sound of that, Ronan said. *What does she mean 'all'?*

They wouldn't make us go back to the space station now. Not after we saved Da and everything. They can't! And Ke-ola saved all of us. They can't send him back too. He likes Petaybee. I know he does.

It's too cold for him, sis, and winter's coming.

Well, but – well, it just wouldn't be fair. He should get to pick.

When the humans returned to Kilcoole, Sky and the Honu stayed behind so the Honu could swim and commune with the sea otters and absorb more information about the place he felt would become his new home. Sky had remained behind to tell his hundreds of relatives and the sea otters all about his adventures,

Sky otters, he told his hundreds of relatives, now

including the sea otter cousins, *know all kinds of creatures, like this big shell one. He is not a big clam and he is not to eat. He is a turtle and a very important creature. He came with his own human from a place far away that is not our home. But he helped keep the volcano from killing everybody, otters, humans, everyone, so he must belong here. So otters can play with him and talk to him but not harm him.*

What happened out there after we left? the sea otters wanted to know. And Sky had a long and enjoyable time of it telling them in great and colorful – and because he was an otter, somewhat smelly – detail of the adventures they missed.

While the others prepared for the latchkay, Johnny Green and Marmie accommodated Ke-ola by taking him out to visit the Honu. When they returned, Sky came with them.

Ke-ola was looking a little more satisfied. Sky scampered off the copter ahead of him.

Ke-ola had no fancier clothing than his bright colored ship suit and the flowered shorts he swam in, but Clodagh said she thought he could wear some of her things.

However, when the drumming began at the long-house and everyone filed past the stew steaming in the cleaned-out fuel drum heating over the open fire, Ke-ola wore his ship suit. One of Clodagh's extra snow shirts was draped over his lap, humped up in the middle.

'We looked for you all day long but couldn't find you anywhere,' Murel whispered fiercely. 'Where *were* you?'

'I had stuff I had to do,' he said, his lower lip squashing into his upper one as he looked down at her to see if she bought it. There was a ghost of the old twinkle in his eye. He was still pretty tired, she guessed, and also sad. He'd miss the Honu. Maybe Marmie would let him swim in her river sometime. Maybe they'd all end up swimming in it together. She decided not to think about that.

Speeches were made, and Clodagh said there would be songs to sing about the volcano, but everyone's throat was still very sore right now, so that night no one would sing of it, except for one repeat of the chant, for those in the village who had not come.

Ke-ola laid aside the snow shirt and what was under it and obligingly sang the chant and stamped the rhythm, as did all of the others who had been there. Then it was time for the smoked salmon to get passed around and a few more speeches.

But finally Ke-ola stood up himself and said, 'I want to do something before it's time to go. This is something my people used to do all the time, and now only at special times, and with special people. These aren't what we usually use but I did what I could with them.'

He lifted the shirt, under which was a mound of flowers, purple and magenta fireweed and lupine, pink wild roses, white wild daisies. Only the flowers, none of the stems. It must have taken him hours and hours, since the fireweed was a cluster flower. Lifting a few in his fingers, he brought up a long necklace made of them and put them around Clodagh's neck, kissing her on both cheeks and saying, 'Aloha, Auntie.'

He did the same for Marmie, Johnny, Yana, and

Sean, and last for Ronan and Murel. The wild roses were for Murel, and she stroked the already wilting petals.

'These are flower leis. In old times they were made of plumeria, frangipani, and other beautiful flowers from our islands, to welcome people. But I made these to thank you for your hospitality.'

'No dance tonight,' Clodagh told everybody. 'Meet in the communion cave in an hour.'

People murmured among themselves. Some folks had traveled from as far away as Harrison's Fjord to attend this latchkay, and the amenities were being dispensed with. Everything was so hurried up these days, what with the offworlders here. Even Clodagh seemed to be losing her feeling for the stateliness of the old ways.

Murel and Ronan grabbed Ke-ola's arms and immediately headed with him down to the hot springs. They knew he'd enjoy a nice warm swim, and they wanted to show off the beautiful waterfall and steaming pools, one falling into the other, where their parents told them they had fallen in love.

The twins dived and splashed for a while but soon fell into the same mood as Ke-ola, who floated on his back and admired the new night sky.

Before long the others began arriving and filing into the waterfall, with the cave behind its shimmering curtain.

The three of them got out, dried off, and dressed. Marmie and Johnny, Mum and Da, Clodagh, Dierdre, and Dr. Fiske were just arriving. Mum put her arm around Ronan, Da around Murel, and Johnny Green clapped Ke-ola on the shoulder. They walked straight through the outer cave and down the winding path into the innermost one.

They stepped cautiously forward as they reached the inner cave. Murel let out a sigh of relief. Ronan said, *Much better than last time, yeah?*

Much. Petaybee is glad we're home. I almost feel like the planet is giving us a lei too.

Yeah, like we're being honored or something. As we should be. Really, we've been wonderful.

She batted at him. *We did good, but Ke-ola was really the hero. He's such a good guy, Ro, and he's just sort of lost.*

Yeah, well . . .

They all sat, and Murel was afraid she was going to have to explain things to Ke-ola, but when the planet began talking, he just snuggled back against the rocky cave wall with a huge grin on his face. So Murel relaxed and gave herself up to the experience.

Maybe it was just the recent volcanic activity, but Petaybee seemed more excited than usual, stimulated, happy even. The cave walls glowed with the cherry red of lava, and Murel felt the beat of her own feet on the shipboard and seemed to hear the chant resounding through the stone. A breeze blew through the cave, the scent of flowers on it – surely not the flowers Mum and the others still wore with their leis? These flowers were as heavily and sweetly perfumed as anything Murel had ever smelled before. She felt something soft under her fingers and looked down. Sky lay beside her, his head cradled on her leg, looking utterly peaceful and happy.

Paradise. Petaybee was already very good, but tonight it felt like paradise. Which, she realized, was a concept from ancient religions found mostly in old books these days. But it meant that a place was the best of all possible places, an ideal place. Tonight Petaybee showed them how it could make a place with no ice, where the water was warm and the wind was balmy.

Great round rolling waves seemed to break at her feet, which felt as if they were bare and buried in something pleasantly hot and gritty. The roar of the water was as great and as oddly comforting as Coaxtl's purr. These rhythmic swells had a completely different feeling than the fierce and frightening crescendos of water that had pounded the yacht.

Then, gradually, the sense of being beside the lovely sea faded, and the only watery roar she heard was that of the waterfall at the mouth of the communion cave. Murel caught one last fleeting impression of foamy pearls left glistening in front of her toes before the seaside sensations washed away entirely.

People began to stir and move. Clodagh was the first to rise.

She smiled beatifically. 'Well, Petaybee has spoken. Did everybody get the message?'

People nodded to each other, though some a little doubtfully.

Murel wondered what the shanachie meant, since usually the communion was somewhat different from person to person. Mum and Da, for instance, were so tightly entwined they seemed to entirely forget where they were.

Ke-ola opened his eyes, blinking, then rubbing them.

'You, young man, you understand what our world is saying?' Clodagh asked.

He shrugged. 'I – I think so.'

'I hope you do, because Petaybee told *me* that you, of all the people here, are the one who understands the need for the warm landmass and the one who wants it. You were the one to welcome it with your song. Soon Marmie's ship will be flying back into space, and before you go, Petaybee has a question. Did you get it?'

He blinked and shook his head uncertainly.

'You, Murel and Ronan, did *you*?'

They exchanged looks, widened their eyes at Clodagh and shook their heads too.

Clodagh began to laugh. She turned to Marmie. 'I thought these kids were getting an education up there in your sky house, Marmie, but they don't even seem to see the obvious.'

Ronan, who didn't have much patience and knew when he was being teased, prompted, 'Which *is*? You're the wisewoman, Clodagh. You tell us.'

'It's dead simple, boy. Petaybee loves your new friend and wants you all to find out if there are any more like him out there that you can bring home.'

Epilogue

I'm not sure which one will take longer,' Da told the twins and Ke-ola, 'Petaybee, building its landmass, or the Federation red tape we have to cut through to invite Ke-ola's people to join us.'

Three months had passed since the latchkay. Summer was at an end and freeze-up would begin soon. Neither Ke-ola nor the twins had returned to school.

Mum, back from her helicopter trip with Dr. Fiske and Dr. Metaxos to check on the volcano, said, 'My money is on Petaybee finishing first. As for inviting Ke-ola's people, a lot of that paperwork is just nonsense they use to keep the punters at bay and the pencil pushers employed, love. Have you never heard that it's easier to ask forgiveness than it is to ask permission?'

'It's my ancestral family motto, actually,' Ke-ola said.

'Which makes it ours too,' Ronan put in.

'See there?' Da told her. 'We're setting a bad example for the children. Pay us no mind, kids. We're just frustrated by the communication glitches. With the equipment banjaxed every other week or so, having to send messages by passing ships is ponderous. Really, you do have to wait for permission for some things. To make it official. To keep from bringing the wrath of the heavens down upon our humbled heads. We've yet to hear back from the Federation or Intergal about our proposal. Neither is there any response from Ke-ola's people.'

'Da, why don't we just go get them?' Murel asked. 'I don't see why we need permission to issue an invitation or why they would need permission to come and see if they like it here or not.'

'They'll like it,' Ke-ola said. 'But they're probably not even getting the messages. The Company Corps monitors traffic in the area, and besides, we have communications problems of our own. Lots of meteor showers. Very hard to keep a com relay up when the sky keeps falling.'

'See what you started?' Da asked Mum playfully.

'Me?' she asked, hand to breast in make-believe innocence.

'No, seriously,' Murel said. 'I don't see why not.'

'We have no spacecraft of our own,' Da pointed out.

'Marmie has lots.'

'Those things cost a great deal to operate, dear,' Mum said. 'Marmie has been a wonderful friend to us and to Petaybee, but we mustn't ask her to beggar herself.'

'We could pay her back. Probably,' Ronan said.

'Besides,' Da said, 'there's no hurry. Winter is coming and Ke-ola's folk don't care for the cold, from what he says. The volcanic area is still way too unstable for them to try to occupy it.'

'But it won't be for very long, right, Mum?'

'We have no way of knowing that, kids. We can't be inviting Ke-ola's people to come and cohabit with active volcanoes.'

'Pardon me, ma'am,' Ke-ola said, 'but that's how my people used to live. That's what they remember from way back. They liked it. It's how we learned the chants I showed you. How we could help Petaybee and everybody else who lives here. If some volcanoes are left all alone, or with people who don't understand them, they get wild, explode all over the place, shake the whole world and make huge waves higher than the treetops, kill everybody.'

'But Ke-ola, your people haven't lived near volcanoes for many generations,' Mum said.

'Don't matter. Honus remember. Some people remember stories and songs. They can help the others.'

'Well, you're certainly optimistic, I'll say that,' Mum said, sounding the opposite of optimistic.

'What's it like out there now, Mum?' Murel asked. The twins hadn't been allowed to swim in the area since they returned, and Da didn't seem inclined to do it either. Sky had returned to his hundreds of relatives on the coast, and the twins hadn't heard from him, or Ke-ola from the Honu, for almost a month. The twins had spent the time teaching Ke-ola to ride a curly coat and showing him around the woods and villages surrounding Kilcoole. When the days were chilly, they swam at the hot springs. But this time they had not ventured beyond the area where their parents said they could wander. Almost losing their father had been an eyeopener. If they got into trouble, he'd come looking for them again, and he or other people in a rescue party could get hurt even if they themselves and Ke-ola were fine. So the twins obeyed the restrictions, though they chafed under them.

Mum said, 'The smoke kept us from seeing a great deal, but the central crater is now elevated to approximately a hundred feet above sea level.'

Da gave a low whistle.

'It is not the only vent, however. What we haven't seen in the past is that another crater has surfaced about fifteen klicks south of the primary one, and there is some activity from a third another forty miles south of that. The landmass surrounding the primary crater covers something like five square miles at the moment, but of course there's still pyroclastic flow from the crater, pumping steadily from it as if it were blood from the heart. I didn't think volcanoes worked that way.'

Da, who had been sitting at his desk while the kids stood around him, reached up, meaning to pat Ke-ola on the shoulder, but only reached his elbow, so he patted that instead. 'Petaybean ones apparently do – especially one that has had a good coach.' With an apologetic glance at the twins, he added, 'Or coaches.'

'Has the planet given Clodagh any idea how long this might take?' Ronan asked.

'I don't think Petaybee wears a watch, Ro,' Murel said.

Ronan colored and said, 'I *meant* that Petaybee seemed to be pretty clear about wanting Ke-ola and his people to live there. I don't think the planet would have been that specific if it didn't have some notion that the land would be ready in Ke-ola's lifetime.'

'The Honu might know,' Ke-ola said.

'How?' Murel asked.

Ke-ola shrugged. 'Honus know many things people don't. Especially about weather and disasters and natural events.'

'It can't hurt to ask,' Murel said. 'And I miss Sky. If the volcano is behaving itself, Mum, don't you think it would be okay if we swim out there to see them?'

'In a couple of days I could take you in the copter,' Mum replied.

'But we want to swim!' Ro protested. 'Ke-ola can swim with us – he's not a selkie or an otter but he's a really good swimmer. Please?'

Mum was looking at Da, but he shook his head. 'I'll never get all this paperwork sorted if I take off now. I see no harm in them going, though. After all, they've already been through quite a bit out there and got through it all right. In fact, the rest of us, especially me, might not have made it without them.'

Mum tilted her head and looked at him questioningly. He smiled and shook his head. 'No, love, I still don't remember what happened or how I survived. I suppose that will always be a mystery.'

Da, Ronan asked. *You don't suppose maybe some special kind of animal who lives under the sea found you and took you into its city – its shelter – and took care of you, do you?*

Now, why would I suppose something like that, son? You have quite an imagination on you, boyo. No, what I suppose, between you and me, is that Petaybee somehow knew it was me in trouble – and me its first selkie and father of the selkie twins – and somehow led me into a safe place with enough air to keep me going until the fireworks were done or you found me.

Yeah, I guess that makes more sense at that, Ronan said.

Murel shot him a look. They had promised the deep sea otters that if they gave Da back, no one would learn of the strange city or its mysterious inhabitants. But Ronan hated keeping a secret from Da, especially one that concerned him and Petaybee. So he'd sort of given his father a chance to remember what really happened. Which he hadn't. Also, it seemed that Da wouldn't have believed them if Ronan and Murel had sworn to what they had seen, so it was okay not to push it. Ronan's conscience was clear.

'So we can go?' Murel asked hurriedly.

'Yes, but take your dry suits. And Ke-ola, you'll want to wear a wet suit. The water is far too cold this time of year for you to swim unprotected. I'll fly out in the copter and pick you up Wednesday afternoon, so be right there at the otter colony. Got it?'

'Got it,' the twins said, and bounded off, Ke-ola in their wake.

I'm dying to know if the deep sea otters and that strange city of theirs survived the eruption, Ronan told his sister.

Me too, but we promised not to go back there.

Yes, but Sky didn't promise. The Honu didn't promise.

The Honu doesn't know about them.

Are you sure? Ke-ola says the Honus know about many things. And Sky might have told the Honu about them.

Nobody said anything about not telling animals about them – just no humans.

The three of them had been swimming hard all day, with one break to portage themselves in human form to the foot of the falls. Fun to slide down when frozen, the cascade was much too dangerous to tackle even for seals and certainly for Ke-ola.

The twins pointed out the site of the former otter dens to their friend before everyone plunged back into the water. Ke-ola dived in first, to give Murel privacy to change from her suit into her sealskin. He was also a little slower than they, so he would find the head start useful.

Poor Ke-ola wasn't much good at eating raw fish either, so he didn't have the benefit of frequent energy-boosting snacks that they did.

Finally they could smell the salt in the freshwater and saw the river broadening as its mouth opened to feed the sea. It came much sooner than they expected and was much broader than they remembered.

I guess the shoreline has risen permanently here, because of the water displaced by the volcano, Murel said.

We're lucky we were out swimming when the waves hit, Ronan agreed. *There used to be a lot more trees here – a lot more lots of things. And look at the sea otter island. It only barely sticks up out of the water now. A lot of it was flooded.* They hadn't noticed any of these things when returning from their harrowing encounter with the volcano, but now, in calmer times, the changes in the landscape were downright unsettling. Perhaps all of the changes hadn't taken place immediately after the first major eruption. The steady pumping of lava Mum described could have accounted in part for the higher water level. What if the otters had lost their dens, become afraid to live here, and moved somewhere else?

The twins began sending mental calls to Sky. It was a good idea to announce their presence and identify themselves anyway, so as not to alarm the hundreds of relatives, lest the three of them be attacked as invaders by angry otters. *Sky, it's us, Murel and Ronan! Can you hear us yet?*

Hah! River seals! The river seals have come! Sky's thought sang out, and before the twins quite knew where they were, they were surrounded by eager, not angry, otters, who immediately wanted to show them a new mud slide they had made.

Ke-ola was also surrounded, but at first the otters weren't too sure about him. 'Hey, what is this with the small, cute, and menacing?' he asked aloud. The twins started to translate for Sky but their otter friend had already assessed the situation.

Mother, sisters, brothers, cousins, aunties, and uncles, do you not recall my story about the Honu? What did I say about this Honu?

Hah! Not food! A sister three litters behind him answered.

Yes! Did I not also tell of the Honu's brave human protector? One who does not eat otters and is friend to the river seals? What did I say about him?

Hah! Not food? asked his uncle five litters before his mother.

Not food and not to be harmed. Friend. Like river seals.

Friend? asked another much younger brother.

Family member who is not an otter, Sky said quickly.

He had evidently given the concept considerable thought since being introduced to it.

At that, the otters around Ke-ola relaxed. One brushed gently against him in apology. The little sister dived down and resurfaced holding a rock in her paws, which she dropped into the water near Ke-ola's hand. He caught it. 'Thank you,' he said, but she didn't hear. She watched him catch it, then dived back under the surface again.

Sky! Murel exclaimed mentally, and dived under him and resurfaced to show her pleasure. *We were afraid you'd moved your dens again, that maybe the bigger waves and higher tides had washed them out.*

Hah! Old dens are all underwater. Sea otter dens too. But riverbank is full of holes. Otters dig holes larger, have new homes. Have to get more rocks, though, he said. *And the sea took back hundreds of clamshells.*

I'm sorry, Murel said. *Maybe we can help you gather more.* The twins pulled and flopped themselves onto the riverbank and shook off the water, then put on their dry suits.

Did the sea otters make new dens too? Ronan asked. *I see their island is mostly underwater now.*

'Hah!' Sky said. *Sea otters don't have dens. They need only the sea. Their back feet are flippers and they blow bubbles in their fur to make it warm and waterproof. When they are on land it is just for hunting food in pools on the beach. They sleep in the sea, wrapped in kelp. They mate in the sea. They have strange ways, but they are our cousins.*

And— the deep sea otters, Sky? Murel asked. *What of them? Have the sea otters seen them since the volcano?*

'Hah!' Sky chittered a moment, plainly disturbed.

No deep sea otters. No deep sea otter strange bubble den. All land now. Underwater land, under volcano land. But no deep sea otters. No.

Oh, Ro! Murel said.

Looks like we got Da out just in time, Ronan said.

But we didn't save the deep sea otters, or whatever they were. They helped Da, saved his life, and now they're extinct and we didn't even try to help them.

We sort of had our hands full. And they didn't want help. They wanted secrecy, remember?

She couldn't help it. She started crying. Everything had turned out fine for everyone except the heroic creatures who had saved their father, and it wasn't fair, it just wasn't.

Ke-ola, who had been sending his own silent calls to the Honu, turned back from the sea in alarm when he heard her sobs. He swept her up in a huge and all-enveloping hug that nonetheless only circled her lightly within his arms, to comfort her but not break her. 'Little sistah, why do you cry? Did someone bite you?'

'No, no, it's just too sad, Ke-ola,' she said. And she told him about the deep sea otters and what they had done and what had become of them. 'If they hadn't been so afraid of us, maybe they would have saved themselves. They wanted everything secret – well, I told you now, but I guess it doesn't matter since they're all dead.'

'I would never tell,' he said.

So she blurted out some of the rest of it, and Ronan finished. While they were talking, the sun completely disappeared and the moon rose. Its shaft fell on the mouth of the river, and within it they saw the head and shell of the Honu swimming toward them. He looked awfully sacred right then, his shell sheened by moon-glow and his wet head glistening with light.

'Except for the Honu, of course,' Ke-ola amended. In a moment he sighed and said, 'And that's okay. The Honu knew all about the deep sea otters. He says we should take them flowers.'

'We can't go,' Murel said. 'We promised Mum.'

'I didn't promise,' Ke-ola said. 'The Honu didn't promise.'

Sky, who had been following the thread through the twins' thoughts, piped up, *Sky did not promise. Deep sea otters did not think Sky could tell scientists about them, since otters cannot talk to two-legs who are not river seals.*

'You should wait till morning,' Murel said aloud to Ke-ola and Ronan. 'We won't be able to find flowers to make leis until then anyway.'

They don't want flowers, Sky said again. *Otters have no use for flowers. Why flowers?*

Because— because they're pretty, Sky, Murel answered, feeling even as she said it that the answer didn't make much sense. Otters weren't great flower fanciers unless they sometimes nibbled certain varieties. And then, she doubted the beings that had helped Da and inhabited the strange city were otters of any kind. Maybe some ancient pre-terraforming denizens of Petaybee preserved by their city and resurrected with the opening of the volcanic vent. Maybe aliens. But they were good, whatever they were, because they saved Da, and if the Honu thought they deserved flowers, then they did.

Rocks. Clams. Food. These are good gifts. Pretty gifts. Deep sea otters would like these gifts. Not flowers.

'He's got a point,' Ronan said aloud. To Ke-ola, he said, 'Sky thinks the deep sea otters wouldn't appreciate a flower lei as much as one made out of something otters value – like rocks or clams.'

'But we can't make a rock lei or a clam lei – can we?' Murel asked.

'Clamshells,' Ke-ola said. 'They used to make leis from shells sometimes. We could net them with seaweed.'

Sky and all of the other otters, including the sea otters who had congregated by the shore to see what all of the excitement was about, agreed that clamshells were best. Dead otters ate no clams but would enjoy the pretty shells. Living otters would have to eat the clams *for* the dead otters. It made sense to them. The tide pools, beach, river mouth, and sea soon frothed around diving otter butts, the owners of which made short work of the whole clams and deposited the shells into huge piles. These they basketed in strands of kelp and other seaweed, enclosing each shell in three or four strands, then tying another strand at top and bottom. It took a very long time. The twins weren't very good at it, so in the end, Ke-ola ended up with three leis, one from each twin and one from their father, which he, the Honu, and Sky would carry to a place as close to the deep sea otters' 'den' as Sky could guess.

Murel didn't think the leis were pretty at all, but she only thought it, so as not to insult Ke-ola.

Sky disagreed. *Pretty. Much pretty. Hundreds pretty.* All of the other otters agreed that the leis were hundreds pretty.

So that was all right. If the otters liked the leis, the self-proclaimed deep sea otters would have liked them.

The day was half gone before Ke-ola, the Honu, Sky, and an otter escort set off for the volcano. Ronan and Murel swam out part of the way with them, but kept their promise and didn't go near the volcano. Well, not very near. Actually, it was hard to judge because, what with all the building up it had done, the volcano sort of met them earlier than they expected to encounter it. At least, the underwater part that was the skirt of the island extended until it was much closer to the northern mainland than they remembered.

It didn't matter anyway. Once they came to the place where the lava flow had cooled on the ocean floor, building it up until the water was comparatively shallow there, nobody stood much chance of getting anywhere near the place where the deep sea otters had so recently dwelled in their peculiar city.

That being the case, the twins watched when the Honu suddenly stopped swimming and turned back to Ke-ola, treading water, and Sky. *Otters talk to other otters best*, the Honu told Sky.

The twins felt relief from Sky. The little river otter had not wanted to go back to the volcano, because it was a long swim, because he was not a sea otter and didn't like salt water very much, and because *his* sort of otter had the intelligence to avoid erupting volcanoes. After a number of 'Hahs,' he dropped his clamshell lei into the sea with the thought, *Deep sea otters, here are your presents – nice shells, only you are not here and are probably dead.* The thoughts were accompanied by vocalized chitterings and mumblings that were otter verbalizations.

To the twins' surprise, the Honu and Ke-ola swam back to them.

'As long as you're here, you may as well represent yourselves,' Ke-ola said, pulling the clamshell lei off over his head and dropping it over Ronan's. The Honu came close enough for Murel to take his lei.

Since the twins were naturally in seal form, Ronan barked acknowledgment, then dived, letting the lei drop over his head to drift slowly downward before he rose once more to the surface. *Thanks for giving our Da back*, Ronan thought.

Murel followed him, letting her lei drop over her head as he had.

Yes, thanks, she said. *And we're awfully sorry you didn't make it too. You could have come with us. I hope you knew that. Whatever you were, you saved our father. We'd have been glad to help you too.*

Then they turned around and returned to the river mouth. Halfway back, they were met by their mother's helicopter. It shadowed them back to the river, where the twins and Ke-ola withdrew from the water and the twins reassumed human shape and pulled on their dry suits. There was no one there to see but Mum, who recently had recertified as a copter pilot, updating the training she had received while in the Company Corps.

Murel expected Mum to be at least a little angry that they had gone out to the volcanoes, but she didn't mention it. 'Get in,' she said to the two of them and to Ke-ola. 'Marmie and Johnny should be docking the *Piaf* in another hour. You'll need to get ready to go.'

Oh, no! Back to school no matter how much more interesting things are at home, Ronan said.

But then Mum surprised them by saying, 'Your father asks if Sky would like another helicopter ride and suggests perhaps the Honu might like to come along on this trip as well.'

Ke-ola's face filled with thunderclouds, but he called the Honu, who had been swimming just offshore, and politely lifted him into the copter and sat holding his shell so the flippers would not have to bear the turtle's weight on dry ground. It wasn't a lot of weight even yet, though the Honu was several inches larger in diameter than he had been when he arrived, but the flippers were delicate.

Mum had her headphones on the whole way so they had no more opportunity to quiz her about why Sky and the Honu needed to come, unless it was to say goodbye.

Of course, there was always the chance that Marmie's school might be starting special classes for airborne otters and psychic sea turtles with extrasensory knowledge of natural disasters, but it didn't seem likely.

The copter set down at the space port just as the *Piaf* was landing. Da and Aunt Sinead arrived, and Clodagh too. They seemed to be trying to look as if they had just been in the neighborhood, saw the spaceship landing, and decided to come and see what was going on, but the twins noticed that their bags and Ke-ola's were strapped across the back of Da's mount. Page and Chapter were nowhere to be seen, nor were other mounts for Johnny and Marmie. But when Mum, Da,

Clodagh, and Aunt Sinead dismounted, Coaxtl and Nanook appeared from behind them, split up and sat down flanking them, one on each side, like good guardian beasts.

Other than the refueling crew, no one disembarked from the *Piaf* except Johnny and Marmie, who waved and hurried toward them.

'Ah,' Marmie said, 'I see the delegation has arrived. What's it to be then, Your Excellencies?' she asked Mum and Da.

Delegation? The twins exchanged startled looks.

Before they could ask, Mum answered Marmie. 'We haven't had a chance to discuss it with them yet.' She turned back to the twins and Ke-ola, 'Sorry, but with the communications problems, Marmie wasn't able to get through until this morning to let us know about this.'

'What?' the twins and Ke-ola asked at once. The Honu was not exactly struggling in Ke-ola's hands, but seemed to want to go somewhere, and poked his head toward the ship first at one angle, then another, his flippers paddling as if he would swim through the air to reach it. Sky stood beneath him, the lower part of his body still but the upper part bobbing inquisitively from side to side as he too watched the ship.

'Are we going back to school then, Mum? What's all the fuss?' Murel asked.

Mum shook her head, and now she did seem a bit angry. 'No. I'm dead set against it, mind you, but Marmie has been pulling all the strings she can and this seems to be the only way. We've received permission from the Federation, though not from Intergal, to send a native Petaybean delegation to invite Ke-ola's people to visit us, and live with us if everyone is mutually agreeable.'

'So, is that what Marmie and Johnny are doing here? Have they found some way you and Da can go after all?'

'Of course not,' Mum snapped, then relented, realizing she was acting angry at a time when she most wanted to be loving. She continued in a more patient and reasonable tone. 'You know that. We're too acclimated by now to leave the planet for any length of time. And we're too old. To my way of thinking, you are too young. And what with everything happening, we haven't had much time to catch up or for you to enjoy being home again. But still, if you're willing . . .'

'We need you to be Petaybee's emissaries,' Da said aloud. 'It's a lot to ask of youngsters, but Ke-ola is your friend, after all, and you brought him and his Honu to Petaybee's notice. Besides, it will be a fine opportunity for you to travel, see other places. I've never been able to do that myself, you know. And of course, Ke-ola must go to introduce you.'

'You mean we're going to go see Ke-ola's people and bring them back?' Ronan asked. 'We don't have to go back to school?'

'Not right now,' Mum said.

'Though I have brought a nice selection of vid courses with me and you can study those if you find yourselves hungering for knowledge on the journey,' Marmie said.

'No!' they both said, but Murel added diplomatically, as befitted her new appointment, 'That is, a journey to a distant world and a real mission to perform seems educational enough for now, thanks.'

'So you don't mind then?' Marmie asked.

'When do we start?' Ronan replied.

Sky suddenly streaked toward the *Piaf*. Otters run very quickly when they want to, as he had told the twins. The Honu's swimming motions seemed to be dragging Ke-ola in the same direction. 'You still got the sacred Honu's tank, Madame?' Ke-ola asked Marmie.

'A bigger one,' she said. 'Of course, if your people or some of them come, we hope they will bring others of his species with them.'

Da handed Marmie a sheaf of paperwork, and Johnny handed the twins some as well. 'Maps and such,' he said. 'So you'll know where we are, and if communications clear up, can get in touch. It's a bit out of the way, on the fringes like Petaybee, but another fringe. Yana, you know—'

'Yes, of course,' she said. There were hugs all around and head butts and rubs from Coaxtl and Nanook, then Da took the packs off the curly coat and handed them to the twins, and Clodagh handed them another.

Da held out Ke-ola's, but the Kanaka boy was already halfway to the ship, so Ronan took it.

More hugs and, amazingly, tears from Mum and Clodagh. Sky streaked back to them, then back toward Ke-ola and the Honu.

'Better we take off pretty quick,' Ke-ola called. 'The Honu wants to go *now*.'

Johnny frowned. 'He seems to be on a tight

schedule. I never thought to see a turtle in such a hurry.'

'Better go now, then,' Clodagh said, waving the twins toward the ship. They turned toward it, and her bemused comment followed them. 'Honus know things.'

THE END

MAELSTROM
BOOK TWO OF THE TWINS OF PETAYBEE
Anne McCaffrey and Elizabeth Ann Scarborough

With three acclaimed novels – *Powers That Be, Power Lines* and *Power Play* – bestselling authors Anne McCaffrey and Elizabeth Ann Scarborough launched a thought-provoking science fiction saga that told the story of a sentient planet, Petaybee. In *Changelings* they returned to Petaybee and introduced the Shongili twins, Ronan and Murel, who have the ability to transform into seals and converse telepathically with the creatures of Petaybee.

In *Maelstrom* Ronan and Murel are on board Marmie's luxury spaceship *Piaf* with their schoolfriend Ke-ola, on a mission to rescue Ke-ola's family, who are marooned on a planet racked by meteor storms. The rescuers arrive to discover another ship already there and its commander, Colonel Cally, makes it clear that he considers the planet his territory. Ignoring the colonel's protests, Marmie, Ke-ola and the twins land on the planet, where they find some survivors and their totem animals, the sharks and the giant turtles, or Honus. Marmie and the twins offer them all a new home on Petaybee. However, Marmie has made an implacable enemy in Colonel Cally and he swiftly plans his revenge.

Back on Petaybee the twins, in their seal form, are escorting the Honus to their new home in the middle of the ocean when, during the long journey, Murel falls asleep and becomes separated from the others. She wakes to find herself surrounded by a pod of Orcas, who, thinking she is a normal seal, try to eat her. She calls Ronan telepathically and he races back, but they are both caught up in an underwater whirlpool and dragged down to the ocean floor . . .

POWERS THAT BE
Anne McCaffrey and
Elizabeth Ann Scarborough

The first collaboration between two of science fiction's mightiest names.

It was a world of ice and snow – a planet that just supported life and that had been terraformed from frozen uninhabitable rock. The people of Petaybee were hardy, self-reliant, friendly – and also very secretive.

Major Yana Maddock, medically discharged from the service, was shipped to Petaybee in the hope that her burnt-out lungs might just recover in the icy air. And at the last moment, she was given a special commission. Unauthorized life-forms had been seen on the planet and, more seriously, geologic survey teams had vanished into nowhere, the odd survivor being discovered abandoned and insane. It was Yana's task to infiltrate Petaybee society and find out who – or what – was causing the eerie events on the planet.

She discovered a primitive ice-bound community of extraordinary people – people who possessed some mysterious quality of surviving – and people who Yana discovered she both liked and revered as she found herself becoming one of them.

9780552140980

CORGI BOOKS

A LIST OF OTHER ANNE McCAFFREY TITLES AVAILABLE FROM CORGI BOOKS

THE PRICES SHOWN BELOW WERE CORRECT AT THE TIME OF GOING TO PRESS. HOWEVER TRANSWORLD PUBLISHERS RESERVE THE RIGHT TO SHOW NEW RETAIL PRICES ON COVERS WHICH MAY DIFFER FROM THOSE PREVIOUSLY ADVERTISED IN THE TEXT OR ELSEWHERE.

08453 0	DRAGONFLIGHT	£6.99
11635 1	DRAGONQUEST	£7.99
10661 5	DRAGONSONG	£6.99
10881 2	DRAGONSINGER: HARPER OF PERN	£6.99
11313 1	THE WHITE DRAGON	£7.99
11804 4	DRAGONDRUMS	£6.99
12499 0	MORETA: DRAGONLADY OF PERN	£6.99
12817 1	NERLIKA'S STORY & THE COELURA	£6.99
13098 2	DRAGONSDAWN	£6.99
13099 0	THE RENEGADES OF PERN	£6.99
13729 4	ALL THE WEYRS OF PERN	£6.99
13913 0	THE CHRONICLES OF PERN: FIRST FALL	£6.99
14270 0	THE DOLPHINS OF PERN	£6.99
14272 7	RED STAR RISING: THE SECOND CHRONICLES OF PERN	£6.99
14274 3	THE MASTERHARPER OF PERN	£6.99
14631 5	THE SKIES OF PERN	£6.99
14762 1	THE CRYSTAL SINGER OMNIBUS	£8.99
14180 1	TO RIDE PEGASUS	£6.99
13728 6	PEGASUS IN FLIGHT	£6.99
14630 7	PEGASUS IN SPACE	£6.99
13763 4	THE ROWAN	£5.99
13764 2	DAMIA	£5.99
13912 2	DAMIA'S CHILDREN	£5.99
13914 9	LYON'S PRIDE	£6.99
14629 3	THE TOWER AND THE HIVE	£6.99
09115 4	THE SHIP WHO SANG	£5.99
08661 4	DECISION AT DOONA	£4.99
08344 5	RESTOREE	£5.99
10965 7	GET OFF THE UNICORN	£6.99
14436 3	THE GIRL WHO HEARD DRAGONS	£5.99
14628 5	NIMISHA'S SHIP	£6.99
14271 9	FREEDOM'S LANDING	£6.99
14273 5	FREEDOM'S CHOICE	£6.99
14627 7	FREEDOM'S CHALLENGE	£6.99
14909 8	FREEDOM'S RANSOM	£6.99
14098 8	POWERS THAT BE (with Elizabeth Ann Scarborough)	£6.99
14099 6	POWER LINES (with Elizabeth Ann Scarborough)	£6.99
14100 3	POWER PLAY (with Elizabeth Ann Scarborough)	£6.99
14621 8	ACORNA (with Margaret Ball)	£6.99
14748 6	ACORNA'S QUEST (with Margaret Ball)	£6.99
54659 3	ACORNA'S PEOPLE (with Elizabeth Ann Scarborough)	£6.99
14749 4	ACORNA'S WORLD (with Elizabeth Ann Scarborough)	£6.99
15076 2	ACORNA'S SEARCH (with Elizabeth Ann Scarborough)	£5.99
15135 1	ACORNA'S REBELS (with Elizabeth Ann Scarborough)	£6.99
15275 7	ACORNA'S TRIUMPH (with Elizabeth Ann Scarborough)	£6.99
15291 9	ACORNA'S CHILDREN: (with Elizabeth Ann Scarborough) FIRST WARNING	£6.99
15150 5	DRAGON'S KIN (with Todd McCaffrey)	£6.99
	AND BY TODD McCAFFREY:	
15208 0	DRAGONSBLOOD	£6.99

All Transworld titles are available by post from:

Bookpost, PO Box 29, Douglas, Isle of Man, IM99 1BQ

Credit cards accepted. Please telephone 01624 677237, fax 01624 670923, Internet http://www.bookpost.co.uk or e-mail: bookshop@enterprise.net for details.

Free postage and packing in the UK. Overseas customers: allow £2 per book (paperbacks) and £3 per book (hardbacks).